Operation Arrow Fletcher

James T. Byrnes

Stoney Creek Press —Shelby Twp., MI
ISBN: 978-0-578-68629-5
Library of Congress Control Number: 2020907966
Title: Operation Arrow Fletcher
Author: James T. Byrnes
Digital distribution | 2020
Paperback | 2020

Acknowledgments

For reading draft after draft after draft I am truly blessed with my awesome wife Marsha and my wonderful extended family. They listened to my endless story revisions without complaint. To my brother Eddie who designed the book cover with his usual flair. He is truly a talented artist.

Special thank you to my editor Cheryl Bogner, *The Tornado*. Cheryl takes my writing and tears it apart but there was always a rainbow after the storm. Cheryl is my writing coach and a gifted writer in her own right. More importantly she is my dear friend.

Prologue

She is alone this morning. Dressed very warmly in her puffy parka and boots. She left so early I barely had time to finish the first sweep. I wish I could run to her and tell her what is going on. I think that would only scare her. I must remain hidden. I must keep the promise.

My partner will be here soon to take over. It has been a long night. The hard snow crunches under my boots as I press against the branches within a copse of pines. The high-power binoculars are zoomed in on her. I see her looking around. Does she sense she is not alone? She looks directly at the pines where I am hidden and pauses. I stand still. She then looks straight ahead. I am buried so deeply in the trees that she cannot see me. It has to be this way. For now.

Chapter 1

The sun barely pierced the ghostly canopy of tall firs and snow-dusted maples covering the nature trail. Long thick branches, like out-stretched arms, arched up and over the path, creating a white tunnel stretching far ahead and disappearing around a bend. An inch of newly fallen snow blanketed the forest floor, undisturbed except for infrequent imprints etched on its crystalline surface.

Through the soft pink and peach light of dawn, Carly Fletcher followed the path with a plan to end her morning walk at Piney Bow, a shady lake surrounded by pines, aspens, and birches.

Armed with her G5 X PowerShot camera, Carly scoured the forest before her, looking for deer tracks—fresh deer tracks. Up ahead, to her left, she spotted some, one set large, the other set much smaller.

She saw the deer yesterday and her goal was to get a snapshot to add to her almost completed forest collage. It was a beautiful piece consisting of woodland objects, ribbons, and fall colors of crimson, gold, and orange, all glued on the background of a backwoods painted canvas. The pictures of the deer would round out the project. Dr. Hayes had suggested this type of art activity as part of Carly's therapy, and she loved it.

As she focused her camera on the deer tracks, she swayed slightly. Again, it was there, like blazing lightning, a cinema of death and carnage careening through her mind. Blurry images of the slaughter. The fiery muzzle flash. Crumpled bodies. White virgin snow. Red bits of spatter, and blood mist.

Why does it seem so real?

With great mental effort, she pushed the troubling images from her mind and focused on happier times when, just over a year before, she had been a twenty-one-year-old art major living the hipster scene in Corktown, Detroit. Her inner circle of close friends was vibrant—bright young millennials, full of dreams and personality, living amidst the tight-knit community full of sushi bars, micro-breweries, and street music that Carly called home.

Detroit was on a comeback from the largest municipal bankruptcy in the country. Victorian-era houses beautifully restored with vibrant colors of purple and blue stood next to dilapidated structures still waiting for their renovation. Gardens filled with day lilies and zebra grass dotted the streetscape.

Home. The word seemed strange to her. Almost alien.

Off the trail and now in deeper snow, the tracks led in the direction of the lake. Plowing through the snow, one slow step at a time, she came to the vast body of water and found it black and still. It was cold, but not frozen. The sun was now above the trees, and Carly could see vapor rising from the water like smoke drifting from a dying bonfire.

Stepping onto the rocks, careful not to slip on the slimy moss exposed from the melting snow, she followed the shoreline and made her way to the deer blind she'd built the day before. She had intertwined branches and woven them into a four-foot-high camouflage wall that blended with the forest background. A dead pine stump worked perfectly as a seat.

Trudging through ankle deep snow, Carly stopped about 30 yards from her blind. She removed five apples from her parka and tossed four of them to the ground. She scraped the fifth on the rough bark of a nearby tree, releasing its irresistible scent to any passing deer. She then sat behind her wall.

The forest was Carly's peaceful time, her lavender, her Zen. This morning, however, was different. Weighing on her mind was today's late morning therapy. Dr. Stephen Hayes, her therapist at Holy Oaks Hospital, had suggested a new procedure. He had enlisted the help of Dr. Alexander Slovak, a leading practitioner in hypnotic therapy.

Carly jumped at the chance. Anything to get her life back. Dr. Hayes explained that she would be placed in a semi-conscious hypnotic state, and Dr. Slovak would attempt to take her back to the time and place she lost her memory. He hoped to find contributing factors as to what Dr. Hayes referred to as her "occasional delusional state of mind" and the amnesia that prevented her from experiencing clear memories.

Carly remembered some things, like living with Bo and riding the downtown *People Mover.* She remembered going to classes at the university and taking Little Max to the dog park. Her arrival at Holy Oaks, though…that memory was completely gone.

She often asked Dr. Hayes, "How did I get here?"

His response always was, "When you remember that, you will no longer need to be here."

Her early morning rise and lack of coffee had taken its toll on her. With her head now bobbing and fighting heavy eyes, she eventually succumbed and gently closed them.

She slept quietly, unaware of space or time until the raspy honking sound of a white swan emerging through a veil of mist made Carly jump and immediately open her eyes. There, with its black masked eyes and orange narrow beak, swam the perfect shot.

Carly adjusted her lens and brought the image of the swan closer. Like a professional photographer, she gently squeezed pic after pic of the graceful bird. Her last photo was of the swan swimming away and the sun barely shining on the lake.

With no sign of the deer, and having plenty of pictures of the swan, Carly decided to head back. Group therapy started at 10:00 a.m. She stood up from the crouched sitting position on the stump, and her back felt tight. Bending at the waist, first to the left and then to right, she heard her bones crack and the tightness faded away.

Leaving the deer blind, she stepped over the jagged limbs and stumps of dead trees and made her way to the shoreline.

The stranger watched as she placed her feet in the compressed boot marks left on her journey in. She followed them, one by one, to the exact place where her morning adventure had started. Lowering the binoculars, the stranger thought… *It's getting late, Carly. Get yourself to therapy.*

Chapter 2

Back at the hospital, sitting in a semi-circle of chairs, Carly waited patiently for her chance to speak. Sitting next to her, as in every group session, was David Farris. Broad shouldered and brawny, his shaggy jet-black beard filled his face. He reminded Carly of a lumberjack. Talking was sometimes hard for him. She remembered one session when he was explaining why he was there and in the middle of it, got up and left.

"Today, I don't have anything I want to say," he said. "I want to be here, but I just can't talk about my sister."

"I get how you feel, man," Jesse said. "There are nights I can't sleep thinking about my dad…how he killed himself in the garage. How I found him…he never showed up to my football game."

"David, Jesse, this is a voluntary group," Ms. Shirley, the group leader said. "It's all about timing, and if the time doesn't feel right, we understand."

Ms. Shirley looked around the semicircle of residents and no one was volunteering.

"I guess if no one has anything to contribute, we can just end our session today."

Carly lifted her hand just above her shoulder. "I have something to say."

"Go ahead, Carly," Ms. Shirley said.

"I have been working on a project for art class—a forest collage. I got up early this morning and went to a deer blind I made yesterday, hoping to get a picture of some deer for my collage. I didn't see any, but I got some great shots of a swan that I am going to use instead.

Ms. Shirley nodded. "Adding the swan is a great idea. Be sure to bring it and show all of us."

"You'll be the first I show…The swan had no idea I was there, and it was singing…if you could call it singing. More like squawking. It moved in slow motion. My heart was beating so fast I thought for sure he would spot me. I could see his eyes in the black mask of feathers."

Carly paused, unconsciously scraping at her worn nail polish. "You know what they say about swans singing, don't you?"

Carly's comment was met with silence.

Ms. Shirley noticed the blank faces and wrinkled eyebrows of some of the residents in the group and quickly said, "Why don't you explain what it means?"

Grateful for her help, Carly continued. "Legend has it that swans do not make any sound until the day they are going to die and leave this earth. Singing is the last thing they do before passing away. They call it their "Swan Song."

She smiled while intertwining her fingers. "People can have a "Swan Song" you know. It doesn't mean they are going to die. It just means that a person is about to do something for the last time. For me, I am getting ready to undergo special therapy with Dr. Hayes. I'm going to be hypnotized.

"This therapy may lead me back to the events that caused my amnesia. If I get my memory back, I can leave this place, just like the swan does…except, I won't be dead."

A couple girls in the group giggled, and Carly laughed with them.

"Maybe this therapy is my "Swan Song," Carly added. "Maybe…just maybe, I can really go home."

"I was chased by a bird one time," Sally, who sat across from Carly said. "They can be really mean, especially if they are nesting. I think I walked too close to her nest. She must have felt threatened because she took off after me hissing and flapping her wings. Scared the hell out of me. I was only around ten."

"I think you're missing the point, S-a-l-l-y," David drawled, bracing his forearms on his knees. Swinging his head back and forth, he said, "I'm desperately trying to connect the dots between Carly's *Swan Song,* and you being chased by a bird."

He crossed his arms and stuck out his legs. Looking up at the ceiling and in a singsong voice, he said, "Ding, ding, ding…no connection. Except that bird was a good judge of character!"

Muffled laughter filled the room. Ms. Shirley looked disapprovingly at David, even though she struggled to stifle a smile.

"I *know* what Carly means," Sally snapped. "But my therapist said to share whatever comes into my mind. So when she talked about the swan coming close to her, I remembered the bird that chased me."

David rolled his eyes.

Carly, fighting her own smile, slid her foot over to gently kick at David's boot.

He looked at her and winked.

"You know Farris…" Sally sneered, "I think those rumors are true. What you did to those boys was sick. They should never let you out of here."

Ms. Shirley quickly interrupted. "Sally…that's enough." An uncomfortable silence fell over the group. "Let's call it a day. Thank you for being here. Please put your chairs on the rack and see you next week."

Grabbing her chair and folding it, Carly turned to take it to the rack when David appeared and took it from her.

"I'll hang that for you."

"That Sally can be such a bitch!" Carly said softly.

"Yeah. Well. I sort of had it coming. I probably shouldn't mess with her so much. She just makes it so easy. On a different note, sounds like you've got a big day ahead."

"I do… I've never been hypnotized before."

David placed the dented chair along with the others on the rack. "So, you went to the lake again this morning. I take it you don't feel like you're being watched anymore?"

"Not totally…I still get that feeling at times, but I've learned how to handle it. It really hasn't gone away. I try not to bring it up with Hayes."

"Do you really believe in that magic stuff?" David asked.

"What?...You mean being hypnotized?"

"Yeah. Do you really think it works?"

"Dr. Hayes thinks so. He said I might get memories back that my mind had me forget."

"Hayes?...I wonder if his degree came in a Happy Meal! He knows I'm not crazy. He knows those boys had it coming. And yet, here I am!"

Carly lightly laughed and continued just above a whisper. "David, hush before someone hears you. You have less than a month to go and could be home. Don't say anything that could get you back up the hill."

"I won't. But it kills me that one man has that power over us."

"It is…what it is. We play the game…and get to go home. We've talked about this."

"I know. Still pisses me off though. You better get going," David said, looking at his watch. "Don't want you to be late for your hocus-pocus show."

Carly smiled, flashed him a wink, and left him standing there, looking after her.

Chapter 3

While walking down the two flights of stairs to the outdoor parking lot, Carly tied her scarf around her neck and zipped up her parka. Dr. Hayes' office was clear across campus. As soon as she stepped outside, bits of snow hit her face like grains of sand. She held the top of her hood over her head, keeping her face protected from the wind.

By the time Carly reached the office building, the overcast sky cleared, and rays of sun glinted against the snow. She pulled the glass door and entered a dimly lit hall. As she stood unzipping her parka and stomping her boots, a musty smell wafted up from the damp rug under Carly's feet.

She passed a large lobby sign listing doctors and offices in the building and headed for the elevator. Her finger had almost touched the UP arrow when she withdrew her hand and decided to take the stairs instead.

Quickly, she headed up to the second floor, leaping two steps at a time. Little clumps of snow fell off her boots onto the steps and hallway carpet as she hurried to Dr. Hayes' office.

All the suites on this floor had large windows with a view into a reception room. Carly stood outside the office and watched a short man standing in front of Dr. Hayes, shaking his head and pumping his index finger into his chest. Susan, the receptionist, had not yet arrived, and they were the only ones in the eight-chair waiting room.

Feeling a bit uneasy, Carly decided not to enter the office. She pulled out her cell phone, leaned up against the wall and thumbed through her screen icons seeing if Meghan had texted her. The voices stopped and Carly looked up to see Dr. Hayes motioning her to come in.

"Carly, I'm sorry you didn't come in right away," Hayes began. "You witnessed two old friends passionately debating their positions on a certain psychological therapy. We were discussing an article in one of our journals where we have a difference of opinion. A *big* difference of opinion.

"It brings back memories of the old college days where Alex and I were on the debate team. Isn't that right, Alex?" he said, addressing his colleague, seeming very much at ease.

"Those were the days," Slovak answered. "I think we debated back and forth more than against the other team."

Shaking hands with Carly, he introduced himself.

"I am Dr. Slovak. Nice to meet you, Ms. Fletcher."

With his short-cropped beard and gray shaggy hair, Slovak looked more like a hippie of the 60's rather than a therapist. He wore a tan turtleneck sweater, black sport coat, and wrinkled khaki pants. She noticed a pink scar on the side of his face from what looked like a recent surgery. His right eye was also noticeably disfigured.

Dr. Hayes helped Carly remove her parka and hung it up.

"Please, let's go to my office." he said.

Every time Carly entered his office, she felt she was in a time warp. Two padded chairs sat next to a brown leather couch. Dark brown paneled walls with thick crown molding reminded her of the style her grandparents had. Grainy, wooden filing cabinets were next to a similarly dark wooden desk. A glass table in the middle of the room was the only piece of furniture that looked as though it had been purchased within the past decade.

Carly chose to sit on the couch while Hayes and Dr. Slovak took their places on the padded chairs in front of it.

Slovak scooted his chair a little closer. Carly's body tensed, and she leaned back slightly, her own gaze flicking toward that eye then looking away, embarrassed at herself.

"Rest assured, Carly, you're not the first to be taken back by my appearance," Dr. Slovak said, unshaken by her reaction.

Gesturing to his eye, he began to speak again. "It was during the Kosovo war. I was a young man in my early 20's, and our house was destroyed. The only thing I remember is a huge explosion and cinder blocks raining down and crushing me. When I awoke in the hospital, my entire face and head was bandaged."

Dr. Slovak paused as if reliving the explosion. "I did not know of my family's fate or how disfigured I was until months later. Being kept in a semi-coma to manage the pain, I was not aware of my family's absence. Looking into the mirror for the first time was a horror I will never forget.

"It took years of reconstructive surgery to get to this point. As you can see from the fresh scarring, the surgeries continue to this day. Learning of my family's fate was devastating, as I am sure the death of your brother Artie was for you."

Hearing Dr. Slovak say Artie's name, tore at the wound that never healed in her heart. "How do you know about my brother Artie?" Carly asked suspiciously.

"Dr. Hayes and I have gone over your files and discussed some of the issues you are experiencing. The death of your brother was part of that discussion. I can see you are upset, and I apologize for not being more sensitive. Would you like me to stop?"

Carly glared at him. "No," she replied. "I just don't see what this has to do with Artie, so I prefer we not talk about him."

"Carly," Dr. Hayes interrupted. "For this therapy to work, you have to discuss everything with Dr. Slovak. You agreed to that. Everything has to be on the table."

Carly nodded. "All right, all right. It's a touchy subject."

"Please continue, Dr. Slovak," Hayes said. "That was a painful time in Carly's life, but it all has to be discussed."

"I'm sure it was," Slovak said, turning his attention back to Carly. "Dr. Hayes informs me that on the day your brother got lost you were watching him."

"Yes."

"Dr. Hayes has also informed me that you blame yourself for his death."

Carly tucked her hair behind her ears. She stared at Slovak saying nothing for a moment. "I was watching him. I should have kept a better eye on him and if I had, he'd be alive today."

Seeing her discomfort, Slovak changed the subject. "Tell me about your memory loss and these images you are seeing."

"I do have memory loss and yes, horrid, awful, images. People being shot and dropping to the ground. It happened again today while I was out by the lake. I don't know if what I see is real or if I'm losing my grip."

"That's why we are here. We need to find out what could be triggering these thoughts. So, do you feel these killings actually happened?"

A line etched between Carly's brows and she paused before answering. "I can't be sure. It seems so real, so vivid. And they leave me feeling scared and knotted up inside. Like I am running for my life."

"Do you know who these people are?"

"That's just it... no faces."

"Do you still get that feeling that someone is watching you?"

Rubbing her moist palms together, Carly struggled to answer. "Not as bad as I used to. When I first got to Holy Oaks, I was afraid of everyone and everything. I was afraid to even go outside or stand in front of a window. I had to take medication daily to keep myself calm. If I didn't, I felt panicked, like I was losing my mind."

"You're not losing your mind, Carly," Slovak assured her. "There is an ability to detect another person's stare. It comes at the fringes of our awareness. Some call it *ESP*. Science calls it *gaze detection*."

"So... maybe I am being watched?" Carly questioned.

Slovak grinned slightly as he shook his head. "I'm not saying that. What I am saying is the brain through evolution developed a mechanism that could sense a stare. It kept us from becoming a predator's prey. This genetic makeup is with us today. If it gets over stimulated, paranoia can set in."

"We use medication to treat this," Dr. Hayes added. "And you no longer are taking any medication."

"Yes," Slovak assured her. "That's why you're here and can do this therapy. If you were on meds, you would not be a candidate for this procedure. Dr. Hayes tells me that he is very pleased with your progress."

Slovak looked at Dr. Hayes who nodded in agreement.

"What I would like to do today is to put you into a semi-relaxed state and find out where your subconscious will go. Sometimes forgotten or repressed experiences can cause emotional wounds that never heal. If we can find and expose the painful memories, then we can treat them and get you well. So, what do you think, Carly? Are you ready?"

"I am," Carly answered, "even if I am scared about what I may find out."

Getting up from the chair and walking to the desk, Slovak grabbed a prepared clipboard of documents, and using a pen as a pointer, showed Carly where to initial. "Ok, Carly. We are going to go over some ground rules. First and foremost, you may stop at any time. Just say STOP and the session will end. Are you comfortable with that word or do you wish to use another one?"

"STOP is good."

"When you say STOP, I will immediately bring you back to the present."

"Also, I will be taping the sessions," Dr. Hayes said, interrupting the conversation. "Are you okay with that?"

Carly nodded her head.

"Good," continued Dr. Slovak. "I would like you to place your legs up on the couch, lean back, and get comfortable. Stephen, will you dim the lights?"

Carly settled into the couch, making herself comfortable. She looked up at Dr. Slovak and then the ceiling. "I'm ready."

"I want you to concentrate on regular deep breathing. As your eyes grow heavy, close them, and allow yourself to become calm. Feel relaxed. Let this feeling flow over you like warm, soothing sunshine."

Slovak stopped talking and leaned back in his chair, never taking his eyes off Carly. He watched as she closed her eyes and began to take deep controlled breaths. Her breathing was slow and deliberate at first but quickly became rhythmic and normal.

Slovak leaned in closer and with a soft voice continued. "Relax your forehead. Let that relaxed feeling spread across your face. Let that feeling flow down your body. Relax your entire body from your chest to your feet. Relax every bone and muscle in your body."

Carly was soon in the deep state that Dr. Slovak wanted.

"I want you to imagine yourself leaving your body through the top of your head. When you have done this, look around you. If you find a path, follow it to see where it may take you."

Carly felt peaceful, content. She was aware of herself, but at the same time felt as though she had left her body.

"I want you to think about that day you lost your brother. Think about Artie and let the memories flow."

Suddenly cast in the awkward years of her adolescence, fifteen-year-old Carly found herself at Ramstein Air Base in Germany. Her father, Colonel Arthur D. Fletcher, was the Chief of the Medical Corps for the Army's Human Resource Command. The family had been living in Germany for almost a year.

Follow the path, Carly. See where it leads.

Within seconds, she was there. On the playground.

Located in the middle of a park was a playground surrounded by a silver 6-foot chain link fence. Lagoons zigzagged their way through the marshy ground spilling into a beautiful lake. The lagoons and tall grasses gave the playground the look of a castle surrounded by its medieval moat.

"I'm at the park," Carly said, and then became silent.

The park was filled with young children, barking dogs, and babysitters of all ages. Gentle breezes swayed flowers back and forth, sending a sweet aroma into the air. With the sun shining on her face and her hair blowing in the breeze, Carly looked at eight-year-old Artie and said, "Little brother, it doesn't get any better than this."

"Hey, Car."

Her best friend approached with two small girls straggling behind.

"Looks like you got your hands full, Emma," Carly said back.

"That's an understatement. Got double duty today. I swear, don't know if my sisters will see their next birthday. Kate is eight, and she thinks she is going on eighteen. Claire is five and feels she should be in charge. I have them until four, and then my mom gets back from work."

Kate and Claire began fidgeting and looking around the playground. "Can we go to the slides and playscape?"

"Sure," Emma answered. "How about you play with Artie. Take the kick ball and go no further than the slides," she continued as they bolted. "I want you to stay within sight of me."

Waiting for the kids to be out of ear shot, Emma turned to Carly and asked, "Did you see that new boy who started yesterday? I heard that he's the son of our new base commander."

"Is he *HOT*? Let me guess, he's got nice buns. I know how you like a nice set of buns." Carly joked.

"I do not!" Emma fired back. "But actually, he does." She grinned. "He reminds me of Justin Bieber!"

"Ooohhh, Justin Bieber. Can't get much hotter than that," Carly said, teasing her. "Maybe you could ask him to the base dance we're having next week."

"I don't even know him. Besides, I'm going with the Frenchman."

"Billy Starnes!?" Carly asked surprised. "Better make sure you triple floss your teeth and bring plenty of mints."

Hearing a dog bark near the kids, Carly turned to search the slides and playscape for Artie. She saw the dog and Claire and Kate, but not Artie.

"I don't see Artie," Carly said. "Where did he go?" Carly hurried away from Emma and to where the two girls were playing. "Claire, where's Artie?"

Claire looked around the playground. "Last time I saw him he was by the bleachers He yelled that he would be back when he got the kickball."

Carly looked at the bleachers. Empty. She ran to the fence where Artie was last seen. Pressing her face against the chain link fence, she saw the abandoned kickball lying on the other side. Her stomach turned.

Emma and the two girls were right behind Carly, following her to the bleachers. "Did he hop the fence?" Emma asked.

Ignoring her friend, Carly bolted to the top of the bleachers, hollering Artie's name. With no sign of him, she jumped over the top of the fence and landed on the grassy perimeter on the other side. As Carly looked out over the wetland, she noticed footprints in the marshy mud. She kicked off her flip-flops and followed them, stepping into each print as she went.

Standing at the edge of the marsh in front of a 10-foot wall of grasses and reeds, she could go no further. The mud had turned to leafy vegetation. Tracks could no longer be seen in the shallow brown water. *Please, God, help me find my brother*!

Parents who were at the park were the first to respond. Base 911 was called and in a matter of minutes, the military police had arrived. The canine unit was brought in and the military dive team headed to the lake. A helicopter joined in the search. The scent the dogs followed, wound its way through the marshy land of beech trees and grasses and ended at the edge of a stream.

Nightfall had come, and there was still no sign of Artie. A small search team remained and continued throughout the night. A full-scale search would resume in the morning.

"I guess we go home now," Carly's mother said, her voice cracking as they watched the emergency vehicles drive away. "We should try to eat something."

Her mother had set the table earlier in the day. They took their places at the table. Her father was not eating, just sipping a bourbon and avoiding her mother's gaze. Carly picked at the food on her plate, trying not to pay attention to Artie's empty place at the table.

Breaking the silence, she broke down. "I'm so sorry, Mom. I should have paid more attention, but I thought it was a safe place with the fence and all."

"Honey, no one is blaming you," she said softly.

"You are wrong, Mom. I'm blaming me!" Carly burst out, pushing her chair back and leaving the table.

Her mom called out after her. "We will find your little brother in the morning, and we will have a good laugh when he shares the night he spent alone in the marsh," she said, making an effort to believe her own words.

The next morning at sunrise Carly was still lying in bed. She had been up for hours, unable to sleep. Hearing sirens, she jumped up and looked out her bedroom window just in time to see a passing ambulance heading in the direction of the lake.

God, please don't let that be Artie, Carly prayed, as she threw on some clothes and rushed out the door.

Arriving at the shore, she found the now silent ambulance along with a group of adults waiting by the docks. Off in the distance, she noticed a military flat boat making its way in. Carly's parents walked through the crowd of adults toward her. Her father's arm was wrapped around her mother who could barely stand on her own. Carly's father guided her mom to where Carly stood and cradled his arms around both of them.

"It's Artie, isn't it?" Carly bawled, burying her face into her father's chest.

Colonel Fletcher remained stoic and self-controlled while Carly and her mother sobbed. His face showed little emotion, and only by looking closely, could one see that in his eyes were traces of tears.

The military flat boat reached the dock, and all three watched as a small plastic body bag carried by two somber military men was loaded onto a gurney and lifted into the waiting ambulance.

Seeing the body bag loaded into the ambulance Carly yelled "STOP!" She then yelled "STOP!" again.

Dr. Slovak gently touched Carly's shoulder and whispered her name. Carly found herself returning from the depths of hypnosis.

Chapter 4

Carly lay on the leather couch without opening her eyes. She was aware of her arms stretched along her sides, and she unclenched her fists to relax her hands.

Dr. Slovak watched as she took slow breaths and low murmurs came from her throat. He was very aware of the distress in Carly's face, and waited until he felt that she had gained control of her emotions and would be able to talk without difficulty. He gently inquired, "What did you see?"

Carly pressed her lips together. It had been a long time since she had seen that day so clearly. "God," she gasped. "I was back at the playground in Germany… on the day that my brother drowned. There were uniformed men and women frantically searching up and down through the marsh. I heard the roar of the helicopter and felt the down draft of the blades."

Carly paused for a moment. "That day was one of the worst in my life. I'll never forget how my mother looked—eyes red from crying, and her white, chalky face… That entire afternoon she aimlessly wandered like a zombie looking for any sign of Artie. Night came and there was still no sign."

Carly sat up on the couch and reached for the necklace around her neck. Opening it, she revealed its contents. "He was a wonderful brother, and I loved him."

Both doctors gazed at the picture of a young boy with brown hair, broad smile, and freckles. "He was my baby doll," Carly said closing the locket.

"Baby doll?" Dr. Slovak asked.

Carly smiled and sighed. "One afternoon my father made a rare, mid-day visit. He said it was sizzling out and to get our suits. We were going to the pool. Artie came running from my bedroom. I had him dressed in my Patty-Play-Pal clothes. She was my favorite doll. Even the black, patent-leather shoes fit him. Not pleased, my dad told me that Artie was not a doll, and if I wanted to play dress up, find some GI Joe military fatigues. He was only two at the time. I called him my Baby doll until he got old enough to complain about it.

"This is the last picture I have of my baby brother. I keep him close to my heart, and I never take it off," she said, her voice breaking. "It was my job to watch him, and I failed."

Lying back on the couch, she closed her eyes, then quickly opened them. A thought had quietly entered her mind, grabbing her attention, forcing her to consider it. In all the years that passed, why had she not seen this before? Mind jumping from one thought to another, she murmured, "Kidnapped? Drowned? Killed? Mr. Etadirhtim."

Dr. Hayes slightly tensed in his chair, edging forward, listening with great attention as Carly rambled and struggled to get her thoughts together.

"Murdered? Kidnapped? Mr. Etadirhtim? asked Dr. Slovak. "What *are* you talking about?"

Carly furrowed her brows, straining to remember what she had seen at the park. The image became clearer. "When I first tried to follow Artie, I was struggling to walk. I remember this sucking sound as my feet pushed through that mud. I began to step into the tracks to make it easier to walk. There was only one set of large tracks," she blurted, raising her voice.

"I'm not following. What does it have to do with Artie?" Slovak asked.

Carly kept talking, more to herself than to Dr. Slovak. "Don't you see?! I was walking in tracks in the mud that were much bigger than mine. My feet fit inside them. Artie's prints would have been much smaller."

Carly's eyes suddenly widened. "Someone else was there. Someone was carrying Artie. What if some son of a bitch killed my brother?" her voice rising with every word. "He needed to ask for Mr. Etadirhtim."

Dr. Slovak raised his eyebrows. "Who is Mr. Etadirhtim?"

"It was the password. My dad was a high-ranking military officer and very busy. He would at times send a driver to pick us up if he was running late. Sometimes we would be driven to the Officers' Club where we'd meet him. Other times we'd just be driven home.

"We were taught if a driver showed up that we'd never met before to ask for the password. My dad would have told the driver the password. If he didn't know it, we wouldn't go with him. Sometimes he would purposely send a driver we never met just to test us. He drilled that name into our heads with this silly rhyming song.

"E is for education; you can never get enough…

"T is for training if you want to get buff…

"A is for active and staying alert…

"You know, it spells out his last name. Etadirhtim. That's so weird, haven't thought-about that in years."

Dr. Hayes sat back in his chair. "Did you get the feeling that your father was paranoid?"

"Now that I think about it, after Artie died, I was never alone in public. It was at this same time my father started taking me to the gun range. We would go super early in the morning and if anyone else was at the range we would leave.

"Carly, in all our talks, you never mentioned shooting a gun." Dr. Hayes said skeptically.

"You think I'm delusional again!" Carly snapped, surprising Dr. Hayes. "I'll prove to you I know how to shoot a gun."

Getting up from the couch, Carly clutched both hands in front of her as if holding a gun. She bent her knees keeping her weight in the front of her stance all the while aiming her index finger out the window. Looking at the doctors, she explained how to fire. "Weight has to be forward or the kick of the recoil will push you back on your feet. Aim the bead at your target and squeeze your finger lightly, never jerking the trigger. Two quick pops, never one." Carly sat back down on the couch then continued.

"The gun was kept in a silver metal case with a combination lock built in. I would see my dad leaving from time to time with the case but never knew what was in it. When we went to the range and he opened it, I realized it was a pistol. We would place sponge earplugs in our ears, load the gun, and practice."

"Did you ask your dad why he was teaching you to shoot?" Dr. Hayes asked.

"Yeah, I did. He said you never know in life when you need to protect yourself. Ninety-nine percent you will never use it. But if that one percent rears its ugly head, put a bullet in it."

"So, he taught you to use a gun shortly after your brother died and you were never alone in public?" Slovak pressed.

"Yes. Ahmed had to be with me wherever I went."

"And who is Ahmed?"

"Ahmed was like my older brother. He was a 22-year-old intern doing his residency at my father's medical facility." A faint smile crossed Carly's tear-stained face. "He always made me laugh. He was one of those guys who was so witty. Once I told him I was cold, and he told me to stand in the corner because it's always 90 degrees there. Things like that. Ahmed stayed with us so much that I really did think of him as my older brother."

Carly paused. "I was curious, though, how he ever got his residency work completed because he spent so much time with me and my folks. I just figured my dad was the boss, and that was that."

"What kind of rapport did Ahmed have with your father?" Slovak inquired.

"It was kind of odd. It seemed more like military protocol than of resident and attending physician."

"Why do you say that?"

"Well, for one thing he was always saying 'Yes, Sir' and 'No, Sir.' Ahmed wasn't in the service. And another thing. He would come over at all times of the day and night to talk with my dad. It would be like ten minutes or so and then he would take off. Always wondered what he was telling him."

"What time at night do you remember him coming over?"

"I remember one summer night, or I should say *morning* when Ahmed just dropped by. It was sometime after 3 and I was up because my back hurt, and I had terrible stomach pains. I heard my father get up and walk down the stairs and out the door. When I looked out, I saw him talking to Ahmed. I didn't feel good, so I didn't think much about it and laid back in bed."

"Hmm, that's interesting," Dr. Slovak said. "Not sure why a resident would come so early to your home to speak with your father when I'm sure there was an attending physician on duty."

"It all changed, though, when he was killed."

"Killed? Ahmed was killed?"

"It was a car accident, or at least that's what my parents told me. I really don't know how he died. Like I said, he was part of the family," Carly's eyes began tearing up. "It was almost too much to handle. It had been less than a year that we lost Artie."

"I am sure the funeral was difficult to endure so soon after losing Artie."

With a quizzical look, Carly continued. "There was no funeral or memorial. When I brought it up to my parents, they said his service was where he grew up. Hundreds of miles away...You would have thought we would have done something. You know, like go to the funeral."

"You would have thought," Dr. Slovak agreed.

"Anyway... I visited my father at the hospital one day and saw Ahmed's car parked in the lot. I know it was his because hanging on the mirror was a cross. I gave it to him one Christmas. He was a Christian. When I told my dad what I had seen, he said I was mistaken and that couldn't have been his car. By the time I left, the car was gone."

"Why, then, did you specify a car accident?"

"My mother. I specifically remember her saying that Ahmed was in a car accident. I left it at that and just figured she had made a mistake or that I misunderstood her."

Slovak turned and looked at Dr. Hayes, then back at Carly. "I think our first session went very well. Let's end it here. I am pleased with the progress we have made. I think it's best that we continue day after tomorrow and start where we left off. It's good to give the mind a rest."

Carly nodded as memories of that day brought back feelings she had suppressed for years. With her stomach in knots and her body numb, she rose from the couch and walked to the waiting room. The doctors followed her. Turning to them she asked, "Could Artie really have been murdered?"

"We can't be sure, Carly," Dr. Hayes said. "We'll talk more."

Totally consumed with her thoughts, Carly left the office. Standing outside the elevator, she pushed the lobby button and waited. Several seconds passed before she heard someone else approaching. It was Dr. Slovak. Motioning with a raised hand to hold the door, he walked briskly toward her.

"Thank you. You miss this elevator and you lose five minutes. I hate waiting for anything."

The elevator was empty except for the two of them. The annoying sounds of metal rubbing against metal could be heard as the elevator made its way down.

"They really need to do something with this elevator. I feel like it could be a death drop at any given moment." Dr. Slovak commented.

Carly smiled and reached inside her parka feeling for her phone. "I can't find my phone," she told Dr. Slovak. "I had it when I came here. It must have dropped out of my pocket. I have to backtrack."

The elevator chimed, announcing the lobby floor. The door began to open, then quickly jerked shut. Slovak pushed the button for the lobby. Nothing happened. "I hate when this happens," he moaned, jabbing his thumb furiously into the open-door button. With open palm, Slovak slapped the door.

Carly jumped. "Should we try the emergency phone?" she asked.

Ignoring her, he continued to jam his thumb into the lobby button. Carly heard the chime and the door opened. Slovak quickly stepped out of the elevator.

"Are you all right, Dr. Slovak?"

"I'm fine," Slovak said, wiping his brow with the sleeve. "See you in a couple of days."

The doors of the elevator closed, and Carly felt the upward motion lifting her to the second floor. *Hope this thing opens up.* She was relieved when the doors burst open without a hitch.

Carly entered the waiting room and saw her phone lying on the carpet under the coat rack. She put the phone in her pocket, and she was almost out of the office when she heard Dr. Hayes either doing dictation or talking with someone from his back office.

"No. She has no clue. She just relived the memories of the death of her brother and now suspects he may have been murdered."

Dr. Hayes paused, listening to someone at the other end of the phone. *"No! She has no idea we know her brother was murdered. Slovak is a pro. He played along as if he was surprised. We are doing another session day after tomorrow. This kind of thing takes time. We are right on schedule."*

Chapter 5

Oh, my God. How could they know? How could they know Artie was murdered? Carly thought as she lifted the scarf over her cheeks and ran back across campus. Entering the cafeteria through a side door of the hospital, she noticed friends sitting at a table, motioning for her to come and join them. "I can't," she mouthed from afar, heading directly to her dorm.

Throwing her parka and scarf on the bed, she headed straight to her bedside drawer and removed a pen and notebook. Hands still numb from the walk, Carly rubbed them vigorously until the sting of the outside cold had waned and the feeling in her hands came back. She then proceeded to scribble what she heard in Dr. Hayes office.

Feeling frustrated, she tossed her notebook to the floor. *I need Meghan to help me sort through this.*

****

Meghan Conner, Carly's closest friend at Holy Oaks, was her confidant. The events of Meghan's troubled life began, she explained to Carly, with the murder/suicide of her father at the hands of her mother. With her only living relative a distant aunt she went to live with her.

From the outside, Lynn and Thomas Brock seemed like a God-fearing, church-going couple. Having no children of their own, they told the congregation about Meghan coming to live with them and how the Good Lord had brought them a child to love and raise.

Psychosis ran in the Conner family and Aunt Lynn was no exception. Blaming Meghan for the death of her brother, she set out to cleanse her.–"The Good Lord came to me in a dream," Lynn told her. "He revealed that I am the instrument to remove the evil that lives inside you. God will set you free."

At first, the "Talks with God," as they put it, only involved Uncle Tom. He would undress fourteen-year-old Meghan and make her kneel at the foot of his bed. She would pray and repent. Each cleansing would end with Meghan remaining on her knees while Uncle Tom stood in front of her untying his terry cloth robe.

Later, Aunt Lynn became part of the cleansing.

With Uncle Tom gone and Aunt Lynn napping, Meghan told Carly, she crept into her aunt's bedroom. Three quick blows to the head turned the white sheets red.

Her state-appointed lawyer argued that she had been physically and sexually abused and feared for her life. If she wanted to kill her aunt she would have used an ax, not a baseball bat.

Meghan Renee Conner was convicted of attempted murder and sent into the juvenile judicial system. Her severe depression and unstable mental health led to a life of being in and out of state hospitals. At the age of 21, she was placed in the adult treatment facility at Holy Oaks. With intense therapy and the proper medication, Meghan felt she was making real progress.

****

Meghan's phone rang. One time. Two times. Three times. *Pick up the phone. Pick up the phone,* Carly thought. *Come on, Meghan. Answer the phone.*

The phone rang the fourth time before Meghan answered. "What's up? Why didn't ya join us for lunch?"

"You've gotta come here right away," Carly said with urgency. "I mean, I need you to come here now. I can't wait. And don't tell anyone else why you have to leave!"

"OK. OK." Meghan said in a low muffled voice. "I'm coming right now."

"Just get here as fast as you can. I'll explain everything."

Meghan stood up looking a little worried, grabbed her half empty lunch tray, and slid out of the booth.

"What's going on, Meghan? Finish your lunch," one of the girls insisted.

"Marsha reminded me that I was supposed to meet her in the chapel. You know, for Bible study. Totally slipped my mind. Got to run… see you tomorrow," Meghan lied.

Knocking on the door and entering at the same time, Meghan rushed in to see Carly frazzled, sitting at the table, and frantically writing. She grabbed both of Carly's hands.

"Stop! Breathe. Chill. You called me. What's going on?"

"I… I think he was murdered and both Hayes and Slovak knew about it."

With a creased forehead, Meghan looked at Carly and said, "What? Slow down. What are you talking about? Who was murdered?"

"Artie. I think Artie was murdered. Yes. Yes," she said, nodding her head. "My little brother didn't drown. He was killed."

"Damn, Girl. You're rambling."

Meghan pulled out a kitchen chair across from Carly and sat on it. "Go ahead," she said as she set her elbows on the table and placed her chin on her clasped hands.

"I had this therapy today…you know, I told you all about it."

"Right…I knew that."

"Well, Dr. Hayes brought in this specialist, this Slovak guy. He hypnotized me and said I should relax and see where my mind would take me. One moment I was in Hayes office and the next I ended up in Germany. I went back to when I was fifteen. I ended up in Ramstein… the day my brother died. I found myself on the playground and then I was in the marsh, standing by the kickball… I saw what I thought were Artie's footprints, but they were too big."

"You're losing me," Meghan said.

"I was having a hard time walking through the mud, so I decided to step into what I thought were Artie's tracks."

"Okay."

"Don't you see?! I was stepping into footprints that were much larger than mine. My feet fit inside them. Artie's prints would have been much smaller."

Meghan's jaw dropped. "Damn! I see what you're saying…someone *had* to be carrying Artie."

"That's exactly what I'm saying. Some son of a bitch killed my brother. It looked like he drowned, but if he did, someone else did it. It wasn't an accident. Someone killed him and left him in the water…like a piece of trash! He was murdered! I realized that when Dr. Slovak brought me back to consciousness and started asking questions about what happened."

"What did Hayes say?"

"He acted interested and surprised. They both did. That's not the worst of it. I left my cell phone in Dr. Hayes office…it fell out of my pocket and when I went back to get it, I heard Hayes talking to someone on the phone. He was talking about me."

"How do you know?"

"Because he was saying 'she' and was discussing my session. I heard him say, 'she had no clue we knew her brother was murdered. Slovak is a pro and played along with it.'"

Carly picked up her notebook. "I wrote down some other things I heard him say."

"Like what?"

"'Tell the team we are on schedule to have the answers by the end of the month.'"

Meghan considered this, then said, "Let's look at this from a different angle. You heard him say that you have no clue. Maybe he was just telling a colleague that you are trying to remember. But at this point, you don't have a clue. That's a possibility."

Carly rubbed her brows. "Yeah, maybe……oh, I don't know."

"And this second thing," Meghan said, "the thing about the answer by the end of the month. Maybe he meant that if you get the right answers and your memory comes back, you'll be able to go home by the end of this month."

"Wouldn't that be awesome," Carly said.

Meghan motioned with her chin towards Carly's notes. "Anything else?"

Carly did one last scan. She checked off each point she wanted to remember and then looked up from her pad. "That's about it. Those memories were vivid."

"I think you better keep what you heard to yourself. If Hayes thinks you're becoming paranoid, he'll never let you out."

Carly nodded. "I agree. I have another session day after tomorrow. Let me see how it goes. I'll keep you posted."

Chapter 6

Driving his Volvo down the winding roads of Northern Oakland County, Slovak yanked the ear bud from his ear. "*Son of a bitch,*" he said aloud then asked Siri to dial Hayes.

"It's a *goddam* good thing we had the room bugged!"

"What are you talking about?" Hayes asked.

"We got a problem. I just listened to a conversation with Carly and some other girl.

"What other girl?"

"Who's that nut job friend of Carly's who bludgeoned her aunt with a bat?"

"Meghan Conner?"

"Yeah, that's her. I just listened to a conversation between the two of them and Carly suspects we know her brother was murdered."

"No way. That's impossible."

"I'm telling you she thinks we knew about it. She heard you talking on the phone. On the way down in the elevator she told me she left her cell phone in the office and was going back to get it. I should've called you. Were you on the phone?"

"Yeah…I called that number you gave me when you left. You told me to. Didn't even know who I was talking to.

"It's better that way. The less *you* know, the better."

"So, what's the big deal?"

"Well, she heard you and now is trying to figure out what's going on. I don't like it. Call her and cancel our next session until we can go over this further."

"What should I tell her?"

"I don't know. Think of something. You're the reason we're in this fucking mess."

"Wrong! You're the reason for this fucking mess… I'll handle it." Hayes ended the call and tossed his phone onto the desk. *What have I gotten myself into?* He paused, then pick up his phone and dialed Carly.

Carly recognized the number as soon as it crossed her phone and her heart began to race. "Hello, Dr. Hayes."

"Hi Carly. I usually don't call patients, but I had to because we need to cancel our session. I apologize, but it totally slipped my mind that I volunteered to chaperone my daughter Savannah Ray's field trip. It's really the only thing I do with her school. I'd hate to miss it."

"No problem," Carly said forcing herself to sound very much at ease. "I'll wait to hear back from you. Meghan will be happy. Now, I can go on that Christmas outing in Welchester."

"That's right," said Dr. Hayes. "The Christmas shopping trip. You and Meghan have worked hard to get to this level of independence. It actually works out better for both of us. I'll get back in touch when I have a new date."

****

What a beautiful crisp morning, Carly thought as she removed one of the large, knobby-tired mountain bikes from the rack and rolled it out of the stable. *First a ride, then a day of shopping.*

Looking over the acres of farmland divided by white wooden fencing she was in awe. "How could one family have owned all this?"

As she stood straddling the bike and adjusting the chin strap on her helmet, she noticed a bronze plaque mounted on the stable door.

Bequeathed to the State of Michigan in 1957 by
Margaret and John Brennen. A Unique Property.
A new home called Holy Oaks.

"This will not be my home for much longer," she said under her breath as she squeezed the hand brakes to test them and gently shoved off. Carly could hear salt crystals crunch under the fat tires as the mountain bike plowed down the asphalt path.

Cabin 2 sat at the edge of a clearing, overlooking a field. The steeple of the clock tower from Welchester University could be seen in the distance rising high above the tree line. Carly peddled to the front of it, squeezed the hand brakes, and put out both feet to stop.

The brakes were sensitive, and the bike shook and pulled violently to the left.

The cabin was tiny. Four wooden steps led to a viewing deck, perfect for deer watching. Two wooden chairs sat against the cabin overlooking the field. A pair of binoculars hung from a leather strap between the two chairs. In a corner was a stack of seasoned firewood covered with a weathered green tarp.

Carly knew that it was here each resident had to prove that they could make it on their own for sixty days. They would cook, clean and live without any help. David had already started his time in cabin 1.

"I'll get in this cabin. I'll make it happen," Carly said to herself. Pulling back the sleeve of her parka, she looked at her watch. *Damn, the bus leaves in 20 minutes.*

As she peddled back, Carly entered a blind curve. Rounding the bend, she saw two deer standing in the middle of it. "Whoa," she yelled as she squeezed the hand brakes. The bike skidded and drifted to the left stopping just short of a tree.

Mama Doe and Baby. "Where were you a couple of days ago when I needed you?" she called out as the two bolted into thicker cover.

Carly dragged the bike away from the tree. She couldn't miss the shopping trip to Welchester.

The Stranger chuckled as he watched her through the binoculars. "You could have broken your neck," he said as the bicycle wobbled and faltered on the way back to the stable.

Chapter 7

The bus was late! Almost 25 residents and personnel wandered around the Gary Jensen lobby waiting for it. Carly and Meghan shared a single chair while they waited.

The girls were outfitted with their backpacks, hospital ID, orange day passes, and phones.

"Do you have much cash on you?" Meghan asked.

"I've got about $75 and $50 on a Visa gift card. I'm hoping to hit some Christmas sales."

Meghan pursed her lips and looked up toward the ceiling, like she was doing calculations in her head. "$75 in cash and a Visa gift card. That should be enough to shop for me, but what about the others on your list?"

Carly groaned, "Santa will bring you exactly what you deserve," she finally answered. "And if you are lucky, he will bring you something you don't deserve!"

"The bus is here," yelled a resident wearing a Santa cap who had been watching out the window.

As soon as Carly stepped outside, she could smell the diesel fumes of the waiting bus. Since she had been at Holy Oaks, she had always liked that smell, equating it with a sense of freedom. The bus was small and had a maximum capacity of 30 passengers. It was used to transport residents to various off campus functions. Climbing the three steps to the deck and stopping, Carly greeted the driver. "Happy Holidays," she said with a smile.

Boarding the bus and nudging Carly from behind, Meghan said, "Go all the way to the back. We can make our shopping plans on the way."

The group was heading to the little village of Welchester. Every year the merchants decorated the Main Street buildings with multi-colored Christmas lights—neon pinks, electric blues, and purples--transforming the village into something that looked straight out of Disney.

Finding an empty seat, the girls sat next to each other.

"Should we eat first or head right to the stores?" Meghan asked.

"Let's shop first. If we wait too long, things may get picked over."

Meghan agreed. "We can shop first, and then go to Dublin's. They have great cheeseburgers and for people watching, it's the best!"

"Almost as good as people watching where we live," Carly said. "They don't call us crazy for nothing!"

Hearing the squeak of the air brakes, the small bus rolled to a stop at the corner of Main and Sixth. Standing and shuffling slowly down the crowded aisle, Carly and Meghan were the last off the bus.

The streets were bustling with shoppers and the familiar melody of "Joy to the World" floated through the air. Carly's heart beat faster as she gazed at shoppers of all ages carrying bulging holiday bags with tissue paper spilling over the top.

"Let's go to Winter's first," Carly said. "I always have good luck there."

As soon as both girls entered the store, they realized that buying anything would take a long time. The sale prices were really good, but the tables that held the gloves and socks were a scrambled mess. Red striped socks and knitted woolen hats were lying on top of leather gloves and soft slippers. One floor clerk worked busily to straighten out an assortment of pajamas while customers came behind her, pulled them out by the stack, and then threw them back onto the table.

Large signs on tables and racks indicated the sale items, and practically the entire store was on sale. Carly found some socks, t-shirts, knitted hats and scented soaps while Meghan picked out pajamas, an alarm clock, lotions, and boxes of chocolates. Their carts were half-filled as they stood in a long check-out line that was not moving very quickly. After checking out, they went outside and stood close to the building, leaning against the brick wall.

"I have a couple of stores I want to shop at yet. Why don't we split up, and meet at Dublin's at 4:00?" Meghan said. "The bus is leaving at 6:00 and we will have plenty of time to eat."

"Sounds good. Dublin's is at Main and Fourth. Right?"

"Yep. Are you good with that?"

"I am. See you at 4:00."

It was 3:45 and Dublin's was four blocks away. Carly weaved in and out like a skier on a slalom course and eventually made it to the

Pub. Meghan was out in front, sitting on a bench when Carly arrived. The girls went inside and stood in line until the hostess came to seat them.

"Merry Christmas, just the two of you?" the hostess asked.

"Yes,…we would like a table by a window, if possible," Meghan said.

Stepping around the yellow caution sign warning of the slippery floor, the two followed the hostess to a table located right in front of a window.

"Enjoy your meal. Your server will be right with you," the hostess said while placing the menus on the table.

Meghan and Carly were enjoying their time together. Their food arrived quickly, and they munched on French fries and devoured Dublin burgers.

"So, Bo really wants a vape?" Meghan asked, somewhat surprised.

"Yep, that's what he told me yesterday. He said he doesn't want to be a bad influence and tempt me to start smoking again once I get out of here."

"That's so sweet. Any guy that would come and visit every week is a keeper."

"I know, right. Sometimes though I get the feeling he is doing it because he feels obligated."

"What da ya mean obligated?"

"Remember I told you how we met when I was a Candy Striper?"

"Yeah. You basically nursed him back to health."

"Right. So now I feel at times he is doing that with me. Just that he is not a hundred percent committed."

"So he's returning the favor," Meghan said. "Least he can do."

Carly shrugged. "Maybe you're right. He's taking me to visit my parents when I get out."

"In Germany?"

"That's what he said. According to Dr. Hayes when I first got admitted to Holy Oaks my parents flew in from Germany. I guess they stayed for a month. My father had used up all his leave, so he had to get back. I don't remember any of it."

"Your dad is a colonel right?"

"Yep. He is the Chief of the Medical Corps for the Army's Human Resource Command. My mom stayed another few weeks, but Dr. Hayes convinced her to go back and join my dad. I really wasn't making progress so why have my mom stay?"

"Wait til she sees you now," Meghan said. "She's not going to believe how much better you are."

"I am pretty much my old self, except for the stuff I can't remember. My mom noticed a change in my letters. She said I was sounding like my old self."

Peering out onto the sidewalk, Carly became silent. A confused look spread over her face.

"Is something wrong?" Meghan asked, puzzled.

Carly looked away from the window and back at Meghan.

"Ahmed? I think I saw Ahmed."

Carly continued to stare out the window, her eyes never leaving the man wearing the stocking hat and long black coat. Surprised by the outburst, Meghan asked… "Ahmed? Isn't he dead?"

Paying no attention, Carly pounded on the glass with her open palm, yelling, "Ahmed! Ahmed! Turn around! Look at me!"

The stranger kept moving and never lost stride.

Forgetting her half-eaten meal, Carly jumped up from the table and rushed down the aisle bumping into a teenage server carrying a heavy tray of food. Annoyed, the server managed to set the tray on the edge of the closest table.

"I'm sorry… I'm sorry," Carly managed to say.

"Wait!" Meghan shouted, ignoring the stares of the people seated around them.

Carly rushed out of the restaurant and zig-zagged between shoppers, pushing her way down the walk.

"Ahmed! It's me… Carly," she called after him.

The stranger stopped and looked then quickly stepped-up his pace. He was getting further and further away when Carly finally stopped. Annoyed shoppers forced to walk around her turned and stared..

As if in slow motion Carly watched the stranger entered the intersection, unaware that the light had changed. The car could not stop. Slick streets from freshly fallen snow allowed for little reaction time. The car hit the stranger. Spider webs of broken glass instantly filled the windshield as he rolled over the hood and dropped to the ground. Carly gasped as he picked himself up and stumbled through the crowd, finally disappearing around a corner.

"Let me through. Please, let me through," Carly pleaded, using her elbows to push people to the side as she tried to slide through the tight crowd. "I have to find him."

Stunned observers stood shoulder to shoulder watching the driver get out of his car and search for the person he hit. "Where is the guy? Is he okay?" a young male driver asked, scanning the crowd. "Anybody see where he went?"

Desperately trying to maneuver, Carly felt strong hands on her shoulders.

"Miss... settle down," the ruddy-faced officer warned. "You can't be shoving and pushing people around." Removing his hands from her shoulders, he said, "Do you know that guy?"

"I think I might," she answered.

"Wait here," he ordered.

Carly read the name "Thompson" on his uniform, but her eyes narrowed as she studied his pistols. *A Glock 17 and a taser?*

"I need an ambulance at Sixth and Main," Officer Thompson talked into the mic attached to his shoulder. "Possible pedestrian hit with vehicle."

Four police cars showed up and rerouted traffic. Captain Starzeckie exited his squad car, but left it running. Squeezed into a uniform that fit many pounds ago, he surveyed the entire scene, eyes noting the damaged car, the driver, and all the commotion.

"Hey, Captain," Officer Thomson called. "When you get a minute."

Captain Starzeckie approached, "What do you got, Thompson?"

"Captain, this is Mr. Stafford. He saw everything. I've already taken his statement."

Looking at the gentlemen dressed in snowmobile bibs and boots, he pulled a small notebook and pen from his pocket.

"Mr. Stafford, I am Captain Starzeckie. Can you repeat what you told Officer Thompson?"

"Sure...it was the craziest thing. I was walking down the sidewalk just in front of Gilman's Sporting Shop and was thinking about buying a snowboard. I was just about to go into the store when I saw this guy get hit. No way that car could stop. It hit the guy, knocked him over the hood and then to the ground. What's crazy is he got up and staggered away, like some kind of stunt man. Scared the hell out of me."

"A stunt man?" the Captain asked, scribbling notes in his notepad.

"You know…he knew how to take a hit…like a stunt man…like he was trained. He actually stumbled at first, but then kept going."

"So, he might be hurt?"

"Maybe. How do you flip up onto a car, break a windshield, then run away? I've seen deer do it, but never a guy."

"Mr. Stafford, I appreciate your time. Officer Thompson has your statement, and we will get in touch if need be."

"You got it," the witness said as he bent over, grabbed the twine handles of his Christmas bags, and went on his way.

Pointing in the direction of Carly standing in the exact spot she was ordered, Officer Thomson said, "See that girl. She was chasing the guy."

Captain Starzeckie saw Carly, her arms crisscrossed over each shoulder, shivering with no coat. "Did you say she was running after the guy that got hit?"

"Yes Sir. Saw it myself."

"Well then, let's go have a chit-chat. Go to the squad car and get her a blanket."

As the Captain came upon Carly he said, "You look like you're freezing. I sent one of my officers to get you a blanket."

"Thank you," Carly said. "I am freezing."

"My name is Captain Starzeckie…and yours?"

"Carly…Carly Fletcher."

"So, Ms. Fletcher…you were chasing the guy that got hit. How do you know him?"

"I don't for sure…I thought it was an old friend, so I was trying to catch up to him."

"So, you're not sure if you even know him?"

"No, not really…thought he might be a friend from Germany."

"Germany?" Starzeckie said, curious for her to continue.

"Yeah, my dad was military…we were stationed there."

Before Carly could say another word, Meghan rushed up to her.

"Are you all right? What happened?" she said. "I've been trying to get to you, but the cops wouldn't let anyone past Fourth Street."

Irritated, Captain Starzeckie spoke. "Ma'am, would you let us continue? You can talk to your friend when I am done with her. Go over by the squad car and wait there."

Officer Thompson returned and handed the blanket to Carly. She wrapped it over her shoulders and thanked him. A tow truck slowly made its way to the damaged vehicle. The car was hoisted onto a waiting flatbed and traffic began to flow as normal. Thompson informed the ambulance driver that she was no longer needed and walked back to where Carly and the captain were talking.

"Anything new?" Captain Starzeckie asked turning to Officer Thompson, interrupting his conversation with Carly.

"Not really, Captain. No blood. The only thing I found was this gold cross," he said, holding it out and letting it dangle from the chain. "Don't even know if it was his."

Carly's eyes opened wide.

Captain Starzeckie took the cross and examined it. "Might have been the thing that saved his life, being a Christian and all." Handing it back to Officer Thompson he said, "Put it in the evidence room… see if anyone claims it."

Turning back to Carly, Captain Starzeckie continued. "You say your dad was in the military, and you lived in Germany?"

Carly adjusted the blanket and was about to answer when Captain Starzeckie lifted his hand signaling Carly not to speak. He turned up the volume on his mic. "Be advised…two females ran from the Dublin's restaurant at the corner of Fourth and Main. They did not pay for their meal. The two females are Caucasian and look to be in their early 20's. One of the suspects ran leaving her purse and coat."

The Captain gave Carly a look that made her feel like a criminal, then motioned for Officer Thomson to follow him out of earshot.

He spoke to him in a low voice. "This kid doesn't seem all together. Find out what happened at Dublin's. I'm heading back to the station. I think you can handle these ladies."

Officer Thompson gestured for Meghan to come and stand next to Carly.

"So, you ladies think it's all right to eat at a restaurant and leave without paying? You think you can just go into a restaurant, order a meal, and leave?"

Feeling desperate, Meghan tearfully answered, "We'll pay. We need to get our stuff back from Dublin's. We both have the money. Just let us go back."

"Where do you live?" Officer Thomson asked thinking this was more of a pain then what it was worth. "Do you have any ID?"

"We are residents at Holy Oaks, and we were on a shopping outing," Meghan said.

Letting out a big sigh, Officer Thompson turned to Carly, "Who is your doctor at Holy Oak's?"

"Dr. Hayes. But please don't..."

Thompson held up his hand and turned away. He radioed dispatch. "Call Holy Oaks and tell them to send someone to the station to pick up a couple of female residents. Ask for Hayes. Tell him they stirred up some trouble in the downtown district."

Still shivering under the blanket, Carly looked at Officer Thompson.

"Turn around Ms. and put your hands behind your back. I'll cover you back up once you're in the squad car."

Thompson removed the blanket from Carly's shoulders and took hold of one of her tiny wrists. He paused and handed the blanket back. "Just get in the back, both of you." Surprised, she turned slightly, and said, "Thank you."

After placing both girls in the squad car and before closing the door, Officer Thompson bent down and said, "We're going back to Dublin's to get your things. You'd be smart if you even up your bill."

Once in front of Dublin's, Officer Thompson accompanied the girls into the restaurant. They paid for their lunch, and then were led back out to the police cruiser parked at the curb. The ride to Dublin's and then to the police station was humiliating and embarrassing as people on the street gawked at them as they passed by. In the station, the girls sat on a detention bench next to the officer on duty.

"The guy I was chasing who I thought was Ahmed got hit by a car and kept running," Carly told Meghan. Moving closer, she leaned in and whispered, "Don't you think that's weird? Why wouldn't the guy stick around. If I got hit, I'd want to know who hit me. What's more bizarre is they found a gold cross that they think was the runner's, and it looks like the cross I gave to Ahmad in Germany."

"So, no blood or anything? Just the cross?"

"Yeah," Carly said just as Dr. Hayes entered the station and headed directly to the front desk. He glared at both girls, saying nothing.

"Hello, Officer. I am Dr. Hayes from Holy Oaks. I came to get the girls. Can you tell me what happened?"

Filing through the police reports issued that day the office removed the one pertaining to the girls and read it silently. “Looks like one of the girls ran out on her bill at a restaurant called Dublin’s. According to the report, she claims she was trying to catch up with some old acquaintance she saw walking down the block. The acquaintance wouldn’t stop and entered an intersection where he got hit by a car. He then got up and ran away. Sounds a little odd to me but that’s her story. That’s the reason she ran out without paying her bill. The manager of Dublin’s called, and they aren’t going to press charges. The girls went back and paid their bill.”

“Thank you, Officer. May I take them?”

“All yours. Happy Holidays.”

Chapter 8

The ride back to Holy Oaks was uncomfortably silent. Both girls sat in the back seat looking out the window and saying nothing. *I blew it. There's no chance of me going home anytime soon,* Carly thought.

After a couple minutes, Dr. Hayes looked into the rearview mirror and asked, "Is there something either one of you want to say?"

Carly and Meghan looked at each other.

"Come on girls," Dr. Hayes said raising his voice. "Which one of you ran out on your bill."

"I thought..." Carly began to say before Meghan kicked her foot and leaned forward.

"It was me, Dr. Hayes," Meghan confessed. "I'm the one that ran out of the restaurant without paying."

"You!" asked Dr. Hayes skeptically.

"I thought I saw my dad...I know that's crazy; I know he's gone."

"Well, if you know he's no longer with us, why would you run after a stranger?" Dr. Hayes asked with hint of sarcasm in his voice.

"You're going to be mad at me, but I haven't been taking my meds for a few days," Meghan continued with her lies. "I thought I could handle it, but I started having these weird thoughts at lunch, and before I knew it, I was on the street running after that guy."

Dr. Hayes shook his head slowly as he looked at Meghan in his rear-view mirror.

"You have to stay on your medication, Meghan. That's what keeps you from having thoughts like those. We'll have to discuss this further. Come in tomorrow morning. Part of your recovery plan involves you being responsible to take your medication."

Looking at Carly with a half-smile and sitting back in the car, Meghan answered, "Absolutely, Dr. Hayes... whatever you want."

Dr. Hayes gripped the steering wheel as he steered the Cadillac down the snow-covered road to Holy Oaks. Without warning, two deer darted from a ditch onto the road in front of the car. They stopped, paralyzed by the mesmerizing light. Hayes slammed on the brakes slowing the car and stopping it. Eyes glowed green while the deer stared at the car. Then, with a flick of their tails, they leaped off the road into the bordering brush and pine trees and disappeared.

Mama deer and her baby, Carly thought as Dr. Hayes continued his slow drive to the hospital. Driving past the horse stables and up to the main entrance, he placed the vehicle in park and left the engine running. Instead of speaking, he merely moved his head to the left letting the girls know to get out of the car. Both girls grabbed their backpacks and bags and headed out into the cold. Their breath rose into the air. "Thank you, Dr. Hayes," each one said.

Rolling his window down, Dr. Hayes said, "See you tomorrow morning in my office, Meghan."

"Yes, I'll be there," she replied.

As soon at Hayes drove out of site, Carly turned to Meghan. "Why'd you do that? I mean you can get more time."

"You're so close to heading to the cabins. That could mean you would be out in 60 days. What happened today in Welchester would have set you back at least six months." Then half-laughing, she added, "As for me, they may never let this *crazy bitch* back on the streets."

"I owe you a ton. Let's go back to my room and we can talk."

"Better yet, let's go back to mine," Meghan said. "Just bought some new teas. I'll make us a cup and you can tell me why you're chasing dead people."

Meghan unlocked the door to her tiny room and stepped back.

"Guests first," she said and followed Carly into the room. They placed their bags on the couch and stripped off their heavy winter garb. Feeling in one of the bags, Meghan removed two tins and asked, "Gentle Night or Diamond Black… these are the two teas I bought."

"After what went on today…I'll take the Gentle Night," Carly laughed as she walked up to the table, pulled out a chair, and sat.

Tossing the unopened teabags to Carly, Meghan grabbed two cups, filled each with water, and placed them into the microwave. She reached in a drawer and removed two packets of sugar and a spoon, setting them into the middle of the table.

"Who is this Ahmed guy again? Meghan asked. "I know we've talked about him."

"He was like the big brother I never had."

The bell of the microwave went off and Meghan grabbed both cups of steaming water and placed one in front of Carly. Taking a seat across from to her, she dropped the teabag into her cup and said, "Continue."

"I could have sworn it was him, but it couldn't be. My father told me that he had been killed in an accident. My mom told me it was a car accident. But it wasn't. I saw his car and when I asked my dad about it, he said I was mistaken. Ahmed never had a funeral or at least I never went to one."

"So, you never saw this guy in a casket?"

"Nope. Never. Nothing was ever said about a funeral or memorial. Just sort of thought my parents didn't want me to deal with any more trauma. He was killed shortly after everything with Artie. He was a resident at my father's hospital while we were stationed in Germany. My father really took a liking to him, and he became part of the family."

"So, if the guy is dead, why do you think it was him?"

Shaking her head with no real answer Carly said, "Not sure; just thought it was him. My heart did that leaping in my chest when I saw him and every bit of me believed it was him. But …then that chain. I gave him a gold cross with a chain just like the one that cop was holding."

Carly appeared puzzled. "And, this is another weird thing, I brought him up in my hypnosis session."

"You did? Why did he come up?"

"Well, after the drowning, I was never allowed to go out in public by myself. Come to think of it, my mother was never allowed to go out by herself either. We had to be either with my dad or Ahmed. It was like he was my bodyguard."

"Bodyguard? You know something Carly? Ever since you started this hypnosis stuff you've had some real crazy ass thoughts."

"Careful who you're calling crazy. I'm not the one who has to go explain to Dr. Hayes that I see dead people."

Meghan dipped her teabag in and out of the steaming water. Always looking for a logical explanation, she said, "Ahmed was probably on your mind from the session with Dr. Hayes, and you just let it get the better of you."

"But, what about the chain?"

"There are thousands of chains like that, I have one myself. I really think this hypnosis thing has got you 'weirded out.'"

"You're probably right. Just a knee jerk reaction."

"You want to talk about a knee-jerk reaction? What about me telling Hayes I thought I saw my dead father. Maybe I'll be lucky to get only six months tacked on to my stay. It could be more!"

"I hope not," Carly said, taking a few steps to the sink. "Hope it doesn't get too heated between you and Hayes. I really feel awful about this."

"Don't sweat it. You didn't make me do it. I just wanted to help the best friend I've ever had."

"You have," Carly said. "You really have."

Chapter 9

Holding the banister with both hands, the stranger hobbled up the stairs of his rented townhouse. Fumbling through his coat and then his pants, he could not find his keys. *Damn, where the hell are they*? Finally, he felt the cold metallic cluster deep inside his coat pocket. Opening the door, the warmth felt good as he limped into the kitchen and tossed the keys onto the table. *No broken bones,* he convinced himself as he proceeded to take the stocking hat from his head and toss it next to the keys. He pulled out a kitchen chair, unbuttoned his long wool coat, and placed it on the back. Lifting his sore knee onto the chair with both hands, he rubbed his calf up and down before reaching and removing his gun from the ankle holster. Placing the pistol into his front waistband, he proceeded to the bathroom where he drew a hot bath. The stranger was never without a gun.

****

When her clock chimed 7:00 a.m., she smacked the snooze alarm and flopped back onto the mattress. Blue flannel sheets lay twisted back and forth in a letter "S". Carly placed both hands on her stomach, quieting the nausea that twisted and turned. Uncontrolled thoughts jumped haphazardly in her brain. *Will Meghan get more time? Could that really have been Ahmed? What will the next hypnosis session be like?*

She let her legs drop to the floor and forced herself out of bed. Shuffling her way to the kitchen, she placed a pod of flavored coffee in its cradle and snapped the unit closed. Water trickling through the coffeemaker gurgled, bubbled, and swished its way into her cup. *Caramelito. Love at first sip.*

Making her way to the bathroom, her eyes widened as the mirror revealed her appearance. Streaks of mascara smudged her cheeks.

Long brown hair hung in separate clumps as if she had come out of the shower instead of being ready to go into it.

"I look like a freak," Carly whispered to herself as she set her Caramelito on the ceramic sink. She took the cold cream from the shelf and massaged a gob onto an eyelid. She removed the black smear with a Kleenex and proceeded to the next. The mixing handles squeaked as she adjusted the temperature of the shower. Carefully stepping over the tub ledge and pulling the plastic curtain, she eased her way into the warm deluge.

****

Carly entered the cafeteria and grabbed a tray from the rack. She placed a warm plate and coffee mug on the tray and slid it along the stainless-steel track. Surveying the breakfast bar, stomach still queasy, she placed one strip of bacon and a scoop of scrambled eggs on her plate before heading to her usual table.

Oh shit. Carly thought when the only one sitting at the table was Sally. "What's up? Ya on a diet?" she, asked, proceeding to move her cell phone and purse, making room for Carly's tray. "No French toast this time?"

"No. Just not that hungry," Carly said, as she slid the tray onto the table and pulled out a–pink plastic chair. "Where's everyone this morning? It's pretty deserted around here."

"I'm thinking therapy or community service," Sally said, proceeding to cut her fried eggs and mix the yellow yolk into her hash browns. "I've been sitting here by myself the whole time."

Carly looked at the gooey mess of egg yolk and potatoes and turned her eyes away from Sally's dish. She pushed her tray to the center of the table. As if a sign from heaven, a text came over Carly's cell, allowing her to avoid interacting with Sally.

"GOOD NEWS! Where are you?" Meghan wrote.

"Cafeteria."

"See you in two."

Carly tapped on the Welchester Post App looking for anything about the accident. It was the first story.

Pedestrian Hit by Motorist and Then Flees

By Mary Beth Meldon

Deputies from the Welchester's Police Department responded to a 911 call at 5:35 p.m. Saturday reporting a pedestrian hit by a motor vehicle. The caller reported seeing a white male hit at the corner of Sixth and Main. According to the caller, the man was hit by a sedan, landed onto the windshield and then rolled off the hood. The pedestrian fled from the scene, presumably unscathed. Welchester PD is asking for your help. If anyone has information as to the pedestrian, please contact the department.

"Hey, there's Meghan," Sally said, causing Carly to look from her phone.

"What's the good news?" Carly asked, as Meghan pulled out a chair and scooted up next to them.

"Well, after you left my place, I got a call from Dr. Hayes. He decided we didn't need a meeting since no one was pressing charges. He felt we could discuss this over the phone."

"Lord," Sally interrupted. "What did your crazy ass do now?"

"Excuse me!" Meghan snapped at her. "I don't think I'm talking to you."

An awkward silence fell over the table.

Standing up from the table, Sally gave Meghan a derisive smile. "Aren't we the bitch this morning?" she said as she abruptly grabbed her tray and proceeded to leave.

They watched as Sally walked to the conveyer belt and returned her tray. She grabbed the apple that was on it and dropped it in her purse. Ignoring them, she proceeded to the cafeteria door, her brown leather boots clicking on the tile floor as she had left the room.

Eyes wide open, Carly turned to Meghan and said, "Well, that was awkward. I really wish you would quit messing with her."

"I can't stand a busy-body. She's always up in people's business and butts in on conversations that have nothing to do with her."

"That's just the way she is. Enough with Sally. Why no meeting?" Carly quickly asked.

"Because I'm brilliant," Meghan proudly said, feeling a little devious. "That's why."

"Brilliant?"

"I sort of got a feeling he thought there was more to the story than we told him. I think he was just going along with it, letting me take the blame."

"Did he give you more time?"

"He was easy on me. No off-campus activities for one month. I told him the reason I didn't take my meds was because of him."

"Him? What's that mean?" Carly asked, taking a bite of her bacon.

"I told him that the sessions with him have been so awesome and made me feel so good that I didn't think I needed the medication anymore."

"And *he* believed you?" Carly said incredulously. "You're such a good liar!"

"I know he loves to hear praise, so that's what I did. I also told him that I didn't think I would have come this far without him."

Carly paused, then said, "Thanks again for taking the blame. You know if Hayes thought it was me running after a dead person, this *would* be my permanent residence. He'd never let me out."

"I can't let that happen. Ever since I met you, I feel I have a future."

Touching Meghan's hand across the table. Carly looked at her and said, "We do have a future. We talked about this. You'll come and live with me."

"That's what's keeping me going."

A text came in over Carly's phone.

Meghan watched as Carly's eyebrows raised and she read the message. "It's Dr. Hayes. He wants to do another session early this evening when he gets back from his fieldtrip with Savannah Ray."

Concerned, Meghan asked, "Are you ready for this? I mean you can't let on what you overheard."

"I know. I am not sure what I'll say once I'm hypnotized. I guess we'll find out."

"Well… text him back. Tell him you'll be there," Meghan said reassuringly. "What time?"

"Five."

"Go in there and act like you know nothing. Play the game, Carly…isn't that what you always tell David? Just play the game and…"

"…you'll get out of here," Carly finished. "I know that's what I say. But this feels different."

"What do you mean, *feels different*?"

"You know, like it's not a game. It feels *more* than that."

"I had that feeling, too," Meghan admitted. "But I was afraid to bring it up."

Carly rested her face on her hand. "Yeah, I didn't want to bring it up either. I guess we won't know until I go back under."

Meghan looked at her watch. "You've got about seven hours until your appointment. Try to stay positive and keep your mind off of it."

Carly gave a half smile, "Easier said than done."

Chapter 10

Hayes had already been at the office for over an hour when Slovak arrived.

"Morning, Alex. There's fresh coffee."

Slovak walked straight to the hutch without saying a word. He poured himself a cup of coffee. Grabbing three packs of sugar and flipping them between his fingers, he opened them one by one and added them to his morning brew. Stirring his confection laden drink, he looked up from his cup and said, "Seems like we have a slight problem, Stephen. Any ideas?"

"I've been thinking. Let's be proactive at Carly's next session. We'll let her know that during her last hypnosis that she, though confused, mentioned that she thought Artie had been murdered. We'll tell her that we already knew. This way we can get in front of her suspicions and ease her mind about what she heard me saying."

Slovak tossed the tiny red straw into the can beside the hutch and took a cautious sip. "I like it. Let's get ahead of it. Can we get her here this afternoon?"

"I already scheduled a session late this afternoon. I told her the field trip with Savannah Ray was going to end early, and I wanted to keep going since we had such a good start."

Nodding in agreement Slovak said, "You know something, Stephen? We may just get out of this alive."

****

When Carly entered the office, she saw Dr. Slovak wearing the same wrinkled khaki pants he wore the day before. Even the vest he wore had deep wrinkles.

"Come in. Come in, Carly. We were just discussing today's session."

Dr. Hayes took her parka and gloves, acting like the shopping trip and visit to the police station had never happened.

"Cell phone turned off?" Dr. Hayes asked.

"Yep. Made sure before I came in."

Dr. Hayes gestured to the unoccupied chair next to Dr. Slovak. "Please, Carly. Have a seat."

"You look well, Carly," Dr. Slovak remarked as she walked to the chair.

Though her stomach was knotted, she kept calm. "I'm feeling pretty good."

"I was very impressed with all the details you remembered a couple of days ago. I'm sorry that there is the possibility that your brother did not just drown, but that he may have been murdered."

Carly's heart wrenched as she forced a reply. "I'm dealing with it. Not easy, but I'm dealing with it."

"You know Carly, it did not surprise me that during our discussion after the hypnosis that you felt Artie had been murdered."

"Why not?"

"Because I already knew."

Carly's face became flushed. Her eyes pinned to his. "How's that possible?"

"You see, my dear, when you were telling us about losing Artie at the playground, you shared placing your feet inside the tracks you were following. Does that ring a bell?"

"Yes."

"I suspected there was more to the drowning than it being an accident. My job as a therapist is not to put things into your mind because it may influence you. I need to let you find the answers and come up with your own conclusions."

"Is that why you acted surprised when I realized Artie was murdered?"

"Exactly! I had to let you discover that, not me inferring it for you."

The furrows in Carly's forehead disappeared, and she sighed.

"Shall we continue?" Dr. Hayes asked.

"Yes. I want to know what happened to me."

Slovak grabbed his notepad that was tucked in the side of the armchair and scanned his notes. A slight pause occurred as his index finger ran down the list until he stopped at a highlighted name; Bo. "Dr. Hayes informs me that you have a boyfriend and his name is Bo."

"Yes. We have a place together in Corktown."

"We thought it might be good for you to go back to the time you first met Bo. Dr. Hayes tells me he was a wounded vet and that you met him at Walter Reed Medical Center."

"Yes, that's right. I was a Candy Striper. It was a very emotional time in my life working with the wounded vets. A lot of highs and lows."

"That's what we want," Dr. Slovak said enthusiastically. "Emotional feelings. Raw feelings."

"I certainly have memories of Walter Reed."

"Perfect! Let's get started. If you will go and lie on the couch?"

Carly unfolded her hands and got up from the chair. Dr. Hayes dimmed the lights as she lay down on the couch.

"Like before, I want you to focus on the soft white light above your head. Dr. Hayes, would you start the recording?

"We are going to go back to the time you worked at the hospital and met Bo. Remember, Carly if at any time you feel the session is getting too intense or painful, you can end the session by saying STOP, and I will bring you out of the hypnosis."

"Yes, I know," Carly acknowledged.

"Focus on the soft white light, then close your eyes. Continue to take deep breaths. Relax and feel that relaxation move slowly down your body."

Dr. Slovak's soft voice relaxed Carly and moved her deeply into hypnosis. Her mind became quiet and soon she was at Walter Reed Medical Center.

Chapter 11

"One of your patients is named Bo Harris," the head nurse informed Carly. "He can be a handful. There are times he becomes really anxious and has episodes of anger. Fighting some kind of demon, I suppose."

"Is he violent?" Carly asked.

"He's never threatened staff or indicated that he wanted to. But he has punched holes in the walls of his room. Bo came from a small town from northern Michigan called Grayling. He was a star player on the football team and led them to a state championship. He was a canine handler in the Corp and was injured in the Iraq war when his humvee hit a mine. He was the only survivor. The battle trauma caused hysterical blindness from which he has since recovered."

Carly looked down at the yellow pad she had scribbled notes on and then back at Nurse Harrington. "I think I got it. I just feel so bad for him."

"Can I give you some advice?"

"Sure."

"Try not to get too emotionally involved. It'll affect your care. These vets need us so much that we have to keep our distance and take care of ourselves. If you don't, you won't last a month."

Taking a deep breath, Carly grabbed her drink and magazine cart, pressed the lever with her foot, releasing the locking wheel and headed to Bo's room. Parking her cart just inside the door, Carly smelled fresh drywall paste and noticed numerous patched spots on the walls. Sitting in the only chair staring at a blank TV screen was Bo.

"Hey," Carly said.

Bo turned, looked at Carly, and said nothing, staring at her in silence, no emotion on his face.

Carly summoned the courage and asked, "Would you like a magazine?" as she held up two *Sports Illustrated.*

As if being insulted, Bo barked, "How the fuck you think I am going to read? I can't even remember my A, B, C's?" He then turned away from Carly and mumbled, "dumb bitch."

Visibly shaken, Carly regained her composure and continued the conversation. "Would you rather have some music? I have a lot to choose from."

Bo said nothing. He kept staring at the blank TV screen and ignored her.

Giving up for the day, Carly bent to push the cart, but it wouldn't budge. In her haste she had forgotten to the release the locking wheel. Realizing this she tapped the pedal and released the brake, then headed to the door. With her guts twisting in her belly, she stopped and said, "I come every Monday, Wednesday, and Friday. See you day after tomorrow."

Every Monday, Wednesday, and Friday was the same. "It's me again," Carly would say in a sing song voice, as she entered Bo's room. She would freshen his water, make his bed, and replace the magazines he did not read. His tortured look staring at that blank TV screen made Carly feel bad for all the wounded vets who returned from the war so broken.

Carly was in her second month at Walter Reed when after filling his water glass she heard something that surprised her.

"Thank you," Bo barely uttered, looking at the floor.

Carly straightened up and looked at him. "It's about time you noticed me. I get hit on all the time by the other vets, and I was starting to think you were gay."

Bo cracked a half smile and told her that since his accident he couldn't remember if he was straight or gay. For the first time, laughter spilled out into the hallway.

"Would you like me to read a *Sport Illustrated* magazine to you?" Carly asked. "I heard you were quite the football player in high school."

After a few seconds of struggling to comprehend the question, Bo said in a low voice, "No one's read to me in a long while. You have any of those books with finger puppets, like that Hungry Caterpillar book?"

Caught off guard by his response, Carly began to laugh.

"It wasn't *that* funny," Bo murmured, even though he felt some enjoyment in making her laugh.

"No, it certainly wasn't," Carly answered, a bright look on her face. "I wouldn't take your show on the road yet."

There was only one chair in the tiny room and Bo was sitting on it. Carly jumped onto the bed, fluffed the pillow, then motioned for Bo to join her. With a surprised look, Bo remained in his chair.

"Oh c'mon," Carly's prodded. "Sit next to me, I don't bite."

Standing up from his chair and tying his robe, he succumbed to her request and dragged the chair next to the bed.

"I never get in bed with a girl on the first date. My daddy raised a gentleman," Bo said smiling.

Through the hospital's rehabilitation program, Bo changed. He took daily showers and worked–out three days a week. The medication she reminded him to take was gradually being reduced. His physical appearance improved as he regained his muscle and strength. As if the planets were aligning in heaven, Bo's brain started making connections. He could recognize letters which blended into words. Words blended into sentences. Sentences bringing meaning to life.

"I am starting to recognize letters and words," he said to her one day. "I'm figuring out patterns the sentences are making. Memories are coming back, and life is making sense again!"

"I knew you would," Carly assured him. "I just didn't know how long it would take."

Bo pulled a chain from around his neck. It was the dog tag of his fallen canine. As proud as a four-year-old reading his first book aloud, he began... "I am Max, and I am a Warrior," the brail embossed graphics said. Bo wore this around his neck and never took it off. He told Carly that a military working dog was considered an (NCO) Non-Commissioned Officer. It was this tradition that kept canine handlers from mistreating their dogs because the dog was always of a higher rank. Rank did not matter to Bo; he loved his beautiful black and white Belgian sheep dog and would never have mistreated him.

Carly and Bo became close. Any free time she had would be spent in Bo's room. They would eat lunch and play board games. They would sit on the edge of his bed, knees touching, while Bo would read to her. On this particular day, in the middle of a paragraph Bo stopped and looked up from the page.

"What? What's wrong?" Carly asked.

"I can't stand this numbness in my heart," a tortured look crossed Bo's face. "Why did I live and all my boys, including Max, did not? Without you, I would have given up long ago. I almost did give up," Bo added, thinking about the plan he had to end his life.

Bo reached and hugged Carly. Carly placed her arm over Bo's shoulder and the two kissed.

"Would you like to talk about it? Sometimes it helps."

"I miss the guys, and I miss Max. He was such a good dog, and I loved him," Bo said, his voice cracking. Grabbing the chain from underneath his shirt, he let it dangle.

"I will never take off this tag. This is the only memory I have of him, and I'll keep it forever."

"It's okay," Carly murmured. "Your feelings are natural, and I am glad you are sharing them with me. I can't even imagine what you went through. But I do know that we will get through this together."

Taking Bo's face with both hands and looking directly into his eyes, Carly said, "Don't ever give up. I feel what you are going through."

Pulling the gold locket from under her smock, Carly showed it to Bo. "I have this picture of my little brother Artie. He drowned when he was eight. It's the last happy memory I have of him, and I never take it off. You'll never forget your men or Max, and I will never forget Artie, but as time passes the hurt will get easier," Carly promised.

"It's already easier since I've found you," Bo answered. "The doctors are saying that I'm close to getting discharged."

"That's fantastic. Where are you going to go?"

"Home, I guess. Back to Michigan. I really don't want to be a farmer, but I don't know much else."

"What about school?" Carly asked.

"Never thought about it. Not sure I could get through it."

"I could help you. I have been thinking about what I'm going to do. Detroit has a great university. We could become hipsters and go to Wayne State."

"Are you being serious or just messing with me?"

Carly smiled. "I'm not messing with you. Think about it. I've been here for almost a year. I think we know each other pretty well."

"We do Carly, we really do." Bo said affectionately. "I know you better than any other woman in my life. Well, next to my mum that is."

"Your mum," Carly chuckled. "I've heard you say that before. Is your *mum* English?"

"No. That's just what my brother and I always called her."

"Well I think that's cute…so is that a yes? Are we gonna live together?"

"Will you take care of me like you do here? If so, hell yeah!"

Carly gave Bo a peck on the cheek. "You take care of me and I'll take care of you. We'll be a team."

"Deal." Bo said, never taking his eyes off her as she walked out of the room.

Chapter 12

It was midnight and Bo was tossing and turning, unable to sleep. His mind raced with the anxiety and anticipation of his discharge. Worried about the impending packing he still needed to do, Bo got out of bed, put on a shirt, and grabbed his old duffle bag from the closet. Kneeling on his hospital room floor shoving socks and clothes into the tattered bag, Bo heard someone outside his hospital room door.

"Who's there?" Bo asked, hoping it wasn't a nurse coming to take some blood or bringing papers for him to sign.

The latch of the door handle turned, and Bo noticed the thin silhouettes of red stilettos just outside his door. Carly walked in slow and sexy, with her index finger over her puckered lips, indicating not to make a sound. She held a cloth bag in her other hand. With a long wool trench coat skimming her body and hair pinned high atop her head, she made her way to the nightstand.

Carly turned to Bo, raised her hand, and released the clip that was holding her hair. Shaking her head slowly, her hair fell into disheveled strands of curls, Carly looked at Bo and said nothing. She reached into the bag and removed two lavender candles, lit them, then walked to Bo. The glow of the candles and the scent of the lavender transformed the dingy hospital room into a romantic getaway. The flickering candlelight accented her delicate features as she slowly unbuttoned her coat exposing her smooth silky skin. The coat slid to the floor, leaving Carly wearing nothing but her locket, Chanel, and four-inch red stilettos.

"Surprise, Baby," Carly said.

Bo jumped to his feet. "What if someone comes in?"

"That's the whole point, Silly. It adds to the excitement."

Carly removed her cell from the cloth bag and began to scroll through a preselected playlist.

"Hear what's playing?" she asked.

"Adele… Love Song," Bo answered. "That's *our* song."

Pouring two glasses of Pinot Noir that she also smuggled in, Carly handed one to Bo.

"Remember the I-Tunes gift card you gave me?"

Bo nodded.

"Well, I made a version of a high-tech cassette tape of our favorite songs. My mom made a cassette for my dad when they first got married, and he was deployed without her. I used to listen to that tape all the time and played it over and over thinking of how romantic it was for her to do that for him. I always thought to myself that I would do the same for my man, the one that I love. It may not be a cassette tape, but it's our playlist. We have music for the entire night," Carly said proudly.

"You see, Mr. Harris, I have this plan to seduce you." Carly inched closer. Seductive eyes blazed into his as she slid her tongue into his mouth.

Bo pulled Carly's lean body tight to him. He could feel her firm breasts pressed into his chest. Carly led Bo by the hand to the bed and the two sat. She lifted her glass and toasted, "Here's to us and our new life in Detroit."

As Carly sat, legs crossed sipping her Pinot, Bo noticed her shiver.

"You're freezing, Babe," he said retrieving her coat and placing it over her shoulders. Draining his glass, he placed it on the nightstand and slipped his hands between her waist and coat. Carly jumped as his cold hands touched her warm skin.

"Your hands are freaking cold," Carly said, pulling them from her waist and rubbing them. By now, both were standing, and Bo's hands were back inside her coat. Caressing the middle of her back, he gently made his way down to her buttocks. Her perfume wrapped around him as he kissed and nibbled up and down Carly's outstretched neck.

Heart beating with excitement, Carly grabbed the bottom of Bo's shirt, brought it above his head, and threw it on the floor. Her hands now behind his neck, she grabbed him by the back of his hair, and pulled him tight against her. Mouth opened; she placed her tongue in Bo's accepting mouth. With raging desire, Carly explored every inch of it.

Bo could barely contain himself as he began to thrust up against her. She felt the firmness coming through his boxers as he pressed between her open legs.

Lips wet with desire; she placed her hands inside Bo's boxers. Moans of pleasure left his body as she dropped to her knees and began kissing his hardened manhood. Gentle rhythm flowed between Bo's moans and Carly's intensity as she was bringing the man she loved to the edge. Carly stood up and pushed Bo down onto the bed. She gently climbed on and straddled him; her locket dangled between her breasts.

With Adele quietly playing in the background and the aroma of lavender filling the room, Carly lowered herself, and the two became one. Whispers and moans of passion consumed the young lovers. Slow pelvic thrusts quickly turned faster as the two simultaneously became more aroused, capturing and holding the feeling as long as they could.

As the lovemaking intensified, and the two could last no longer, Carly arched her back which brought Bo to the brink of explosion.

"Bo" is all Carly could whisper as the two erupted simultaneously into orgasmic ecstasy.

With him still inside her, she leaned forward and put her head on Bo's chest. Reaching down and stroking her hair, Bo whispered, "I'm alive because of you, Carly."

As they held each other, Carly nuzzled her face into Bo's chest. Not another word was spoken, and they both fell asleep.

The rattling sound of a gurney rolling down the hallway woke Carly. She jumped out of bed.

"Bo," Carly said as she vigorously shook a deep sleeping Bo.

"We got to get up. Damn… you're being discharged in less than two hours."

With his eyes open and the realization of what Carly said sinking in, Bo too jumped to his feet.

"Okay, okay," Bo answered almost falling over putting on his boxers.

Throwing on her wool coat and frantically grabbing the empty wine bottle, glasses, and candles, Carly tossed them in the bag and made her way to Bo.

"You have to take a shower and get ready to be discharged. I will be back by eleven and pick you up in the lobby like we planned."

"Sounds good. I'll be ready."

Walking down the hall, a disheveled Carly was getting more than a few looks.

"Looks like someone had a good night," Judy the head nurse cackled.

As Carly walked by the nurses' station, she saw four of her close colleagues smiling at her. Trying to look dignified in her 4-inch red stilettos and wearing her long wool coat, Carly stopped and replied, "As a matter of fact, ladies, the night was not good...It was awesome."

"Good luck in Detroit," Nurse Judy said as Carly headed to the elevator.

Bo's room was neatly packed. His duffle bag lay in the corner of the room, and his bed was made. He was watching TV when Dr. Bennett and his nursing aid walked in.

"Good morning, Bo. Looks like you're ready to go," Dr. Bennett said.

"I am, Sir. So ready."

Shaking Bo's hand and going over the outpatient therapy he would be receiving in Michigan, Dr. Bennett wished him well.

"Thank you for everything, Sir," Bo said as he placed his discharge papers in his duffle bag and headed to the lobby.

****

What could be taking her so long Bo thought chewing on his bottom lip. He peered out the lobby window looking for any sign of Carly. A ruckus in the hallway caused him to half turn and look behind him.

Running around the corner was a beautiful black and white Belgian sheep dog puppy. The puppy ran to Bo's feet, circling his ankles and nipping at his shoelaces.

"Surprise, Baby!" Carly shouted.

Bo knelt on one knee and picked up the pup who squirmed and wriggled-- wanting to be let down. He held the little guy close and ran his fingers through his thick fur.

“This is a direct descendant of Max.” Carly said, beaming with pride. “It turns out that dogs of Max’s caliber that prove themselves in the theater of war have their semen harvested for future breeding.

“This pup has Max’s DNA! I used my Dad’s good name and pulled some strings and got a Little Max! It’s good to have a colonel for a dad at times.”

Chapter 13

Still under hypnosis, Carly turned from side to side. "Bo, meet me at the student center," she whispered then suddenly fell silent as memories of Corktown became vivid.

Slovak scratched a note on his yellow pad and showed it to Hayes. *I think she's back in Detroit!*

The upper flat was silent, dark and cold. Dragging herself from the warmth of Bo's bed, she climbed down from the loft and wrapped herself in an afghan. It was 4 a.m. She grabbed the pack of Marlboro lights from the sill and opened the window, lighting her first cigarette of the day. This was Carly time, a time of no interruptions and no distractions. Just Carly and her thoughts. She scratched designs in the partially open frosted window while staring at the streetlights illuminating the cars below.

Today was "harvest day" as Carly called it, and she hated it. Donating blood at least once a month, she would do what she needed to.

Still wrapped in the afghan her grandmother had crocheted years ago, Carly walked to the cupboard, she grabbed a box of cornflakes and two glass bowls. She filled both with cereal, then lowered one to the floor.

"Sorry, Max. Dog food is on the top of my list."

She opened the refrigerator and moved aside the juice, grabbing the soymilk. A sniff proved that the milk was fine, even though it was three days past the expiration date. On a coffee table in the far corner of the room sat the Victor H4000. Bo had borrowed it from the computer science department at Wayne State. He was a computer science major and convinced his professor of "ethical hacking" to let him borrow it.

With cereal in hand, she walked to a rocker next to the coffee table, lifted the computer, and sat down. Balancing the bowl on her knees she began to open the laptop until the bowl started to tip.

Cornflakes and soymilk fell to the floor. She sat the Victor H4000 back on the coffee table.

"Damn," Carly said, a whole lot louder than she should have. Grabbing Bo's shirt which lay on the couch, she knelt and began cleaning up the mess.

Awakened by the commotion, a disheveled Bo clambered down from the loft and stood at the bottom of the stairs. "What's going on?"

"I spilled my cereal. I'm cleaning it up."

"Where are the cigarettes?" Bo asked with thinly disguised annoyance.

Motioning with her head and saying nothing, Carly nodded towards the still open studio window. Bo walked to the window, lit a cigarette and inhaled deeply. He then let out a long sigh, along with a thick trail of smoke.

While Carly snatched his milk-soaked shirt from the floor to toss in the wash, a card fell onto the floor. She picked it up and read it.

CyberSteal LLC
Cyber Security and Ethical Hacking
Dr. Tatyana Nikolaev

"The professor gave all of us her card yesterday," Bo explained. "I guess she has her own business and she may hire some of us to work for her. There's an internship for vets only."

"That'd be fantastic," Carly said. "Let's hope it pays good."

****

Jumping on the Detroit People Mover and then transferring to the M1 Rail, Carly was heading to the donation center. As she walked to the corner of Rosa Parks and Michigan, she noticed a long line and stood behind a thin woman wearing a blue and white scarf. The line moved slowly as people shuffled in. When it was her turn, she removed the bag hanging from her shoulder and looked for her donor card.

"Have you given before?" asked the grayed-haired staffer. "If so, I need to see your Red Cross card or some ID."

Back on the M1 heading to Wayne State, Carly proudly wore her "I Gave Blood Today" sticker. She didn't need the brown paper bag. She drank her juice, ate her cookie, and never once did she feel faint or nauseous. She had a rendezvous with Bo at the student center.

Flinging the long strap of her bag over her shoulder, she hopped off the M1 to walk to the University Center. Her sunglasses helped temper the brilliant sun. The Michigan air was crisp. Wearing a long black wool scarf wrapped several times around her neck, Carly was going for "the artist" look. She had a matching black beret, gloves, and knee-high boots. A sweater dress clung to her body covered by a wool Indian poncho. The look was great, but not real functional. This was January, and it was freezing outside.

She trudged through the snow, keeping her head down and tilted to lessen the sting of the wind across her cheeks. Finally, reaching the University Center, she pulled the door open and instantly felt relief. "God, I hate this weather!" Carly exclaimed to anyone that was close by. Stomping the snow from her boots, she panned the center looking for Bo. Unable to spot him, she took the first seat she found.

Fifteen minutes passed, but it felt like so much longer. It was not like Bo to be late because he was such a stickler when it came to being on time, a trait he brought with him from the Marine Corp. "Never be late for a fire fight or your buddies could get killed," Bo would always say.

She decided to take a more thorough look to see if by chance she had missed him. Walking by the taco bar and past the ice cream station, she spotted Bo sitting on a couch in the reading section. He was not alone. Sitting next to him was a very attractive woman. Feeling a tinge of jealousy, Carly walked over to the two of them.

"Hi, Baby," Bo said, quickly standing up from the couch.

"What's going on? You were supposed to meet me," Carly snapped as she looked inquisitively at Bo and then to the woman.

Surprised and a little embarrassed, Bo fumbled over his words, "I… I lost track of time. This is Dr. Tatyana Nikolaev, my Cyber Security Professor. I have some great news. Dr. Nikolaev has just offered me a *paid* internship at her firm. We were going over the details."

Carly's face flashed red with embarrassment. She remembered seeing the doctor's business card earlier that morning. "I am so sorry!" is all Carly could muster as she held out her hand to introduce herself.

Shaking Carly's hand, Dr. Nikolaev said, "We are very excited to offer this position to Bo. Our firm is so proud to have partnered with the university. This internship program for returning vets is the least we can do for the sacrifices they made for this country."

Turning to Bo, Dr. Nikolaev said, "I have one more request...Outside the classroom you must call me Tatyana. Dr. Nikolaev makes me feel so old."

"Ok then... Tatyana," Bo managed to say. "See you in the morning."

As Dr. Nikolaev walked away, Bo turned to Carly and gave her a big hug, picking her up off her feet and whirling her around. Totally wrapped in Bo's arms, Carly opened her eyes in time to see Doctor Nikolaev turn and check out Bo from behind. The doctor's eyes travelled quickly up and down, then met Carly's. She stared boldly at her and turned away, not missing a step on her way out of the reading section. Carly noted the look but decided to say nothing, not wanting to spoil the moment.

Dr. Slovak watched Carly's expression change. She moved her head from side to side and clenched her fists. Carly was whisked from Bo's arms to the open door of an office. She gazed down from her out-of-body experience and watched as Bo helped Professor Tatyana up from her knees, his pants still hanging around his ankles. "You son of a bitch, Bo!"

"STOP!" Carly yelled.

****

"Carly...Carly," Dr. Slovak spoke, gently coaxing her to wake.

Slowly opening her eyes, Carly at first didn't realize where she was. Taking a deep breath, she said, "This felt so real."

"Hypnosis can make you feel like that. Tell me...what happened this time."

"I was in Bethesda at Walter Reed taking care of wounded vets. Bo happened to be one of them. I was there when he was going through all his rehab. Really more like fighting it. He was rude and so filled with anger that at times I was afraid of what he would do."

"At first, you felt relaxed, and I detected some happiness. Did you remember something that changed that feeling?" Dr. Slovak prodded.

"Everything changed! One minute I was at the hospital, giving Bo a puppy and the next I saw them in an office. Her…getting up from her knees."

Carly became more and more agitated. Abruptly, she swung her legs off the couch and stood. "I'm leaving now. I have to get out of here."

"Wait, Carly," Dr. Slovak insisted, placing his hand on Carly's shoulder. Carly jerked away. "I said I'm done for the day."

She snatched her parka from the coat rack, jammed her arms into the sleeves and pulled her hat over her head.

"Definitely enough for today," Dr. Hayes said, attempting to soothe her. "I can see that you are upset…" His voice trailed off.

Not bothering to even look at him, Carly left the office, saying nothing.

Chapter 14

Carly lay in bed thinking of nothing else. Her dark room was lit only by Bo's contact information on her cell. *Did I really see them, or did I imagine it?* With a long sigh, she tapped her phone and listened to it ring…

"Hi, this is Bo…sorry, I can't get to my phone right now. You know what to do…do it after the beep."

Secretly relieved he did not answer, Carly hung up and placed her phone back on her chest. It was 9:30 and she wondered if it was too late to text Dr. Hayes. *Oh, what the hell…*

She began to type and then stopped, and then started again. "I left your office too upset today…can we set up another session for tomorrow?"

Carly was surprised at how fast Dr. Hayes responded. "Absolutely! How about 9:00 am?"

"Could I have imagined walking in on Bo with that professor?" Carly typed back.

"That's a possibility. Hypnosis doesn't always produce truths," he explained. "Try and get some sleep. I'll let Dr. Slovak know the time."

Feeling better, Carly texted back. "Thank you," then set the phone down and closed her eyes.

****

Waking energized and feeling better than she had the day before, Carly ate a granola bar and headed out the door. *I am better than this. I need to find the truth.*

Carly entered Dr. Hayes office feeling confident about her decision.

"Good morning, Carly. Are you feeling better today?" Dr. Hayes asked, noticing that she appeared calm and at ease.

"Actually, I am," she answered. "Been spending a lot of time thinking about Bo. I tried calling him yesterday, but it went to voice mail and I didn't leave him a message."

"Well, maybe it's good thing you didn't leave a message. I might have some good news. Please come in and have a seat on the couch. Let me take your coat and get my notes."

Pulling up a chair, Dr. Hayes placed a thick binder on his lap that held all the notes he had since Carly came to Holy Oaks. Turning to a pre-marked page separated with a yellow sticky note, he silently read, then looked over at Carly.

"When you first came to Holy Oaks, you were very scared and confused. We had to sedate you. Do you remember any of this?"

"Not really," she said, thinking back to when she first arrived. "I remember being disoriented and not wanting to talk to anyone. Answering questions… almost impossible."

"Do you have any memory of Bo being here?"

"No."

"What do you remember NOW that makes you feel Bo cheated on you.?"

"I remember getting up in the morning and getting ready for the day. I was sensing something wasn't right with me and Bo."

"Explain, sensing?"

"You know like a woman's intuition. Bo was distant. Like he wanted to tell me something."

"Okay, continue." Dr. Hayes said.

"Bo left around 7 o'clock. I took a shower and then decided to go to the professor's office. She offered him a paid internship the month before. I saw the way she looked at Bo when she was leaving. She actually turned around and looked him up and down … I didn't like it… I know that look. I was going to let her know I appreciated the internship, but that my boyfriend was off limits. I left my house around 9:00, and that's about all I remember."

"I spoke with Bo the afternoon you were admitted. He told me he left for class and that was the last time he saw you. Does any of that ring a bell?" Dr. Hayes asked.

"Yes, pretty much the same routine every Monday morning."

Looking down at his notes, Dr. Hayes said. "I did some checking, and I believe the class Bo was going to was Cyber Security. Is that correct?"

"It was Monday, so, yes, you're right."

"And Cyber Security was a two-hour block?"

"Yes, 9:00 to 11:00 a.m."

"Is it true that only one professor taught that class, and that was Dr. Nikolaev?

"Yes, I guess so. What does that have to do with anything?"

"You see, Carly. You never made it to Dr. Nikolaev's office. You were admitted to Detroit Receiving Hospital at 10:30 in the morning, so Bo and Dr. Nikolaev were in class. You never could have walked in on anyone because they weren't there. Something happened before that.

"Remember what Dr. Slovak said about hypnosis being like a dream, no end and no beginning? I think you were upset about the professor looking at Bo—that was real, but what you *thought* happened in the office..... It never happened. It couldn't have happened. You imagined it!"

Carly sat in silence, trying to make sense of what Dr. Hayes said. "How can that be? During hypnosis, I remembered it so vividly. Are you saying I did not walk in on them?"

"Not only am I saying that, but I also feel that memories are being jarred in your mind. The timeline just doesn't add up. You couldn't have walked in on them that morning. The events that you're remembering whether real or not are getting us very close to the time when something happened that caused your memory loss. This is a good sign, Carly," Dr. Hayes said, "A very good sign."

Dr. Hayes looked at his watch. "My next appointment is probably waiting for me."

Carly stood from the couch, while Dr. Hayes retrieved her coat. She wanted to believe what he told her...wanted to believe it was true. But, doubts, thoughts, and questions without answers bothered her. More than anything she wanted her old life back.

"As soon as I know Dr. Slovak's schedule, I will get back in touch," Dr. Hayes said handing Carly her parka. "I'm meeting with him later this morning."

"Thank you," Carly said, forcing a smile. "I do feel better."

Chapter 15

As Slovak walked into the office, Susan was busy retrieving files from a cabinet and placing them on her desk.

"Good morning, Dr. Slovak. Coffee for you?"

"No but thank you. Is Dr. Hayes in?"

"Yes. He's in his back office." Susan smiled, then proceeded with her filing.

Hayes scowled as Slovak entered the room and threw his folded coat onto the couch, then sat in a chair in front of his desk.

"Rough night?" Slovak said sarcastically.

Saying nothing Hayes bolted from his desk and went to the front office.

"Susan," Dr. Hayes stopped her. "Why don't you take an early lunch and just get out of here for a while?"

"Are you sure, Dr. Hayes?"

"Also, transfer any incoming calls to the answering service. Better yet, take the rest of the day off. Maybe get in some early Christmas shopping."

"Well Merry Christmas to you too, Dr. Hayes. Thank you."

Seething, Hayes returned to his office and slammed the door.

"You bastard! My wife was off limits," he said before settling into his chair.

"Why are you yelling at me?" Slovak asked. "I'm sure the US government doesn't know your wife has ties to a terrorist group in Israel."

"She doesn't and you know it. You or your people tied it to her, so I had no choice but to help. Now every day we live in fear of her being deported. Savannah Ray would be devastated if anything happened to her mother."

"Well then, I suggest you continue to help, and that little secret will never get out."

Hayes opened a lower drawer and removed a shot glass and bottle of Ouzo. He poured a shot and threw it back. The warm sensation of black licorice traveled down his throat and then settled in his gut. With a firm stroke, he slammed the empty glass on the desk and leaned back. He folded his arms and glared at Slovak.

"Tell me everything," Hayes said. "I can't get the information your people want if I don't know it myself."

Slovak manipulated the combination on his briefcase. Fumbling through its contents, he removed a World News article and tossed it on the desk. "Read this."

"Zombie Anthrax" Outbreak in Siberia: How Does It Kill?

by Allen Marshel, Science Age 1989

An outbreak of anthrax that has killed more than 4,000 reindeer and left two dead in Siberia has been linked to 75-year-old anthrax spores released by melting permafrost. It's an event of the sort many scientists have warned about. Dormant deadly disease, perhaps even long-thought extinct pathogens are being revived by warming temperatures.

The anthrax currently infecting reindeer and people in Siberia likely came from the carcasses of reindeer that died from an anthrax outbreak 75 years ago and have been frozen ever since---until an unusually warm summer thawed the permafrost across the region. According to local officials. The current outbreak is likely to end quickly, said James Hartwell, a medical bacteriologist at the University of Michigan.

Hayes tossed the article onto the desk. "This happened over 20 years ago. What am I missing?"

"Have you ever wondered what killed the Neanderthals? You know like, why they went extinct?"

"Never gave it a thought," he said, eyebrows furrowed.

"Some scientists believe that ancient peoples, perhaps the Neanderthals may have been wiped out by deadly pathogens. The kind of deadly pathogens locked in the permafrost. It's sad when you think of it. Nature sentenced this mass murderer to tens of thousands of years in a frozen prison and we humans are setting it free with climate change."

Slovak went through his briefcase and removed a manila envelope. Inside was a picture of a gray cylinder resembling a cigar tube with screw caps on both ends. Tossing the picture in front of Hayes he said, "This is what we're after."

Hayes took the photo and viewed it. "It looks like a pipe bomb."

"It's mithridate."

"Mithridate!? What the hell is that?"

"An antidote to poison. Fletcher developed it along with a weapons grade line of pathogens. If you're a maker of poison, the first job of a poison maker is to create an antidote. Who wants to poison himself? We have reason to believe he hid some of the antidote shortly after his son was murdered."

"Poison? Mithridate? Fletcher? I'm lost."

"Carly's father was actually CIA operative Second Lieutenant Arthur Fletcher. In the United States, he was trained as a doctor and bacteriologist, overseen by the CIA. His cover, Abraham Ehrlich, was created by the US government and Australia's ASIS. They fabricated his credentials. His documents showed that he graduated from the University of Melbourne and attended the University of Newcastle. He was there when the village was poisoned."

"In Siberia?"

"Yes. He was there under the cover of a humanitarian mission. School of Medicine."

"So, he researched pathogens that have been frozen in the permafrost?"

"Yes."

"I thought the United States banned those weapons. America led the way, for God's sake."

"Indeed, Stephen. The United States wasn't after bioweapons, they were after mithridate."

"And what's that again?"

"It's a universal antidote against disease. The problem is, you must first milk the serpent before you can get the anti-venom. Fletcher was there to harvest and create weapons grade deadly pathogens so that an antidote could be developed. The fear was that a rogue nation or terrorist group could get their hands on these types of pathogens and cause a disease pandemic never seen before. It could kill millions."

"So, why the antidote? What's that do for you?"

"Pathogens! We can reverse engineer the antidote. The same pathogens that went into the creation of the mithridate, could be used to recreate a deadly line. We need to find it."

"What does Carly have to do with all this?"

"We have reason to believe Fletcher gave or told Carly where he hid some mithridate. Our only option was to stake out Carly to see if he would get in touch. If he did, we were going to kidnap both of them and use Carly to make him talk."

Hayes stared in silence as the realization of what was happening became clear. "God, is that what this is about… mass murder!?"

"Mass murder! It's a negotiation tool." Slovak leaned in. "It's about leveling the playing field. Why should some countries have weapons of mass destruction and the power that goes with it and others not?"

Hayes stood from behind his desk and began to pace nervously. He looked at Slovak. "Are you that terrorist group? Am I helping a terrorist group?"

"Does Savannah Ray have her piano lesson today, or is she going to Nanna's for dinner?" Slovak scoffed at him. "Wait, it's Tuesday…that means dinner at Nanna's, right?"

Visions of his little girl filled his thoughts. Hayes sat back in his chair, defeated. "If anything happens to her I'll..."

"You'll what? Kill me?" Slovak jeered. "If something happens to me, your family will suffer the same fate as Carly's brother… May I continue?"

Hayes sunk deeper into his chair and nodded.

"Like I said we had staked out Carly's house. There was no sign of Fletcher until one morning Carly left and went to a park in Detroit."

"You mean Belle Isle?"

"Yes. He must have called or texted her. She left her house and drove there with her dog.

"Carly must have known where she was going. She went to a trail and began to walk the path with her dog. There were four of us. We drove around to the far end of the trail and entered the woods. We broke up into two groups and spread out. Kozlov came with me and the other two went further down.

"Carly had her camera and snapped pictures. We think that was a sign because instantly, Fletcher appeared. The two hugged and continued down the trail. Things happened fast. There wasn't much time to think.

"We lowered our ski masks and walked on the path, acting like hikers. When we got about 20 feet from them, we pulled our weapons. That's when the dog broke free and came charging at us. Kozlov shot it dead. That gave Fletcher time to react. He drew his weapon and shot Kozlov. I fired, hitting Fletcher. As I turned, I saw Carly holding a gun and before I knew it, she shot, hitting my face and knocking me unconscious. Lucky for me it was a small caliber gun."

"So, she isn't delusional… she saw these killings," Hayes blurted. "And your face? It was Carly?"

Slovak felt the bone and scar tissue around his sunken eye. "Oh, yes! It was Carly. By now my other two men heard the shots and came running. They saw Carly drop the gun and run off. Fletcher and Kozlov were dead, and I was badly wounded. The boys loaded us into the van and left Fletcher. They even took the dog."

"Why wasn't this in the news? It would have made the front page."

"Really, Stephen. Hardly the first time this has happened in Detroit. They left Fletcher as a victim of a mugging gone bad."

Both men sat silently in the darkened office.

Slovak was taken slightly aback when Hayes said, "It's a wonder she did not recognize you. There you were… right in her face…sitting next to her, comforting her, smiling, asking her to trust you, for God's sake!"

Then with disgust, Hayes added. "And you would have killed her on the spot, if you didn't need something from her. Just like you did her father." Hayes' voice broke off.

Slovak smiled, his next words chilling. "Yes, all for the Cause. It's a lucky thing for us that she did not recognize me. I did have a mask on, so she did not see my face. But I still needed to confirm she had no clue who I was. There was not even a flicker of recognition on her face or in her eyes at our first meeting.

"Eyes reveal much. Pupils enlarge when a person lies because the brain works hard to maintain the lie. Her eyes remained the same when she saw me and heard me. I am confident she has no idea who I am."

Pursing his lips, Slovak stared at his briefcase still on his lap. "Our plan is moving along. We think in that walk her father may have told Carly where the mithridate is or given her a clue. She needs to remember. You need to make it happen."

Slovak placed the picture of the cylinder and anthrax article back in his briefcase and set it to the side of his chair. Leaning forward he continued.

"We need to get Carly alone. Your discharge program with the cabins will work perfectly. That's your job. Let her know she will be moving into a cabin and then home in sixty days. She'll like that. Don't move her until I tell you. I am going to meet with Sarah and the people that can make things happen. I'll include you in that meeting."

"And who is this Sarah?"

"Sarah Hass. You'll meet her at the meeting."

Long after Slovak left, Hayes sat alone, slouched in his chair. He grabbed the Ouzo, stared at it, then placed it along with the shot glass back in the lower drawer.

Shoving himself away from the desk, he walked to the coffee hutch and ran his fingers up the inside frame of the woodwork. A key fell to the ground. He squatted, picked it up, and unlocked the bottom drawer. A small revolver lay on the bottom. He reached in and removed it. Holding the pistol by its grip, he turned it from side to side, staring at the chrome etching on the barrel. He then placed it in his suit pocket and relocked the drawer.

Chapter 16

Sarah Hass arrived at Dr. Hayes office the following morning accompanied by two brawny men wearing suit jackets nearly busting at the seams. She motioned them to take a seat and approached the receptionist's desk. "May I help you?" Susan asked.

"I'm Sarah Hass… here to meet with Dr. Hayes."

Before Susan had a chance to call them, Hayes and Slovak came out of the back office. Slovak rushed by Hayes pushing him aside and held out his hand to shake hands with Sarah. She glared at him, keeping her hands at her side.

"Let's talk somewhere privately," she said, noticeably irritated.

Slovak lowered his hand and waved with an open palm to the back-office door. Her footsteps struck the floor as she walked into the private office. As soon as Hayes closed the door, she began. "This is the last fucking time! I don't do this anymore. I have a kid. I have a new life."

Slovak met her anger with his own. "New beginnings. A new life! Ha!! There will never be a new beginning. Not for you. Not for me. No sweet little home with a sweet little family. Not for us! We'll always be owned, always… the Cause. Until there is no longer a breath. You made a pact with the Devil and the Devil is a calling…" The words, full of spite and malice, flew like venom out of his mouth.

Slovak's words chilled her. She had known for years that *they* would never free her but refused to accept it. Her life was not her own, but theirs. No end. Forcing that reality down, her cold demeanor resurfaced, settled over her body, and she became the interrogator once again, completely in charge

Sarah stared at Dr. Hayes. "And you are?" she asked, scrutinizing his thin frame, pale face, and long slender fingers. His gray suit, obviously expensive, hung a little loose on his shoulders, and the pants bagged on his legs.

"Sarah, this is Stephen Hayes. He is the head psychiatrist here at Holy Oaks. He is the only university affiliate who is working with us regarding Carly Fletcher."

"What does he have on you!?" Sarah blurted out, then calmed herself when she saw a confused look on Hayes's face. "I'm sorry, shouldn't have said that. It just came out. I'm a little upset."

A brief silence fell over the office. Finally, Sarah spoke again to Slovak in her strong, confident voice. "Does he know how this works?"

"No," Slovak said, then walked over to the bookcase and removed a thick textbook from Hayes's library. It was a clinical terminology book he had referenced before. As he walked back, he began to thumb through the index looking for a particular word.

"Got it," he uttered.

Handing the book to Dr. Hayes and pointing to the word, he asked him to read it.

"Flashbulb memory," Hayes read aloud.

"Are you familiar with this?" Slovak asked.

"I've heard of it but explain."

"This is a memory that is very vivid and highly detailed. It happens the moment a piece of surprising or emotional news is heard.

"Some clinical trials have been conducted using *fear* to bring back memory. The logic is people with Situation specific amnesia can sometimes get their memory back if they are basically scared to death. The trauma the brain goes through can trigger memory that is being repressed deep inside the mind. These trials have never been conducted in the U.S. That's why you haven't read any research on it."

"So, what are you saying? We need to scare Carly to death?"

"Not to death, at least not at first. But experiencing terror might just be the thing that jogs her memory. Would you continue, Sarah?"

Sarah began to explain. "We expose the subject to frightening stimuli. Get her into her hysterical state of mind. We found this very effective in Poland. Even though they were trials, mind you, they worked. Our tests showed the more frightened our subjects became the more adrenaline was released into the bloodstream. The theory is this overload of adrenaline not only increases the heart rate and blood pressure but can also stimulate suppressed memories locked deep inside the brain. When you attack the brain relentlessly and never let it rest, forgotten memories can return.

"It is very important that we keep our subject in that state of hysteria as long as possible," Sarah continued. "If we don't, her memory may stay recessed. We need her under our complete control. Alex, you said there was some type of cabin where we can get her alone?"

"Follow me," Slovak told Sarah, as he led her to the rear window and pointed. "See that opening in the tree line?"

"Where?"

"There, where that clump of ferns opens to the left."

"Oh, I see it."

"That is the drive that leads to the cabins. Cabin 2 is presently unoccupied."

"We'll need to prepare it. Is it locked?"

"Yes," Slovak said gesturing Hayes to give Sarah the keys to Cabin 2. "It's about a quarter mile into the woods."

Hayes opened the top middle drawer of his desk. He handed Sarah a flashlight keychain with one key on it. "Here you go," Hayes said.

"Any surprises out there?"

"Cabin 1 has a resident. He won't give you a problem."

"Good. Problems we don't need. I need to know everything about her. What schools she attended, whom she dated, friends, family, every detail, even if it seems trivial. We'll develop a profile."

With her attention now back on Slovak she asked, "Did you record her hypnosis sessions?"

"Of course."

"Good. Get me those transcripts by tomorrow. You told me this Carly was very disoriented, much confusion, blocks of memory totally lost when she first arrived."

"That's correct," Slovak replied.

"We want her back in that state, back to the same trauma that caused her amnesia. That will give us a better chance to get at those memories."

"Then what do you do? How do you get her to tell if she remembers?" Hayes asked.

"She'll be monitored 24-7. When we feel she is traumatized enough, we'll abduct her and take her to a new location."

"New location?" His brows drew together.

Sarah glanced at Slovak and then back to Hayes.

"Stephen," Slovak said. "She's not coming back. You need to make it appear she had a relapse of her delusional state and disappeared, ran away, or she was sent to another facility for additional intensive treatment. Whatever brings the least attention."

"Jesus Christ," Hayes muttered to himself wanting to get away from them.

"One more thing," Sarah said. "Let security know there will be contractors doing renovation in Cabin 2. We'll start tomorrow. Also, have a talk with the guy in Cabin 1 so he doesn't come snooping around."

"You'll take care of that for us, Stephen?" Slovak asked.

Dr. Hayes paused, the words *No new life, no sweet family playing in his head.* "I'll take care of it today."

Chapter 17

The cabins at Holy Oaks sat a quarter mile into the woods, accessible only by a tree lined blacktop road just wide enough to fit a midsize van. They were self-contained housing units barely visible to each other, a hundred yards of trees and bushes separating the two. Six-foot tree line fencing ran the perimeter of each cabin. Dark silhouettes of gnarly weathered branches showed their irritation at the presence of the barriers as they moved in and out of the cyclone fixtures, bending and deforming the once proud metal structures.

Dr. Hayes made his way down the blacktop road which led to Cabin 1. A short path led to the front of the cabin. Holding onto the wooden banister, he carefully climbed the icy steps and knocked on the door. He braced himself, waiting for David to answer.

"Who's there?" boomed a voice from the other side of the door.

"David... it's Dr. Hayes."

The locked door suddenly thrust open and David greeted Dr. Hayes with a wide smile. He wrapped his beefy arms around him, squeezing like some big old bear.

"Jesus," Dr. Hayes said. "Are you going to squeeze me to death!"

David laughed loudly. "Sorry, Dr. Hayes. Sometimes I get carried away...Carried away with myself," he said, laughing. He gave Dr. Hayes one more squeeze before letting go. As his hands brushed the doctor's suit pocket, a quizzical look came over his face.

"What the hell, Doc? Are you packing? It feels like you got a piece in your pocket."

"I always carry it when I drive," Hayes answered. "I've had my CCW for over a year. I keep it locked up during the day when I'm on campus. I'm heading home from here."

"Well, hell. I learn something new about you every day...So, what brings you out here?"

"I just wanted to let you know that we are doing a little renovating in Cabin 2. If you see people in the area, don't be alarmed. They're just part of the construction crew."

"Glad you told me. I would have confronted them otherwise."

"Oh, I know you would have. That's why I came out to let you know. Carly Fletcher will be moving into Cabin 2," Dr. Hayes explained.

"Is she on her 60?" David inquired.

"Yes. If she makes it, she'll be heading home."

"Good for her."

"Now remember, when people are living in the cabins, you can't give them any assistance. This might be a challenge at first for Carly."

"Not to worry, Doctor Hayes," David assured him. "I'll keep to myself."

Dr. Hayes smiled and shook David's hand. "You've come a long way."

On the way to his car Dr. Hayes began to recall the events that landed David at his hospital. In all his years of practice, David's story was the most bizarre.

Chapter 18

Hayes drove his Cadillac onto the circle drive of his two-story colonial and waited for the garage door to open. The garage was empty, his wife's car gone. Savannah Ray's toboggan leaned in a corner next to the Flexible Flyer saucer she got for her birthday, some last bits of snow melted into a pool around it. Rana had taken her to a dentist appointment and then to Grandma's house for an overnight.

On the way into the kitchen, Hayes' stomach felt twisted. He tossed his coat on the back of a kitchen chair and read the note lying on the counter.

Date night, and we have an overnight sitter. I am picking up your favorite Chinese and I can't wait to get home and have you all to myself.
Love, +Me.

Hayes smiled slightly and tossed the note back on the counter. He left the kitchen and went to his personal office. On the way to his desk, he passed the portrait of Rana, Savannah Ray, and him standing in front of their summer cottage at Torch Lake. He fished through his pants pockets looking for the slip of paper on which he had written Carly's number. He took a deep breath. It was time to make the call.

Carly's cell phone vibrated and hummed in her purse. She reached into her handbag and pushed her wallet, Kleenex, a package of peanuts, and a paperback aside until she found her phone at the bottom.

The name of the caller ID surprised her. Her forehead creased.

Apprehensively, she answered. "Dr. Hayes, is something wrong?"

A few moments passed before her face changed from anxious to excitement.

"Are you telling me that I may go home in 60 days?"

"It's a possibility," Dr. Hayes said.

"Any idea when this will happen?"

"I have to check, but I figure it will be sometime next week…near the end of the week."

"OMG! Wait until Meghan hears this." The image of the cabin with the viewing deck was fresh in her mind.

"Even though we are still conducting our hypnosis sessions, I feel you have made enough progress to move into the cabins." There was a brief pause. "I have some plans this evening, so I have to run. Congratulations, Carly, you deserve this."

"Thank you, Dr. Hayes. Thank you so much."

Hayes lowered the phone. He sighed and shook his head. He felt empty.

****

Throughout the morning, a white van with the letters J&S Restorations sat parked in front of the cabin. The open sliding door revealed several seemingly unimportant boxes labeled *Fragile, This Side Up, and Electronic Device.* Two men efficiently moved them into the cabin while a middle-aged woman with short dark hair barked orders.

Quickly, hidden cameras, listening devices, and powerful electromagnet door and window latches were installed, equipped with remote access. Ordinary wall clocks, photo frames, and mirrors were replaced with ones designed to listen and watch. The TV became a monitor and a means to broadcast. The panic alarm was disabled.

Instructions would be sent from the van to an operative lying hidden outside the cabin. Inside the van, which served as the nerve center of the operation, Sarah Hass sat on her padded office chair adjusting the screens.

All good, Sarah thought.

She called Slovak. "Everything's a go."

****

"I should be hearing any day now when I can move into the cabin," Carly said as she and Meghan walked to the cafeteria. "Can you believe it's been five days since I got the good news?"

"What's taking so long?" Meghan asked. "Does your sixty start from the day you learn you are going to the cabin or from the actual day you move in?"

Laughing, Carly reached into her pocket for the cabin key and dangled it by the chain. "Surprise! Just got this from Dr. Hayes," she said, still dangling the key. "My things have been delivered. Do you want to check it out after we eat?"

"Oh, you sneaky be-yotch." Meghan said with a grin. "Hell, yeah, I'll check it out."

Carly drank coffee and ate cereal as Meghan worked on her breakfast. "You should really eat something more than cereal. This could be your last meal in this cafeteria."

"I'm not that hungry. My stomach is just a bit queasy," Carly said, looking a little gloomy.

"What's wrong? You should be over the top with getting to go home."

"That's just it. Where *is* home?"

Meghan, surprised by the question, struggled to answer. "I don't know. You know… with Bo or maybe your parents."

"My parents are in Germany. The only way I am going there is for a visit. And Bo? You know I'm still not a hundred percent sure there is nothing going on with that professor. I never told him what I brought up in hypnosis "

"Don't worry about her; she sounds like a skank. I thought Dr. Hayes explained that you could not have walked in on them in her office."

"Maybe that didn't happen, but I know I caught her checking out Bo's ass."

"I'm not the one to advise on men, but I think if it's meant to be, it'll work out. You two have a lot of history."

"Do you think I'm nuts?" Carly asked.

"Well, of course you're nuts! Or you wouldn't be here. I wouldn't sweat it, though. Obviously, Dr. Hayes isn't worried otherwise you wouldn't be going to the cabin. Crazies don't get to go to the cabin."

"I know that, but lately I feel like I have more in common with David than Bo. We get each other. His sister, my brother. Dead instead of alive."

"Oh," Meghan said teasing. "You and David *get* each other."

"It's not like that," Carly said, fighting a smile. "I can really relate to his loss."

"Hey, I understand that you and he have things in common. I see it every time we are in group. David is cute in a quirky kinda way. If you have feelings for him, go for it. But I'd also talk to Bo. Guys tend to lose their mind if they think with the wrong head. Maybe that's what happened with Bo."

"The wrong head!" Carly laughed, the devilish bad girl coming out. "I get that big time!"

Meghan stared; her eyebrows raised.

"C'mon,"... Carly said, "Haven't you ever just looked at a guy and thought, 'Come get me now and do me however you want?'"

Carly wiggled in her chair. "When I got to know Bo, the wrong head in *my* pants took over. My other brain went on vacation!!!"

Meghan laughed with Carly. "And not to the Virgin Islands, either!" she added. "But Carly, you and Bo committed to each other. I think that makes it different."

"Maybe you're right. We'll see what happens."

Carly finished the last sip of her coffee. "You ready to go?"

"I sure am. Can't wait to see what living a normal life looks like. Here on the hill I feel like a bug. Every move being watched and if we get out of line we get squashed."

"Hang in there. You'll get to the cabins...that is if you quit chasing dead people."

Meghan crumpled her napkin and tossed it at Carly.

****

The temperature was just above freezing as Meghan and Carly headed to the cabin. The bright sun softened the nip in the air and was already hard at work melting a freshly laid blanket of snow. As the two strolled along the narrow road, the rays of sunshine felt good on their faces.

"Can't wait for summer," Meghan said, stopping for a second, closing her eyes, and looking directly into the sun.

"Would you mind if we said 'hi' to David?" Carly asked. "He's in Cabin 1."

"Humm, how convenient...David in Cabin 1...You in Cabin 2. Just saying," Meghan said, trying to hold a straight face.

"Stop it! It's not like that."

Slushy snow squished under their boots as they climbed the steps to Cabin 1.

"Hey, Carly," David said, as he flung the door open and walked out onto the porch. "I saw you coming up the steps. I heard we're going to be neighbors."

"Oh, you already know?"

"Yep. Dr. Hayes came for a visit last Friday and told me. Come in, come in." He gestured to them. "I can make some coffee. I just took some chocolate chip cookies out of the oven."

"You bake?" Meghan asked.

"Oh, hell, yeah, I bake. Calms my nerves. So how about it? Wanna come in?"

"We're heading to check out my cabin," Carly said. "We wanted to stop and say hi since we were going by."

"Well, at least come up on the deck. I want to show you something." Walking back into the cabin, David returned holding a Scrabble game. "I checked this out today. If I remember right, I beat you like a drum last game."

"Oh, my God. You're too funny. Where do you get those hokey expressions anyway?"

"They just come natural to me. No extra effort required."

"I believe it. I guess we will have a Scrabble marathon later today," Carly said.

"That sounds good to me. Do you need any help movin' in? I can't give you any help after 8:00 at night. Holy Oaks rules. Doesn't mean I can't help you now."

"Nope. I think we're good. I was told my stuff was delivered. Not much to unpack."

"Ok, no problem. I don't want to bug you."

"You're not bugging me. You could never. Really, stop by later and bring the Scrabble game. I may as well start kicking your butt right off the bat."

"Game on. Loser cooks breakfast," David said, pumping his fist into the air and grinning.

The tree-lined road gave way to a snow-covered clearing. Carly and Meghan strolled past a mangled cyclone fence, nearly covered by crawling woody vines. In the distance, the steeple of the clock tower from Welchester University peeked above the treetops. Sitting on the edge of a clearing, overlooking the field, was Cabin 2. Just as Carly remembered four wooden steps led to a small viewing deck. A set of binoculars still hung off one of the two wooden chairs leaning up against the cabin wall. The girls climbed the cabin stairs and stopped in front of the door.

"This is it, Meg," Carly said, then placed the key in the lock and turned it. Stepping to the side, and signaling to her she said, "You go first."

Rustic, but renovated, the cabin had modern appliances. Huge pine logs harvested years before, were interlocked and stacked one upon the other. Notches cut into the ends kept them in place and formed the inner and outer walls. A stone fireplace with a hearth was built into the far end. A small tile bathroom was just off the bedroom.

The bedroom was tiny and only large enough for one chest of drawers. A log-framed bed split the tiny room with its headboard pushed up against the wall. Next to the bed was a small closet.

Mounted just outside the bedroom door in a glass case was a panic alarm. A steel mallet dangled from a chain next to it. If the glass case was smashed and the alarm pulled, Holy Oaks Security would be out within minutes.

The furniture looked to be handcrafted. Branches of knotty pine formed the dowels of the kitchen chairs while stained pieces of grainy white oak made up the seats. Wooden beams hand-honed and hung high, crisscrossed the A-Frame ceiling. Hung in the center was a four-bulb light and ceiling fan. The kitchen had a four-burner stove and a sink that sat under a window and looked out onto the field.

Carly's suitcase and khaki duffel bag sat in the front room on a braided rug next to the couch. Bags of groceries purchased the day before were left on the kitchen table. Perishables were already in the refrigerator, placed there by the maintenance staff who delivered her belongings.

"Cozy," Meghan said, as she looked around the place.

Hearing a snowmobile sputtering outside, the girls sauntered out onto the deck. A Holy Oaks security officer straddled his machine by their front steps. He remained seated and kept it idling, while taking off his helmet.

"Hello, Ladies. Just wanted to introduce myself. I'm Robert Martin, Head of Security. I like to meet the new residents that come to the cabins. It's normally pretty quiet out here. The most you get is some of the college kids wanting to have a bonfire."

"Glad to hear it's quiet," Carly said.

"You must be Carly Fletcher," the security officer replied. "We got the notice earlier today that you will start living here. Congratulations! That means you'll be leaving us in a couple of months."

"I sure hope so," Carly said. "It's good to know you watch the place."

"Yes. Want to make sure our residents are safe and sound."

"Thanks. I hope I won't need your services."

"I'm sure you won't," he said putting on his helmet, revving his Yamaha, and wheeling it back down the path.

Carly and Meghan watched Office Martin drive out of sight. Meghan turned to Carly, "Let's get you moved in."

When everything was unpacked, Carly surveyed the groceries still in bags on the counter and the produce that was packed in the refrigerator. It had been awhile since she had done any kind of cooking.

"How about some good old Mac and Cheese?" she asked Meghan.

"I love the stuff," Meghan answered. "And I saw salad in the fridge."

"Yeah, and what's Mac and Cheese without applesauce?"

"You know, Meghan, cooking makes me feel like a normal person. Kind of how it makes David feel."

"You better get back in the swing of things. Eating in the cafeteria has spoiled you. Not like it was fine dining or anything."

"Fine dining? Only if you call powdered eggs and tater tots fine dining!"

Meghan set the dishes on the sink still holding bits of mac & cheese along with snippets of salad. "Hey, you don't have a garbage disposal," she said as she removed the garbage can from under the sink and scraped the plates into it. Growing up in Kentucky I never knew what a garbage disposal was until I moved in with my Aunt and Uncle. God how I hated them."

Carly saw the tormented look on her friend and quickly changed the subject when she heard footsteps coming up the stairs. "Sounds like David."

David entered the cabin holding the Scrabble game. Meghan rushed up to him. "How would you like to do us a favor?"

"Depends on what it is," David said with a grin. "One of the first things I learned in the service is…"Don't Volunteer! Don't volunteer to do anything unless you know what it is!"

"Would you make us a fire, please. We tried but as you can see, it didn't take."

"I can handle that," he said, handing Meghan the game. "It's all about how you stack the logs."

David took a couple of logs from the firewood cradle and showed Carly how to stack them.

"Logs have to sit so that air can breathe between them. When you add a log always make sure it sets crisscrossed over the other log. It'll burn forever."

The fire quickly warmed the cabin while the Scrabble game went on. Each of them focused on their tray of tiles. A word popped into Carly's head. She dropped the wooden squares into place as David and Meghan watched.

"Chutzpah!" Carly said, smiling smugly on her chair.

"Oh, come on! Chutzpah!" Meghan exclaimed. "That can't be a word."

"It is," David said. "It's like someone who says and does outrageous things. Like the guy who murders his parents and then asks the judge for mercy because he is an orphan. They used that word to describe me during my trial."

"You do have chutzpah, David," Carly said. "One more game?"

"Not for me. But there's something I've been meaning to ask you. What are you going to do once you fly this cuckoo's nest?"

"Oh, I don't know. Maybe finish my art degree. I could become one of those starving artists selling my artwork on the streets of Corktown."

"What about you?"

"Geez, I was supposed be an Army lifer before all this went down." Shaking his head and looking at the floor, he said, "One thing for sure, I gotta go see my Baby Girl."

"Baby girl?" both girls blurted at the same time.

Their reaction took David by surprise, and he smiled when he realized why.

"No, I don't have a daughter! It's Penny, my sister. That's what I called her growing up. Baby Girl. Haven't been to the grave since I got locked up. Penny was so young when she took her life. My folks aren't doing very well."

Standing and taking a deep breath, David said, "Enough with this sad crap…this should be a happy time. Sorry if I brought everyone down."

"Don't apologize," Carly said. "I understand that talking about sad stuff helps with healing. I'm here for you."

"I am too." Meghan added. "I don't believe those rumors."

David looked at Meghan and then to the floor. Just above a whisper he said, "They're not rumors, I did that to those boys."

Meghan's eyes shot to Carly and then back to David. "You did?!...you cut it off?!"

"No!" David said emphatically. "Now that's a rumor. On the ranch when you castrated a bull you would band their balls, or you do it chemically." A smile grew on David's face. "I have to admit though, I had those boys believing I was going to cut off their nut sack."

"Maybe you should tell us what really happened," Carly said.

Nodding, David began…"I was on deployment in the Middle East when I got this letter from Penny. It was a suicide note. These frat boys drugged and raped her and streamed the whole thing live. They came from wealthy families and had high price attorneys. They were acquitted. Said my baby sister was a willing participant in a sex film."

"God David. Now I know why you hate frat boys," Carly said.

"I was devasted. I finished my remaining month of tour and moved back home. Penny had asked me in her note not to seek revenge. I tried; I really did…but then I snapped. I staked out their fraternity house and discovered they often took a short cut to class down a path through a wooded lot. I decided that's where I'd get my revenge."

"Did they know who you were?" Meghan asked.

"Not until I took off my ski mask. I walked them out by gunpoint to a tarp I had laid out in the woods. In the middle of it was a pile of rubber bands. I ripped off my ski mask and asked if they saw a resemblance to Penny Farris. They did!"

"God that had to freak them out," Meghan said.

"I lifted my pant leg and showed them my knife in my ankle holster. I made them strip naked and they were convinced they were going to have to cut off their balls. Instead I had them band them. I used one of their phones and streamed the whole thing live. Just like those pukes did to Penny.

"I drove to the nearest cop shop and turned myself in. Didn't want to put my parents though anything more. I was found [NGRI] Not Guilty by Reason of Insanity. Hospitalization, not incarceration, my attorney argued would better fit this crime and the judge bought it. So here I am…less than sixty days until they unleash my crazy ass back into society."

"You're definitely not crazy, those boys had it coming," Carly assured David.

"Well thank you, that means a lot. Even though the diagnosis is coming from a patient at a mental institution."

"Ha, ha," Carly said.

David turned to Meghan. "You ready?"

"Yep," Meghan said, taking the three cups from the coffee table and setting them in the sink.

A melancholy feeling came over Carly. "Wish me luck tonight. It's been awhile since I've been on my own. I am a bit nervous. What if I can't even make it through the first night?"

"You'll do great," Meghan assured her.

"You'll be fine, Carly," David added. "I know there isn't supposed to be any contact after 8:00, but if something happens, call me. I keep my cell by my bed and I'm a pretty light sleeper."

"Thanks, Guys, and I always have the panic alarm," Carly said.

"God! Don't pull it!" David laughed. "Hayes will have you back up the hill and sitting in group therapy in a split second."

Carly watched David and Meghan plod down the snowy road home. David's low deep voice floated back to Carly's cabin along with Meghan's squeals of laughter. When they were out of sight, Carly lingered in the doorway, savoring the quiet and charm of the woodlands around her.

Alone ... I've forgotten how that felt.

Chapter 19

Inside the van, Sarah and Józef, watched the monitors. She scribbled notes on a spiral pad. *Good. Everything good... Things are working out.*

Carly removed a book from her backpack. It was a gift from Dr. Hayes to celebrate her progress. "What a long day," she mumbled, as she flopped onto the couch, with a big sigh, then turned to where she left off in Accidental Heroes, Danielle Steel's newest book. She couldn't focus; her mind wandered from everything brought up in hypnosis.

She thought of Bo and Max and how the three of them were building a life together.

She remembered the night they were sitting in front of the TV. She was reading a book and Bo was watching a documentary on artificial intelligence and out of nowhere he asked her, "Why do you read that fake stuff!? It doesn't make sense. Wouldn't it be better if you read something real that you could learn from?"

"I like books like this," she told him. He just shrugged his shoulders and looked back at the television. His cutting remark upset her, taking her back to Walter Reed and the ugliness he unleashed on nurses who entered his room. She didn't want to be around him and took Max for a walk.

She pushed those thoughts to some other place in her brain and forced herself to read. At last, one chapter involving a father who abducted his infant son sparked her interest. She soon found herself, as she had so many times before, engrossed in a world not of her own.

Carly shivered on the couch. The fire had dwindled and was smoldering. Placing the book beside her, face down, she slipped on her shoes and walked onto the deck to grab a couple logs, leaving the cabin door open. The sun was nearly below the horizon when she noticed movement at the far edge of the clearing. *Could it be Mama Doe and her fawn?*

"Binoculars. I know I saw binoculars," she said to herself, as she looked around, then spied them hanging from a wooden chair.

Carly brought them to her eyes and focused the adjustment knob until the image came into view. *Spots are gone, so much bigger*. She continued to focus the glasses, keeping the best view, captivated as the doe stretched her neck and twitched her ears. Within a split second, the doe raised her head, snorted, and both deer bolted across the clearing.

What spooked them? Carly wondered as she stood looking through the binoculars. Seeing more movement, she continued to focus.

A dog?

Crawling on hands and knees was a dark silhouette moving slowly along the tree line. As Carly peered through the binoculars, the silhouette stopped and sat crossed legged, facing the cabin. She stood there, turning the knob ever so slightly bringing the figure into sharp view.

Jesus…who is that?

As she watched, the shadowy figure unzipped his white and black camo jacket and removed his own small pair of binoculars. Bringing them to his eyes, he saw Carly with–binoculars looking at him. Instantly he rolled to one side and disappeared into the darkness of the woods.

Paralysis, like cold fluid, flowed through Carly's body rushing to her feet. Her knees weakened. She stood like a statue until the binoculars dropped from her hands and thumped against the wooden floor, tearing her out of her frozen state. Without thinking, Carly tore down the stairs in the direction of David's cabin.

Her boots pounded the hard-packed snow trail leading away from her cabin. Images of leaf barren shrubs and tall twisted poplars barely imprinted on her mind while she focused ahead, intent on getting to David.

Upon reaching his cabin, she leaped two steps at a time.

"David…David… open up," Carly screamed as she pounded her fists on the door. "It's me…Carly. Open the door! Open the door!"

Quickly, the door opened, grating against the wooden floor, and David stood in front of her.

"Carly…Jesus…" He placed both hands on her shoulders.

"I... I saw someone…someone looking at me from the woods."

"From the woods? What do you mean from the woods?"

"Someone. Someone in the woods. Looking at me with binoculars."

Hearing the panic in her voice, David placed his arm around Carly and led her into his cabin. He guided her to an easy chair and helped her onto the seat. He took a stool for himself and placed it in front of her. Keeping his voice calm and low, he said, "Ok. Go ahead. Tell me what happened."

"God, David! It was so freaky," Carly began. "I saw someone come crawling out of the woods like an animal. He looked at me."

"Crawling… like on all fours?" David asked.

"Yes! I was watching Mama Doe and her fawn in the clearing with my binoculars, and they got spooked. I wondered what it was that startled them, so I kept scanning the tree line. I noticed what was a dog—I thought it was a dog-- or something crawling to the edge of the woods."

Carly got up and stood behind the chair, placing her hands on the top of it.

"Are you sure it wasn't a dog?" David asked.

"Yes, I was using binoculars. Once he came into view, I saw him crystal clear. He was wearing a camo jacket. I saw someone…some person, some man…looking at me."

"So, what did he do?"

"He sat on the ground and pulled out his own binoculars and looked toward the cabin. He must have seen me looking at him because he rolled and vanished so fast into the woods."

David took some time analyzing what Carly said, his eyes staring straight ahead. His face showed no emotion as he pursed his lips and then tightened them. A low hum from his throat was the loudest noise in the cabin.

"You saw a scout," he said.

"A scout? Like a Boy Scout?"

With a small chuckle, David said, "No, not a Boy Scout. It's a college kid looking for a place to party."

"Seriously? You're not kidding?"

"No. I'm not. I've seen them myself. Walked up on a couple."

"What? What do you mean walked up on a couple?"

"A couple of college boys. There's a lot of down time in the cabin. You got to keep yourself busy or you can go nuts. No pun intended. I'd go looking for Ali Baba. That's what we called the enemy during the war. I'd walk silently through the woods without making a sound. I practiced stealth to keep my recon skills sharp. See if I can sneak up on deer and birds before they see me. It's a game. It kills the time."

"What's that gotta do with a scout?" Carly asked.

"This one day when I was conducting reconnaissance… that's what I call it when I go on my walks, I came upon a couple of guys looking at my cabin. I snuck up right behind them and I-asked them what they were doing.

"They whirled around. I know I startled them at first. But, once they looked me up and down, they got this insolent, brazen attitude.

"You a cop?!" one of them sneered at me.

"Then the other punk chimed in real smart like. 'Yeah, show us your badge!"

"Oh, God? What did you do?"

"I got a crazy-ass look in my eyes, lowered one shoulder and shuffled towards them kind of dragging my feet. I spoke in my deepest, gruffest voice, 'Badges, to god-damned hell with badges! I don't have to show you any stinkin' badges.' You know, like the Mexican Bandit said in the Sierra Madre movie."

Carly stared at David, picturing the encounter in her head. She chuckled, then said, "Those goddamn frat boys."

"I told them I was doing time in Holy Oaks for almost axing Chucky to death, but that I was pumped full of lithium and nearly cured unless something set…me… off! By this time, they didn't know what to think. That's when they changed their tune and told me they were checking if any cabins were empty so they could party and build a bonfire."

"That's got to be it!" Carly said. "Security was around already today and told me that they were watching for college kids wanting to party on the grounds. I never thought of that."

By now darkness had fallen. David walked to the cupboard, feeling around inside until he found a flashlight. He grabbed a tan jacket from the coat rack as he went by and tossed it to Carly.

"Let's get you back. It's past eight, and we don't want you to blow your first night."

"Funny how your mind plays tricks. Makes you think of all crazy things." Carly said.

"Hold onto the banister," David said on the way out of the door. "These steps get iced up this time of night."

On the way down David's eyes followed the powerful beam of his flashlight. He noticed a disturbance in the snow just inside the wood line and off the trail. *Footprints-- not mine.*

"May I have this dance?" David asked, sticking his elbow out like he was standing in a line at a square dance. "It'll be easier for us to walk since we both need to share the light."

Carly kept hold of David's arm as they walked back. They could see the lights of her cabin glowing through the trees.

Finally reaching her cabin, David said, "I want to check your place out before I leave."

They climbed the steps and David walked through the still open door. "Come on in, follow me."

David walked into the bathroom then the bedroom. He pulled the shower curtain aside and got down on his knees to look under the bed. "Looks good to me," he said. "Nothing here but field mice. You have nothing to worry about."

"Yuck," Carly blurted. "Do you think there are mice in here?"

"Sure, but they don't eat much," David wisecracked on his way to get more wood.

He returned to the living room cradling five logs. He placed them in the fire box, then knelt and stirred the bed of embers with the poker. A red-hot glow filled the fireplace as he crisscrossed two of the logs. He stood and wiped his hands on his jeans. "That should do you for the night."

"Thanks for everything," Carly said. "Seeing that guy really freaked me out."

"It would freak anyone out. Seeing someone watching you with binoculars is creepy."

David pulled the door open, then stopped. "You do know they do wellness checks on us don't you."

"No. What's that?"

"Security sends a staffer to come out after 8:00 to check up on us. Checks are random and unannounced. It's usually the rookie on duty who does it. They just do a drive by. Wanted to let you know so if you see someone in a vehicle checking out the place it'll be security. I better get back before junior finds out I'm not in my cabin."

Carly watched David hurry down the steps and heard the snow crunch as he began jogging to his place. *Now to those footprints.*

****

"The male from Cabin 1 has just left," Zev, the operative stationed outside Carly's cabin whispered into his radio. "The subject is alone."

"So, what happened again?" Sarah inquired.

"She came to the deck and was looking at what I think were deer," Zev answered. "Then the crazy bitch bolted down the steps and ran right past me."

"Did she see you?"

"Of course not."

"Did you follow her?"

"I did. She went to Cabin 1 where the male came out and the two went inside. She stayed for about 45 minutes, and then they walked back. She's alone now."

"Okay. Keep me posted." Sarah waited patiently, letting time pass before giving any new orders. Wearing headphones and watching an array of monitors in the van, she said, "Lock the doors. We don't want her running anymore."

She watched the monitor as Carly grabbed her book, fluffed a couple of pillows, then stretched out on the couch. After just a few pages, she marked her page and tossed the book on the floor. She then folded her arms to the middle of her chest and closed her eyes.

"If she doesn't wake up, we can start in about ninety minutes," Sarah said to her operative.

"An hour and a half ma'am?" he asked with a confused look.

"Yes, at least an hour. We need her in the rem phase of sleep."

Józef turned his swivel chair from the monitor, reached down in the side pocket and grabbed a cigarette. Lighting it, he took a deep drag, exhaled, and stretched back in his seat.

"Józef, put the window down," Sarah said. "Those things stink."

"You're such a pain in the ass," Józef said, lowering the window.

Sarah's face buckled, as her crow's feet tightened. "Pain in the ass," she derided him. "Don't forget where your paycheck comes from. I'm not one of your Ukrainian bitches too afraid to talk back."

"Relax, Sarah. Don't get your panties in a wad."

"Nix the sweet talk, Chump, before you find yourself back in the Ukraine. I gotta get some fresh air."

"Go ahead, Boss, I've got this," Józef said. "I'll keep an eye on her."

Sarah returned about an hour later with a cup of coffee and a sausage biscuit in her hand.

"How's our girl doing? Has she stayed asleep?"

"It's been at least an hour and she looks like she's in a deep sleep. You can hear her snoring."

"Perfect! Start with her brother calling her. Make sure it is real low at first."

With a few keystrokes, Józef piped in a low, ghostly voice.

Carly. It's me. Artie. I'm alive. Carly. It's me. Artie. I'm alive.

Carly began to fidget. She did not wake up.

"More volume," Sarah ordered.

Carly. It's me. Artie. I'm here."

Carly's eyes shot open. She looked around the cabin in a slumber haze trying to figure out if she was dreaming.

"Flash her brother's picture on the TV. Do it. Do it now! Keep the volume the same."

For a millisecond, an image of Artie flashed on the TV.

"Artie? Artie, is that you?" Confused, Carly darted from the couch and grabbed the fire poker. Gingerly walking toward the TV, she paused when she heard faint sounds of laughter coming from outside. Moving to the front door, Carly lifted a slat of the blind and peered out. Flashlight beams bounced up and down as two people approached her cabin.

"Stop!" Sarah yelled as she ripped off her headphones and grabbed the radio attached to her belt. "What do you see?" she asked, speaking into the radio to Zev who was hidden outside the cabin.

"Looks like a couple people pulling a sled with a keg strapped to it. Should I stop them?"

"Stay put. See what happens."

Carly could hear the thud, thud, thud of snow boots climbing up the steps. The sound of footsteps stopped, followed by the stomping of feet. She still held the poker and waited.

The door shook as someone knocked. A woman's voice came from the other side of the door.

"Hello. Anyone home?" There was more knocking, then Carly heard the doorknob being pulled and rattled.

"Get away from the door or I'll call the cops," Carly warned her.

"The bathroom. Can I use your bathroom?" the female on the porch pleaded. "I really have to go. I live in the dorms. It's too far to walk."

Carly pulled the cord on the window blind and peeked through the slat. Seeing it was a young woman, she turned on the porch light. A man stood at the bottom of the steps wearing a black winter parka with the hood covering his face. Again, with bent knees, the girl pleaded, "I gotta pee."

"I'm sorry. Can't let you in."

The woman walked closer to the window and as she did, she removed one of her mittens, placing her palm on the window. Staring straight into Carly's eyes, the woman motioned with her chin to her hand. **THEY'RE LISTENING. THEY'RE WATCHING** was written on the girl's palm.

With a half-smile, she turned to her friend and shouted, "Gotta pee in the woods…let's get out of here."

Carly watched the woman scuttle down the steps to join the man waiting at the bottom. She grabbed the rope and the two pulled the toboggan away. Once the flashlight beams were out of sight, she switched the porch light off. And then, thinking better of it, turned it back on.

"There're gone now," Zev informed Sarah. "Looks like one of them wanted to use the bathroom. Should I follow them?"

"No! Wait another half hour and then come in. We are finished for the night."

Shaking her head in disbelief, she wrote notes in her binder. Not looking up, Sarah said, "Un-freaking-believable. What's she doing now, Józef?"

"Back on the couch. Just sitting there. Still holding the poker."

Throwing the binder to a side chair, Sarah slid the van door open and stepped onto the pavement. "I'm bringing your comrade in from the field. Take shifts and watch her tonight. We'll start again tomorrow."

She tromped to her Jeep and sped out of the lot, sending unmelted salt crystals flying from her tires.

Chapter 20

The rope became taut as Ahmed and Porsche pulled the toboggan across the university parking lot. They could hear the crumbling of the rock salt grind beneath their boots as they dragged the wooden sled to the 2012 Taurus. Breathing heavily, he pulled his heavy wool hood from his head and pressed the remote starter. "Let's get this keg in the trunk," he said, as he aimed the clicker and hit the trunk latch.

It had been over twelve months since Ahmed received that frantic text from across the Atlantic. Within 48 hours he had arrived at Detroit Metro Airport. It was too late. His friend and former CIA boss, Colonel Arthur Fletcher was dead. The last text from him…Help Carly find Mr. Etadirhtim.

Ahmed already had been to her place in Corktown. The door was not locked and when he pushed it open, he saw drawers pulled out and their contents spilled on the floor. The couch had been overturned and cut with long slashes. Stuffing spilled from cuts in the couch. Cushions were strewn on the floor and books lay in heaps having been knocked from their shelves. Someone had been there. Someone was looking for something.

Porsche maneuvered the toboggan next to the car where Ahmed lowered himself to remove the straps. With a grunt he lifted the barrel and dropped it in the trunk.

"Damn, those seemed lighter back in the day."

"What are you talking about, Babe?" Porsche Berliner said. "You still got it. I would put my money on you against any one of these frat boys."

Ahmed looked at Porsche and said, "I think you're a little biased, wouldn't you say?"

She smiled. "Maybe."

Ahmed scanned the parking lot, then opened the back-passenger door. He dumped out crinkled food wrappers from a fast food bag, smoothed it out and wrote FREE TOBOGGAN! HAPPY HOLIDAYS! He handed it to Porsche.

"Leave it over there," he pointed, "by that bike rack. I'm sure some frat boys or sorority will have a blast with it."

"A regular Kris Kringle," Porsche said. "That's why I love you."

She pulled the toboggan to the empty bike rack and leaned it up against the bars. She stuck the note between the ropes and the padded seat, angling it so it could be seen from the sidewalk.

"Turn up the heat, Babe," Porsche said, as she drove Ahmed down a two-track road and headed back into the woods.

"Something could go down tonight. Someone was outside the cabin when you were on the porch."

"Really. How'd you see 'em?"

"I didn't. Smelled the smoke of a cigarette. Wonder where that dumb ass got his training? I want you to drop me off and head back. Pull over here," he said pointing to a small carved out spot in the side of the road. "Hey, I meant to tell you what an awesome job you did. A regular Angelina Jolie."

Porsche pulled over and put the Taurus in park. She reached over, turned the heater blower down, then looked at Ahmed. "It's my shift. You need to get some rest. You've been up over 24 hours"

"It's getting too dangerous. It's one thing to watch Carly as she makes her way around the hospital campus. It's a totally different thing if the bad guys show up."

Porsche stared at Ahmed. "I know what this is about. It's about me being seen, isn't it?"

"Seen? What are you talking about?"

"You know what I mean. Don't play dumb. She caught me. She caught me watching her. It was a rookie mistake, and I messed up. You trained me better than that. One of the best instructors Deutsche Hochschule ever had."

"Really? Best instructor? I got fired for sleeping with one of my students. I think the administration might disagree."

"Any regrets?" Porsche asked.

"None."

"You better say that. But really…I'm sorry."

"Sorry? You have nothing to be sorry about. I call you for help and you fly across the Atlantic. I'm the one that should be apologizing to you."

Ahmed stopped talking and chuckled. "Speaking of rookie mistakes. I got hit by a car and almost killed in downtown Welchester. I may be retired, and my skills a little foggy, but I never should have let Carly recognize me. I should have crossed the street before passing the restaurant. Who knew she would be looking out the window and recognize me?"

Porsche unfastened her seat belt and scooted closer to Ahmed. She placed her hands over the back of his neck and said, "Doesn't matter where I am… America or Germany, just as long as it's with you." She gently moved in and gave him a kiss.

"I love you, Porsche," Ahmed whispered into the side of her neck, then gently pushed her away. "Gotta go. I'm about a half mile from the cabin. I'll stay until daybreak and once I see Carly moving about, I'll come back out of the woods. Don't think they'll try anything during the day. Too risky. Can you find this spot again?"

"Sure. I'll wait for your text. You be careful out there."

"Always am," he said, as he removed his gun from his holster and made sure he had chambered a round. Stepping out of the car, Ahmed leaned down and looked at Porsche. "When I get back, I'm going to show you just how appreciative I am of you."

With a slight grin, Porsche said, "The only thing you're going to appreciate is a warm bed, without me in it. See you in the morning."

****

The rumble of a snowmobile passing the cabin forced Carly to open her eyes. She had been awake for several minutes, lying on the couch with her eyes closed thinking about the night before.

THEY'RE WATCHING. THEY'RE LISTENING. *What's up with that?*

She moved her shoulders and felt an ache in her neck and a twinge in her back, brought about by sleeping on a couch that had more lumps than support. Getting herself to a sitting position, she rubbed the back of her neck, turning her head from side to side to loosen her cramped muscles. Standing and arching her back, Carly groaned and stretched as the stiffness eventually left her body.

She headed to the kitchen and put on a kettle of water and then moved about the cabin turning off the lights left on the night before. Rays of sunlight seeped through the cracks of the blinds as she twisted the grooved rod hanging from the blind. Carly squinted as she pulled on the cord sending the blind up and filling the room with sunlight.

Outside, charcoal-colored bare trees with a coat of newly fallen snow created a striking black and white contrast. *Perfect pen & ink sketch day,* she thought as she watched the Blue Jays, and Cardinals struggle to land on the snow-covered birdfeeder. Slipping on her jacket and fur-lined boots, Carly shuffled to the door and unbolted the locks. She turned the knob, but the door wouldn't budge. *Damn.* Then she double checked the dead bolt and pulled again.

"Bet it's frozen," she said to herself.

Returning to the kitchen, she decided to have tea until the door unfroze. She poured scalding water over her Samurai Chai tea. The onslaught of boiling water released the scent, filling the room with the aroma of sweet flowers. She stood, blowing in her cup, watching the birds still attempting to land on the feeder. Six inches of newly fallen snow had left the woods white and tranquil.

She saw someone walking awkwardly coming to her cabin.

David?

Wearing snowshoes and walking high above the snow was David. In his left hand he held a pan covered with a kitchen towel. Carly laughed as she watched him shift from foot to foot with the huge netted footwear. It reminded her of Artie, taking his first baby steps. At the base of the stairs, he knelt and unlatched each shoe, all while balancing the tray with one hand. Carly set her tea on the stove and headed to the door.

"I can't open it," Carly shouted once David reached the top of the stairs. "I think it's frozen."

He turned the knob and pushed on the door. "Are you sure all the locks are undone?"

"Duh… Yeah… Really?"

"Sorry. Dumb question," David said. "Maybe the wood got wet and swelled. Go over to the window by the sink. I'll hand you your breakfast."

Carly moved to the window and turned the latch. She grabbed the upper frame and pushed against it.

"It won't move either. Good thing there wasn't a fire or something. I'd be trapped in here. Should I call and try to get maintenance out here?"

"Maybe," David shouted through the closed window. "Let me try the door one more time."

Sarah, from many miles away, watched on her I-Phone. *Those idiots! They didn't unlock the cabin!* She pressed hard on the accelerator and dialed Józef.

"Is the cabin locked?" Sarah yelled into the phone, rage in her voice.

"Yes, Ma'am." Józef replied over the speaker phone. She could hear his fingers frantically typing, trying to remedy the malfunction. "The system defaulted. When it defaults, it defaults in a locked position. I am rebooting now."

Panicked, Sarah listened.

"Come on. Open. Open baby", Józef mumbled. "The system is re-booting. Come on. Come on. Open. Open, you son of a bitch.

"Got it," Józef yelled to Sarah. "It's open. The door and windows are open."

"Damn!" Sarah said relieved. "Check everything out before I get there!"

David walked back to the door and set his pan of muffins on the rail. He turned the doorknob, leaned back, and with all his 280 pounds thrust himself into the door. Smashing through like a fullback, he lost his balance, toppled, and fell to the floor with a loud thud. Out of breath, he laid there spread eagled, belly to the floor, looking like he was ready to make a reverse snow angel.

Carly, fighting a smile, said nothing and looked on. After a few seconds, laughter rose from deep inside. David continued to laugh with no sign that it would soon end. As Carly watched, she too started laughing. Which led to more laughter. And when she snorted a couple of times, both of them had a hard time stopping.

"Let me help you up," Carly said, extending her arm toward David.

"No, I got this," he answered as he easily stood up next to her. "Obviously the door was frozen. You may want to keep the heat up a little more at night, so this doesn't happen again. On a different note, I got something for you."

David stepped back out to the deck and retrieved the muffins. Slowly slipping the towel off the pan like David Copperfield, he showed his masterpiece. Arranged perfectly in a pan were four muffins. Chunks of walnuts topped in sugar crystals adorned the pastry. An aroma of banana and walnuts tickled the senses as Carly lowered her head and took a good whiff.

"Banana nut with a hint of coffee. I call it my own recipe because I add strong brewed coffee for flavor and the recipe doesn't call for it, so it's mine."

"Holy Oak's own Wolfgang Puck," Carly kidded.

"I guess so. As I told you, I like to bake. Holy Oaks was offering a baking class, and I signed up for it. At first, I felt a little awkward because I was the only guy in the class, but it didn't take long to find out that I loved it, and I was pretty good at it, too."

He then grinned and boasted, "I was better than the girls. At least they said I was. This baking stuff really calms my nerves."

"I think that's awesome," Carly replied. "Women love guys who can cook."

Heading to the cupboard, Carly grabbed another cup and insisted, "You have to stay for a cup of coffee and have one of these muffins with me."

"If you insist…" David said, glad that he brought four muffins.

He took off his jacket and started to take off his boots.

"Don't worry about your boots. A little snow won't hurt these wooden floors. I think they have seen better days."

While the coffee brewed, Carly placed two plates on the table, each holding a muffin. David inhaled and then exhaled. "Ahhh… the smell of fresh perked coffee. Can't get that from a coffee maker."

Carly poured David's coffee into an oversized brown mug. As she placed the coffee in front of him, she said, "I got to tell you this weird thing that happened last night."

"Other than seeing a scout in the woods?" David asked.

"This is something different. Remember you told me that the guy was probably a frat boy looking for a place to party."

"Yeah."

"Well, you were right. I woke up from a dream where Artie was talking to me. I swear I heard his voice. I was still half asleep, so I wasn't sure. I grabbed the fire poker to protect myself.

"I heard voices coming from the clearing and went to the front door. There were these two college kids, I guess that's who they were. They were pulling a toboggan with a kegger on it. I saw their flashlights. I heard someone walking up the steps. There is a knock on the door and this girl asks if anyone was home. I then see the doorknob rattling and being pushed."

"It was a girl?"

"Yes, and she's asking if she can come in and pee. I tell her no, but she keeps begging to come in. So, I open the blind and turn on the porch light and see her bending at the knees showing me she has to go."

"Did you let her in?"

"Hell, no! Then she comes right up to the door and she looks straight at me, takes off a mitten and puts her open palm on the window. Written on it was ***THEY'RE WATCHING. THEY'RE LISTENING.*** How crazy is that!!"

****

Parked by the entrance leading to the cabins, the van sat undisturbed. Sarah and Józef watched Carly and David on the monitors while listening to the conversation inside the cabin. From her seat in the van, Sarah's shoulders stiffened.

"What did she say…. turn up the volume."

Sarah listened intently as David spoke to Carly.

"***THEY'RE WATCHING. THEY'RE LISTENING.*** That's strange. Wonder what that meant? I bet she wrote that for someone else, like a joke or something, and you just saw it."

Carly took a sip of her tea. "Why would she take off her mitten if it was meant for someone else?"

"Good point. So, what did you say?"

"I said, 'Sorry, I'm not letting anyone in.' It really did seem like she was trying to tell me something. I don't know. She yelled to her friend that she had to pee in the woods. She went down the stairs, grabbed the toboggan rope, and the two pulled it away."

"Maybe you should let security know? It could be that fraternity trying to scare you into leaving."

"Yeah… maybe. I'm not going to say anything just yet. I just got here, and I don't want Dr. Hayes thinking I'm losing it already. I bet it was college kids. They want this place to party and I'm ruining their plans."

"I bet you're right. College kids," David said. "They don't give up, do they?"

"Not lately," Carly answered. "So, what are you planning for today?"

"I'm going to do some snow shoeing and walk the grounds. It's the first time I've ever been on those things. I have to get used to them."

"Really, you looked like a pro walking up here," Carly said, biting her lower lip. "So, you're going on recon?"

"Yep, it's my forest therapy. What about you?"

"I'm not sure. I'm meeting Meghan at 10:00, and later, I plan on doing some sketching on the deck.

David walked down to the bottom steps, knelt, and strapped on his snowshoes. He looked up at Carly who was standing in the doorway.

"I'll see you later today. Have fun getting your artist mojo on."

"DAMN!" Sarah said out loud as she ripped off her headphones and stepped out of the van. She had to let Slovak know. She needed to meet him and not anywhere near the campus. She called and they agreed to meet at Starbucks in Welchester.

When he got out of his Volvo, Sarah was already there, leaning against her jeep. Slovak made sure his door was locked and his gun hidden from view. "Please, don't tell me we have more problems," he snapped.

She glowered at him. "Walk with me," Sarah said as she led the way down the freshly plowed sidewalk.

"Sarah, stop," Slovak insisted. "Why are you acting so paranoid? You're bloody unhinged!"

"Just keep walking. We may have been compromised."

"Compromised? What are you talking about?"

"I don't know. I'm not sure. FBI. CIA. Pick one. I think we are being watched. You know those drunk college kids… they may not have been college kids at all."

"What the fuck are you talking about? Drunk college kids!!?"

Sarah stopped midstride and faced Slovak. "Sorry…I know I'm rambling. Last night two people who we thought were college kids went to Carly's cabin. They were pulling a toboggan with a keg on it."

"So, if they weren't college kids, who were they?" Slovak asked.

"That's the problem, I don't know." Sarah pulled her iPhone from her pocket. Józef had sent her a video of the conversation.

"Here, see for yourself," she said and handed it to Slovak.

He watched with concern, shaking his head in bewilderment. "When you bugged the cabin, I'm sure you scanned for any other listening devices before you put in yours."

"Of course."

"Good. So, whoever gave her that message, if indeed it was a message, could not have heard the conversation this morning between David and Carly."

"That's true," Sarah said. "They would have no clue we suspect something. But if it's the CIA, FBI, or whoever, why don't they do something? What are they waiting for? Take us out, for God's sake."

"That's the strange part," Slovak said, seemingly in deep thought. "Unless?"

"Unless what?" Sarah said impatiently.

"Unless they're not the government."

"Not the government! Who then? Who the hell else could it be?"

"I don't know," Slovak answered. "Now's not the time to let emotions get the better of us. You get back to the van and keep monitoring from there. I'll head to Hayes's office and meet with him. Keep everything the same until you hear back from me."

"You know, I hate you, Alexander. I hate you for putting me in this situation. I wish I had never met you."

"The feeling is mutual, Sarah. I can assure you, once this is over, you'll never see me again."

Chapter 21

Józef watched Carly toss her shirt and bra on the bedroom floor. Wearing only a lacey bikini, she stopped in front of the full-length mirror before slipping her thumbs under the waistband of her panties and sliding them down her thighs.

"Niiiiiiiiiice," Józef said softly, as he savored Carly's curves.

Sarah looked up from her spiral. "You're such a pig, Józef. Always trashy thoughts when it comes to women. I wouldn't give you the time of day."

Under his breath, Józef muttered, "Not to worry, Sarah. I wouldn't ask you for it."

"When she gets in the shower, play the conversation between son and mother. Wait about a minute before you do it. Wait until she starts to wash her hair."

Carly turned on the shower and waited until steam spiraled over the top. She stuck her hand into the flow, then cut back on the hot before stepping into the stall. She stood with her eyes closed, face directly under the flowing stream, enjoying the warm water rolling over her back and chest. Grabbing the shampoo, she squeezed some into her palm and massaged it into her hair.

"Now!" Sarah ordered. "Play the conversation now. Make it as loud as you can."

Carly's eyes shot open, then shut again from the sting of the shampoo. She immediately turned off the water and listened, head hanging, hair lathered and dripping. Her adrenaline spiked. From out of nowhere, her thoughts jumped to a walk in the park. A walk with her father… not so long ago. Panic, fear…the sound of her running footsteps on the snow packed trail. It was quick, fleeting, there and then gone. A flash.

"Cut it off," Sarah shouted.

Carly yanked back the shower curtain and stood motionless. She wiped her eyes, then listened for a while. Hearing nothing, she turned the water back on and quickly finished her rinse. She grabbed the towel hanging on the sidebar next to the shower and patted herself dry. Sliding her arms and body into the bathrobe, she carefully opened the bathroom door and peeked into the cabin's open living room. Nothing had changed. She was alone in the cabin.

****

Carly quickly dressed. Forgoing her hair and makeup she just needed to get out. The unplowed road from the cabin to the hill made Carly's walk grueling. Her boots sank into the newly fallen six inches making it exhausting to lift each one. It was 9:45 when Carly knocked on Meghan's hospital dorm. No one came. She waited, but it took a second knocking before she heard footsteps coming to the door.

Meghan wore a robe and her hair was wrapped in a towel. "It's not 10:00 yet Early Bird," she said, holding the door open. "Get yourself in here and make yourself at home, while I finish up."

Carly followed her through the hall and into the living room. She unzipped her parka, threw it to the side and flopped down onto the couch.

After blow-drying her hair and putting on her last touches of makeup, Meghan returned to the room. She noticed a distant stare on Carly's face and sat down next to her.

"Hey, what's going on? You having second thoughts about the cabin and your 60 days?"

"No," Carly answered quickly. "Never. Not a chance. But, on a serious note, do you remember me talking in the group about my memory loss and how Dr. Hayes said that it could come back all at once or in short pieces?"

"I do. Did you remember something?"

"I remembered something about my dad. Something he was saying to me."

"What was it?"

"We were walking along a wooded trail… I had Max with me. There were lots of trees. It's so weird…I could see my breath in the air. Like it was really happening. Dad and I were walking and talking, and he seemed really upset. He said things like, "Don't trust anyone until you know they can be trusted," and "be suspicious of whatever anyone does."

"That's really strange, like he was trying to warn you," Meghan said. "Did he say anything else?"

"Yes, the last thing was...If anything happens to him, I had to find Mr. Etadirhtim and to look to Artie for direction."

"Etadirhtim?" Isn't that the made-up guy you used as a safe password when you were a kid?"

"Yes. My dad made Artie and me memorize this riddle to remember his name."

"Could this guy really exist? Maybe he was a friend of your dad's. It could be someone he worked with."

"I don't know. I never met him. He was always just a password. A lot of good it did for Artie."

Reaching down, Meghan picked up a crossword book lying next to the couch. She opened it and removed a pen sitting in the spine. Looking at Carly, pen in hand, she asked, "How do you spell it?"

"What?"

"That guy. The password."

"Hmm... "It's been awhile. I got to start with the song.

"E is for Education, you can never get enough...

"T is for training if you want to get buff...

"A is for active and staying alert...

"D is for dodging, or you might get hurt...i-r-h-t-i-m

"Sorry. E-t-a-d-i-r-h-t-i-m." Carly then spelled it out.

"Sounds like it's pronounced Et-a-dirt-im," Meghan said. "Does that sound right?

"Yes. That's it. Et-a-dirt-im."

Meghan grabbed her cell phone sitting on the coffee table. "Let's just see if there's any "Et-a-dirt-ems" in the country. She spoke into her phone and read from the crossword page, saying each letter slowly and distinctly. "Siri, find the address of Mr. E-t-a-d-i-r-h-t-i-m."

"Searching" the voice shot back. Various white pages filled Meghan's phone. She tapped one after the other and read the results. "No address found... No address found... No address found."

Disappointed, she tossed the puzzle book back onto the coffee table.

"He's *not* a real guy," Carly said. "He was just a password."

"All right. What else did your dad say?"

"He said look to your brother for direction." Biting her lower lip and shrugging her shoulders Carly said, "How am I to look to Artie for direction? He's dead!"

Look to Artie for direction, Meghan thought. "Did he say anything else?"

"He said other things. I remember him asking me if I still had the locket he gave me."

"Why would he ask you about that?"

"He bought one for my mom and me. We came back from Germany to bury Artie and were staying at my grandparent's lake house. The house was in Lexington. I think we were there for a month."

"Oh, that's right. Artie's buried a couple hours from here."

"Yes. We had just buried him that morning and the funeral luncheon was at the lake house. My aunts and uncles were there. Everyone was standing around, teary eyed, talking quietly.

"My dad wanted the three of us to go for a walk. He led us down to the lake and handed my mom and me velvet boxes. Inside each box was a locket—the exact same locket. Same picture inside and everything. I didn't think I had any tears left until he gave us those lockets. My dad told us never to take them off. He said Artie is in heaven with Gabriel."

"Gabriel? That's an odd thing to say. Who's Gabriel?"

"He's a guardian angel. The messenger angel. My dad said if we ever get in trouble to look to Artie and Gabriel. The two of them will give us a message and keep us safe. Some people believe, some don't."

Tapping the pen on her teeth, mulling over what Carly told her, Meghan's face suddenly lit up. "There's gotta be something here. Your dad was trying to tell you something. Let me see your locket."

Carly reached inside her shirt and pulled the heart shaped locket out by its chain. She then let it dangle from her neck.

"If he wanted me to know something, why not just tell me?" Carly asked.

"I don't know. Maybe he was going to but didn't have time. Maybe he was worried about you saying something that needed to be kept secret. Or maybe he was worried about someone hurting you."

"Hurting me? How? Like torture!?"

"Could be. Your dad had to know Artie was murdered, right? Just follow me on this. He wanted to give you information about something, if anything, happened to him. So, it has to be something pretty important. At the same time, he wanted to protect you and not tell you everything. Are you following so far?"

"Yes, I think so."

"If your dad said Artie would be like Gabriel. What if Artie is the messenger? How could he give you a message? It may have something to do with the locket."

Lifting her hand and holding it, Carly flipped it from side to side.

"Take it off and open it," Meghan said.

Carly felt behind her neck until she found the clasp. She unhooked the delicate chain and held it in her hand.

"Open it. There could be a clue in it from your dad."

Carly took her thumb nail and placed it in the tiny slit. Her eyes watered as she stared down at the picture of Artie. "He was such a good brother." She held the locket under the bright light of the lamp, holding it different ways, rubbing the golden surface as if she expected a message to appear.

"Nothing… it looks the same."

"The only thing we haven't done is to take the picture out. Maybe there's something behind it? "Can you pop it out?" Meghan asked.

"I need something like a pin or a toothpick. Do you have one?"

Meghan left the couch and went to the kitchen. Carly watched as she rummaged through a drawer. "I have a paper clip, would that work?"

"Sure. Anything with a tip."

Carly lowered the locket onto the coffee table as Meghan walked back straightening the paper clip.

"Try to pry it out," she said handing it to her.

Placing it on the upper right side of the heart shaped picture, Carly gently pried. The picture popped and landed face down. Nothing was written on the back. Carly's eyes grew wide. "There's writing engraved in the locket."

"What does it say?" Meghan asked, not being able to contain her enthusiasm.

Carly placed it under the lamp and squinted. "I can't read it. It's too small."

"Hold on…use my phone."

"How's that going to help?"

"Click the home button three times and it'll become a magnifying glass. If you have an Apple, yours can, too. Just have the magnifier turned on under settings."

Carly hit the home button three times and held the camera lens over the locket. The writing became enlarged and clear. "I never knew you could do that."

"What's it say?" Meghan asked eagerly.

"White Rabbit song
White chess piece."

"What?"

"White Rabbit song
White chess piece."

"Can I see that?" Meghan asked, taking the locket and her phone. She hovered over the writing.

"White Rabbit song
White chess piece."

"I don't get it. Why would your dad have that engraved in the locket? I bet the same thing was in your mom's locket."

Carly shrugged her shoulders. "I don't know…There's so much I don't know… Ask Siri what is the White Rabbit song"

"Siri, what is the White Rabbit song?" Both listened to what Siri had found…

"White Rabbit" is by Jefferson Airplane."

The creases in Meghan's forehead deepened as her brows drew together. Let's find the song and listen to it."

"Yeah, we have to."

Meghan found the song and tapped the red arrow in the middle of the screen. The song came up and the two sat and listened. When the song ended, Carly asked, "Should we play it again?"

"No. Let's get the lyrics."

"Siri… find the lyrics to *White Rabbit, Jefferson Airplane."*

Meghan tapped the first site she came to. "Gotta get to the lines that talk about chess," she mumbled to herself.

Carly watched as Meghan used her index finger and scrolled down the lyrics until she said, "Here we go."

"When the men on the chessboard get up and tell you where to go.
And you've just had some kind of mushroom, and your mind is moving low
"Go ask Alice, I think she'll know
When logic and proportion have fallen sloppy dead.
And the white knight is talking backwards
And the red queen's off with her head..."

"That's it! The white knight. That's the white piece. It's gotta be," Carly said, as she took the pen and puzzle book off the coffee table. "Let's see where we're at."
She began to write down each thing they knew.

"Number 1. *Look to Artie for direction.* We did."

"Number 2. "*The White Knight is talking backwards*. We found it."

"Number 3. *Find Mr. Etadirhtim.* Haven't yet."

"Talking backwards? What could the white knight be saying backwards?" Meghan asked.

Carly's mouth dropped slightly as she held out her hand, "Give me the phone and the page where you wrote Etadirhtim."

Meghan saw the look on Carly's face. She handed her the phone.

"What if Mr. Etadirhtim speaks backwards," Carly said. "I'm going to spell Etadirhtim backwards and see if Siri tells us anything."

"Oh my God."

"Siri, what does m-i-t-h-r-i-d-a-t-e mean?" She spoke each letter into the phone.

Both girls watched as the screen filled with definitions. She tapped the first one and read it out loud.

"**Mithridate** - A universal antidote against poison."

"Poison!" Meghan said in a raised voice. "What's he trying to tell you about antidotes and poison?"

"I don't have any idea."

Meghan grasped Carly's arm and looked right at her. "There's something here. Your dad had that engraved for you and your mom. He gave one to each of you with the same instructions-- to look to Artie if you get into trouble."

Meghan hesitated. "What if the trouble has already started?"

Carly flinched. "What should we do? I mean, if the trouble has already started. And most of all, what kind of trouble?"

"At this point, neither of us know. I definitely wouldn't tell Hayes. If it's just our imaginations playing tricks, so be it. If it's not, we have to be careful."

Carly nodded. She placed the picture of Artie back into the locket and gently pressed on it with her thumb. She re-clasped the chain around her neck, her hands shaking slightly.

"Meghan, I feel so tired. I don't know what to do. Today, little bits of my world crumbled around me. I am remembering things my mind had me forget. All this stuff about my Dad and Artie. It's starting to scare me."

"Oh, Carly," Meghan said softly. "I know you're scared. I am, too. I also know you will make the best decision about what to do. You are one of the strongest people I know. You're stronger than you think. I believe in you."

Carly's face remained expressionless. It took a long time before she began speaking. "There's more to this. There's gotta be more my dad was trying to tell me. Or should I say warn me?"

Chapter 22

Advancing from the woods, Ahmed waved at Porsche and was relieved seeing her driving down the dirt road. She stopped, allowing him to jump in.

"So glad to see you, Babe," he said. "It's so easy to get turned around on these back roads. My cell doesn't work when I'm off the ridge. If you didn't show, I'd have to hike back up to call."

"Everything good?" Porsche asked as Ahmed fastened his seat belt and removed his white camo hat and gloves.

"Yeah, all good. That guy from Cabin 1 came over first thing in the morning. The door must have been frozen; he had a hell of a time getting in. He managed to and that's when I left."

"Good," Porsche said, as she came to a paved road and made a right. "I turned left, yesterday and got lost. Thank God for Google maps. I think I'm directionally challenged."

"You found me."

"No, actually you found me," she said, chuckling. "I had no clue where you were. The woods all looked the same." She merged onto M-59 heading back to their rented townhouse. "So, tell me again… why are you letting Carly go through this. Why not snatch her up and hide her?"

"She has to go through this. It's the only thing keeping her alive. There's something Hayes wants from Carly. I need to know what it is."

Porsche looked at Ahmed and then back to the road. "What aren't you telling me?"

Ahmed didn't say a thing. His face soured. Porsche asked again. "Why don't you just kill that son of a bitch? There's something you not telling me."

Ahmed then blurted out… "It was me! I killed Artie! It was no accident."

Porsche's heart lurched. With her brows knitted she stared at Ahmed. A blaring horn startled her, sending her back into her own lane. She focused on the road looking straight ahead. "What the fuck are you talking about? You said he drowned."

"That was the official Army report. All manufactured by the CIA. Trust me, it was no accident."

Porsche placed her hand on Ahmed's knee, never taking her eyes off the road. "Please, tell me what happened."

He paused and looked straight out the window. A deep sorrow resonated through his voice as he began to explain. "I was a young CIA field officer, stationed in Germany. I was assigned to a small group of operatives that kept the country's clandestine operations safe and secret. The United States was developing deadly pathogens that could be used in bioweapons. This research was banned under an international treaty the U.S. had signed onto."

"Why research bioweapons if your government would never use them?"

"Because we knew other countries and regimes would and we needed an antidote. You first have to make the poison before you can make an antidote. We are talking about pathogens so deadly they could wipe out entire cites simply by introducing them into the public."

Porsche cracked the window and reached for the pack of cigarettes. "I got it," Ahmed said as he beat her reach then fished two out. "Where's the lighter?"

"Glove box."

He placed both cigarettes in his mouth, lit them and handed one to Porsche. Inhaling deeply, he continued. "Fletcher had been working on this project for years. He went to Siberia and mined the pathogens that were used in the weapon development."

"Why Siberia?"

"Because there are deadly pathogens buried deep under the permafrost. Pathogens so toxic they could start a pandemic. Modern humans have never been exposed to these pathogens. They've been buried for tens of thousands of years."

Porsche flicked the ash of her cigarette out the window, then said. "I still don't understand why you're saying you killed Artie. I mean you told me you loved the family and would give your life for them. Isn't that why we're here?"

"I didn't stop it. I tried, but I failed."

"So, you blame yourself for not protecting him. It's not your fault some son of a bitch killed him?"

Talking to the floor mat, Ahmed forced the words out. "I used Artie as bait. Just like I'm doing with Carly."

Porsche pulled off the interstate and into the lot of their townhouse. She shut off the engine and tossed her cigarette out the window. She unbuckled her seat belt and turned slightly towards Ahmed. "Sounds like an operation that went sideways and you're totally blaming yourself. Tell me more."

Still not making eye contact, Ahmed continued. "Intelligence knew there was a terrorist group working in Germany and that this group had breached the weapons program. They wanted to get their hands on the pathogens and would do anything to get them. My job was to keep tabs on the Fletcher family and protect them. Fletcher himself was kept in the dark.

"We uncovered a plot where the plan was to kidnap one of Fletcher's kids and use them for ransom. The ransom being the pathogens. Some of my team wanted to hide the kids in a safe house, but I insisted on using them to flush out who was behind this."

"So, why was it your fault?"

"I was at the playground the day Artie was taken. We took shifts. It just so happened that this went down on my watch. The kids left their house, and I followed them. They headed to the base playground. The playground was built in the middle of a marsh and surrounded by a fence. A dirt path led to it. I stood just outside the fence hidden by tall grasses. Everything was fine until I saw him."

"Saw who?" Porsche asked.

"The guy who killed Artie. I watched what I thought was a teenager kick the ball Artie was playing with over the fence. But I soon found out he wasn't a teenager at all… he was someone dressed as a teenager and he was part of the operation.

"When Artie jumped to retrieve his ball, another man wearing camouflage pants darted from the grasses and snatched him. He placed his hand over Artie's mouth and ran.

"I immediately radioed in and entered the marsh from the far side. I was so sure of myself… Big, bad officer making a name for himself. Within minutes officers were scouring the marsh. I never imagined a waiting canoe."

"Canoe? Is that how he did it?"

"Yes. That marsh had shallow canals no bigger than four feet wide and only inches deep. Deep enough to float a canoe with a 50-pound little boy in it. The vegetation was thick…it made it almost impossible to walk. The kidnapper knew this. We think he bound and gagged Artie and placed him in the canoe. He simply floated him down the canal to the lake. It was diabolical but at the same time brilliant. The dogs followed the scent to the edge of the canal and then lost it."

"Sounds well planned and thorough," Porsche said. "These people really sound professional."

"They sure weren't rookies. We found their abandoned canoe in the woods on the edge of the lake. One of Artie's shoes was in it. Tied to a tree next to the canoe was a rope long enough to reach the water's edge. It must have held a boat of some kind which they used to cross the lake. The abductor was probably halfway across when we were still trudging around in the marsh."

"So? What happened to using him for ransom?"

Ahmed rubbed his eyes, his face somber as he continued. "Artie was fished out of the water the next day. His hands were zip-tied behind his back and his mouth gagged. Somehow, he went over. Don't know why. The kidnappers surely didn't want him dead. Maybe they panicked when they saw the helicopter. Who knows? I was sent to ID the body before they brought him ashore."

Ahmed looked up from the floor with an expression Porsche had never seen before. Maybe it was the shadow cast across his face from the ambient light of the parking lot. Maybe it was the sleepless nights from the nightmares of an eight-year-old's bloated body. Maybe it was just the long day. He looked older… tired. Porsche took hold of the sides of Ahmed's cheeks and looked him in the eyes. He tried to look away, but she held firm.

"You don't own this. This was not your fault. Evil exists in this world and you are trying to do something about it. You can't keep beating yourself up. You gotta let it go."

"I can't let it go. From that day, the image has haunted me. After Carly's brother was murdered, I had this terrible guilt. Fletcher knew it was not an accidental death but kept it from his wife and daughter. He was never made aware that his son was used in our operation. I was now assigned to be with the family at all times. If the Colonel was not with them, I was. I became very close to them."

"Is this when you started training Carly how to shoot and do the martial arts?"

"Yeah, she became a little bad ass."

"I thought this was all behind you when the Colonel got transferred to the states. Right? The program was over?"

"No. It continued. The fear was that more and more rogue groups were getting closer to developing a pathogen line. We needed to keep developing a mixture of antidotes."

"So, what made you leave Germany for the states?"

"I got some distraught texts from the Colonel. From what I could tell, he felt someone, or a group might be after the pathogens, and they were hunting for him. Sort of like what happened in Germany with Artie."

"So, are these the same people watching Carly?"

"Can't be. We killed them all and then some."

"What do you mean? And then some?"

"If you were a friend of a friend or a family member and had any affiliation with the group, the CIA took you out. If it was determined that you were the least bit involved or could have been involved, you were killed."

"Then who are these people that are here and what do they want with Carly?"

"It's gotta be the pathogens. I can't think of anything else. The group we took out in Germany were not the only ones wanting it. Plenty of bad guys out there. The Colonel knew that his texts were probably compromised. He didn't want to spell out what was going on, so he only said so much. He said, if something happened to him, he wanted me to help Carly find Mr. Etadirhtim."

"So, who is he?"

"That's just it, he doesn't exist. It was a password he set up with his kids that if a stranger ever came and wanted you to go with him, you first had to ask for the password. Artie never had a chance. He was grabbed in a matter of seconds."

Porsche pushed the window button on the Ford Taurus and closed it. She grabbed the latch of the door, pulled, and started to exit when a thought entered her head. Turning to Ahmed, she said, "Aren't you worried the same thing could happen with Carly…using her for bait and all?"

Hearing those words, Ahmed sighed. It was a truth he did not want to face. "Don't you think I have thought of that? Part of me wants to avenge Artie and the Colonel's death, and part of me wants to protect Carly at all costs. The way I see it, Carly is in danger one way or the other. She's in that cabin for a reason. I have to find out why."

"You gotta get some sleep," Porsche said opening the car door. "What time do you want to go back?"

"Noon," Ahmed answered. "I want to be back by noon."

Chapter 23

"The town of Aston was quiet, appeared asleep," the narrator's voice droned over the speakers, rising and falling as he read the story. "The light posts in front of the library dimmed, and the sidewalks were bare except for a shadowy flash of feet skittering to nearby bushes."

Drake Adams gripped the steering wheel of his Chevy Tahoe, driving it slowly past the ice cream shop."

Hayes listened to the audio book as he drove down the freshly plowed road to his office. They were an indulgence he allowed himself, something to keep his mind off the ongoing chaos in his life.

An incoming phone call interrupted the reading. He glanced at the instrument panel and let out a sigh. "Alex," Hayes said, noticeably irritated.

"We need to meet."

"Ok…I should be at the office by 8:00."

"Umm…right. I don't want to meet there."

"Why? What's going on now?"

"I'd rather not say. Just meet me at Dunkin's. Downtown Welchester. How long until you can get there?"

Looking at his dashboard clock, Hayes said, "Let's see…7:40. How about 15-20 minutes? Is everything all right? I'm sensing something is not right."

"Just hurry it up. I'll be waiting at a table."

The line for drive-thru wrapped around the building as Hayes pulled into the lot. He quickly saw the Volvo and parked next to it. Warm smells of cinnamon, vanilla, and coffee welcomed him when he pushed through the doors of the coffee shop. Scanning the restaurant, he saw Slovak raise his hand and motion to him. Two cups of coffee with lids sat on the table.

"Why are we meeting here?" Hayes asked. "Why are we meeting at all?" he added, then scooted in his chair.

Slovak suspiciously scrutinized Hayes' chest. "Are you wearing a wire?" he asked.

"A wire? Are you fucking nuts?" he snapped looking from side to side, realizing he spoke too loudly. Lowering his voice, he leaned in. "It never stops with you. Am I wearing a goddamn wire? What the fuck!"

"Take your coat off and flatten your shirt up against your chest."

"Are you kidding me?" Hayes asked in disbelief.

"Do it," Slovak insisted.

Hayes stood, unzipped his winter coat, and dropped it on the chair next to him. He pulled his shirt at the bottom, making it taut against his body.

"Turn around," Slovak ordered.

Hayes turned awkwardly around, feet slowly shuffling on the tiled floor.

Slovak motioned for him to sit.

"What the hell's going on?" Hayes burst out, a scowl on his face.

"Our plans have changed."

"Why?"

"Sarah suspects our operation may have been compromised."

"Compromised?" he said leaning back in his seat. "Why does she think that?"

"That doesn't concern you."

"Doesn't concern me!" Hayes protested. "You call me up and tell me to come here for something you can't discuss on the phone and then tell me it doesn't concern me! It all concerns me!"

"Lower your voice." Slovak surveyed the coffee shop noting two teens up at the counter, a black-haired woman sitting by the window punching in a text message, and a senior eating a doughnut and reading a newspaper before he started speaking again. "We need to get her to another site. We are going to see if we can get some answers there."

Hayes shook his head. "Answers? You want answers? What part of this don't you get? She doesn't remember. You can't torture information out of people if they don't remember. She's not hiding this from us."

Slovak lifted his coffee cup, then abruptly set it down. "Do you have a fucking better plan?" he fumed. "Our backs are against the wall. We may have the FBI or who knows breathing down our necks. At least the black site will be more secure."

Hayes placed his head in his hands and massaged his temples. "A black site now? How can I possibly have anything to do with that?"

"Sarah and I have a plan. We'll meet in your office at noon to go over it."

Sliding the cup towards Hayes, Slovak said, "Take this with you."

"Fuck off," Hayes replied. Then he stood and left, leaving the coffee. A few tables away, a woman pulled up her collar and lowered her head making sure not to make eye contact as he passed.

****

Slovak slowly cruised the lot looking for a place to park. He spotted a Tahoe backing out near the playground and put his blinker on, claiming the space. The municipal park was bustling with people as families dressed in winter clothes carried toboggans, sleds, and hot chocolate. Lifting his collar, he opened the door and instantly felt the bite of the cold. He grabbed the gloves and stocking cap sitting on the passenger seat and put them on. While he stood beside his car, he scanned the area looking for anyone who might be a *tail.* His contact did the same for him. Satisfied none was present, Slovak removed his gloves, signaling everything was a go.

Outdoor locations were the best for clandestine meetings, and there had been several of them. Meeting outdoors made it easier to spot telephoto lenses or surveillance cameras and impossible to plant a bug. Each encounter ended with setting up the next place, date and time. Slovak arrived in the general vicinity, never a specific location at first. The two knew each other by sight and strolled the area eventually making eye contact some distance away. In reversing roles, his operative continued the walk, checking for people loitering that seemed to be in an advantageous position to watch. Finding none, the agent removed her sunglasses and sat on a bench, signaling Slovak to come and join her.

He took a place beside her and held his smart phone in front of him, pretending to surf.

"I need you to find a 'black site'. We are moving in a new direction."

"New direction? What? I still can't believe they're letting you continue after the fuckup with the Fletcher operation," Tatyana Nikolaev replied, never making eye contact, and looking straight ahead at the families skating on the frozen pond.

"My operation was a bit harder than yours; wouldn't you agree? How much skill does it take to seduce men and lure them into your bed just long enough for your goons to come in and subdue them? Not much in my opinion."

Dropping her head and playing in the snow with her boot, Tatyana continued, "Skill! Seduction *is* my skill and over the centuries it has brought down more powerful men than any weapon."

Placing his phone in his side coat pocket, Slovak leaned back on the bench, folded his arms, and pretended to also watch the skaters.

"I've brought in a colleague of mine. Sarah Hass. I worked with her in Poland after 9/11. She's an expert interrogator and got results. She did things that would never be allowed in the U.S. I need you to find a place not far from Holy Oaks. A place where Sarah can work her magic. Maybe an hour north. Check on some cottage rentals that are secluded. It's the off season, shouldn't be tough. Are you still sleeping with Carly's boyfriend?"

"Of course, I've got my orders," Tatyana replied.

"Good. It's time to bring in your thugs. We'll need him and audiovisual at the site too. Make sure it has Wi-Fi."

"Got it," Tatyana replied, smiling at a couple walking their dog past the park bench.

Slovak stood and continued to observe the families frolicking in the snow. "We'll meet in two days. Same time. Welchester's Farmers' Market. Drive to whatever cottage you find and check it out yourself. I'm not trusting anyone at this point."

****

"I know I packed them somewhere." Carly said to herself as she scanned the boxes looking for her pen and ink supplies. *Oh, here we go...*

Heading out the door, Carly walked down the steps to the bird feeder mounted on a pole a few yards from the deck. She brushed off the newly fallen snow then headed back up. She cleared one of the two snow covered chairs and sat down.

With her pad on her knees, she began to sketch the background of the forest. Dipping the quill into the ink bottle she began. Black leafless trees stood in the background as the forest picture came alive. Outlines of winter birds eating from the feeder would have color added once she was back inside the warm cabin.

"So, how's your art mojo going?" a familiar voice called out from the bottom of the stairs.

Carly looked up from her sketch and saw David holding a pair of snowshoes and wearing a backpack. Lifting the snowshoes up above his head he said, "Come on. Come give these a try. The forest is beautiful today."

Sticking the nib of the quill in the baby food jar of rapidoeze, Carly recapped the bottle of Indian ink and placed both atop the pad. "I've never gone snowshoeing before."

"Neither have I…until this morning. It doesn't take long to get used to it."

Carly looked down from the deck. "Let me put this stuff away and grab some gloves. Be back in a flash."

She cautiously walked to the bottom of the steps, holding on to the banister as she did. David knelt and positioned the snowshoes and opened the bindings.

"Step in…I'll adjust."

She lowered her boots into each binding, holding onto David's shoulders. "Push straight down with your foot. I need to get the straps tight." David instructed and then stepped back.

"It'll feel a little clumsy at first, but you'll get used to them…ready?"

"Ready not to break my leg." Carly took a step and then another. Picking up the pace, she glanced at David and then quickly back to the ground.

"See? You're getting it," David started, before the tip of one shoe buried in the snow and she fell. Lying in the snow, Carly strained to look up. "Now what? How do I get up?"

David grabbed two of the four walking poles he had stuck in the snow and snow shoed to her. He helped her to her feet and placed a pole in each hand.

"You have to remember to pick the shoe straight up when you walk, otherwise the tip will get caught when you start picking up the pace. I've already fallen a half dozen times."

David placed both hands under one of his bent knees. "Watch this," he said pulling his knee straight up and casting his leg forward. "You gotta keep the tip above the snow."

Carly lifted her shoe, then lunged it forward. Another lift, then forward. The poles steadied her as she walked.

"Follow me. I'll go slow. You'll feel like you're gliding over water."

"I am gliding on water!" Carly laughed. "Frozen water!"

The two hiked into the woods, forging their own trail on the freshly fallen snow. After a quarter mile or so, he stopped and looked up at a huge boulder sitting high upon a ridge. The boulder looked foreign, out of place. It was the only thing not covered in a blanket of white.

"There. We're going up there. We'll sit and take a break. I bet the view is unbelievable."

"All the way up there?" Carly gasped. "It looks pretty steep."

"That's right. Follow me," David said, his mouth curving into a smile.

Carly leaned her body forward and took one step at a time, using the poles to push and steady herself. She did not look back to see how high she was until safely making it to the top of the ridge.

As the two sat on the boulder, stripping off their sweaty hats and gloves, Carly whispered, "Look David, Mama Doe and her fawn. They're down by the creek at the base of the ridge."

In a whisper David replied, "Why are you whispering? They're a couple hundred yards away."

Laughing, Carly bent down to take off her bindings. As she did, David reached into his backpack and pulled out a small wicker basket.

"I wonder who put this in here?"

Carly grinned when she saw the picnic basket. "Oh, my God, David. Are we having a picnic?"

"As a matter a fact, we are."

Grabbing two napkins, he handed one to Carly. He sat the basket on the rock and pulled out two bottles of water. Four fried chicken legs neatly placed in a zip lock bag followed.

"Did you swipe that basket from my coffee table when I wasn't looking?" she teased. "The one with the ugly, fake, plastic flowers?"

"Nope, both cabins have 'em. Obviously, they didn't hire an interior decorator when they furnished the joint."

Holding up the bag of chicken legs, he said, "Fried these this morning...before I made your muffins."

Carly was speechless. Taking hold of the chicken legs never losing eye contact, she asked, "Are you courting me?"

"If I was courting you, there would be chocolate and roses. It's just you, me, and fried chicken. Go ahead give it a try," David said, grinning slightly and nodding toward the chicken legs.

Holding the napkin under her chin, she brought the leg to her mouth and took a big bite.

"It's good," she mumbled through a full mouth then swallowed. Carly finished the leg and held out the bone.

"What should I do with this?"

David snatched it from her and tossed it into the woods. "It'll be gone by morning. Raccoons like chicken, too."

"Well aren't you the ethologist," Carly joked.

"A what?"

"An ethologist. It's a person who studies and understands the behavior of animals. You know like *Crocodile Dundee.*"

"Not sure about Dundee, but growing up on a farm, I learned early what raccoons will do for food. Had one almost kick my ass."

"You got into a fight with a raccoon?"

"Yep. I was about fourteen and I was working in the back of our barn one night. I heard these garbage cans tip over and when I turned I saw this huge female with her kits. She had three of them. The kits could have cared less about me, but Mama Coon was walking towards me hissing."

"Oh, no. What'd you do?"

"Backed off, picked up a shovel and just stood there. Eventually she went back to the garbage cans and started eating too. The only exit was past those cans. Every time I tried to move toward the door, she would come back at me. Probably thinking I would hurt her babies. I was in that stand off for what felt like an hour until my dad came looking for me and let the dogs out. Once they heard the dogs, they ran like hell."

"How funny," Carly chuckled, then dug into her other piece of chicken. When it was finished, she tossed it into the woods. After she wiped her greasy chin and fingers with the napkin, she balled it up and shot it into the open basket. "Bet you didn't know I played basketball."

"Anything else you play?" he asked mischievously.

"Just keep hanging around," she remarked. "You may find out other things I'm good at."

"If that's true," David replied, "I can't wait until your memory comes back."

The mention of her memory coming back caused Carly to squirm on the rock. Her happy demeanor changed. She lowered her head and moved snow around with her boot. She began to talk, not looking at David. "I think I am getting sick."

"What? My cooking?!"

"No…not your cooking. My delusions are coming back. My mind is playing games with me. I'm hearing voices."

"Like what? What'd you hear?"

"I was taking a shower this morning, and I swear I heard a woman and young boy talking. I mean it really sounded like a conversation."

"A woman and a kid?"

"Yeah. Then last night, I heard Artie calling, telling me he was here. I thought it was a dream at first and didn't think more of it."

Saying nothing, David moved closer to Carly. Close enough for their legs to touch.

"You might not be getting sick. There're some weird things happening around here. You know that girl…that girl with the message on her palms? What if she was really trying to give you a message? Maybe she was trying to tell you something. I don't want to freak you out, but if someone is listening and watching, we need to know how they are doing it and why. I didn't want to tell you that in the cabin, just in case someone was listening."

Carly's eyes grew wide. "What if the person looking at me from the field wasn't a frat boy. Maybe it was someone else?"

"I gotta tell you, I saw footprints that weren't mine. After I checked out your cabin last night, I got curious and followed them. They came from just outside your place and I traced them back to mine. Once you ran from your cabin, someone followed you to my place. I'm sure of it."

"This really is freaking me out."

David reached and took hold of her hand. "This could all be in our heads. I mean, who would be watching you and why? Maybe it's just two crazies letting their minds get the better of them."

"But you did see those tracks." Carly slowly shook her head. "No, I think there's more to it. You know, David, all this weird stuff started happening after I met Slovak and started getting hypnotized. Realizing that Artie was murdered. The conversation I heard between Dr. Hayes and someone he was talking to about me and getting answers. There's one other thing I'm going to tell you. I wasn't going to at first. Meghan thought I should keep it to myself but I'm going to tell you anyway."

"What's that?"

"Remember I told you I was going to see Meghan this morning."

"Yeah"

"Well, while I was in the shower, I had this flash of memory. I was walking on a trail with my dad and he was talking about Artie. He said if anything happens to him or me, to look for Artie for direction. It was like a clue."

"A clue? For what?"

"This is going to sound bat-shit crazy, but do you know what mithridate is?"

"Myth-a-what?"

"Mithridate."

"No idea."

"I didn't either until Meghan and I solved the clue. Mithridate is a universal antidote for poison." Carly unzipped her parka and pulled out her locket. "My dad inscribed a clue on the inside of my locket. It was underneath Artie's picture. He gave me and my mom the exact same locket, the day we buried Artie."

"Why would your dad give you a clue about mithridate? I mean why do you need an antidote?"

"I'm trying to figure that out. There's something more to it."

"You know," David said, "I think Dr. Hayes has started carrying a gun."

"A gun?"

"Yeah. I noticed it the day he came to tell me about you moving into Cabin 2. I gave him a hug and when I put my arms around him, I felt a revolver. I asked him about it and he just played it off. Said he has his CCW but never carries on campus. The reason he had it that day was because he was heading home from my place and not going back to the office. Said he never drives without it. It really didn't sound legit, but I went along with it."

A worried look filled Carly's face. "Dr. Hayes and a gun? Doesn't seem like him. I could sort of feel him out this afternoon when we head to town."

"What's this afternoon?"

"Duh, don't you remember? Secretary of State. Dr. Hayes is taking me to the Secretary of State's office to put in the paperwork to get my license back. I could bring it up when we're driving."

"Oh, that's right. First day after a night in the cabin. You get your license back."

"So, should I? Should I try and get some answers about the gun? I'll make it real nonchalant."

"I wouldn't mention a thing. If Dr. Hayes is involved you don't want him to think you suspect something. If I were you I would act like nothing in the world is wrong. Act as if you're excited to get your license back and that's it."

Carly nodded in agreement. "I can do that."

Dark, grey storm clouds blocked the sun as Carly and David felt a northerly chill. "Look what's coming" Carly said. "My phone says we're in for a storm, maybe a couple more inches."

"I know. I've been following it, too. Let's get heading back."

"Lead the way," Carly said.

Ahmed lowered the binoculars and looked to the sky. *More snow, Damn!*

Chapter 24

Seated in Hayes office, Sarah had already swept the room for any type of listening device. She needed every bit of self-control to keep her gun concealed. She wanted Hayes dead and his whining voice silenced. Instead, she squeezed her fingers into fists, released them, nodded her head in agreement when he spoke.

"Keep him calm and don't say anything that will set him off," Slovak had warned her. *"We need him to pull this off. The bastard could wreck everything if he doesn't cooperate."*

"Where's Slovak?" Hayes asked for the third time, leaning back in his chair. "He said he was coming here. He should already be here."

"He'll be here," Sarah said calmly, glancing at her cell phone. "I'm sure he will be here shortly."

Hayes reached down into his lower drawer and pulled out the bottle of ouzo. His face tensed when he realized it was empty. He tossed the bottle into the small trash bin next to his desk. "I want this to be over!" he shouted, taking his arm and recklessly sweeping everything off his desk. "I want to be done with all of this… and with both of you."

Sarah looked at the stapler, ballpoint pens, and paperclips scattered on the floor. "I know you do. It's been difficult for all of us. A change of plans was needed," she replied, shifting her weight in the uncomfortable chair.

"Who do you think it is?! Why won't anyone tell me who is watching us?"

"Stephan, we're almost done. You'll be back to your normal life, and Slovak and I will be out of yours."

"And Carly will be dead!" Hayes snapped as he abruptly pushed himself up from his desk and stood.

The outer office door swung open, and Slovak appeared. He glanced at the items strewn on the floor and Stephan standing behind his desk. He looked quizzically at Sarah.

"Stephan was just letting off a little steam," Sarah said. "Nothing to worry about."

Slovak removed his overcoat and tossed it on the couch.

"Stephan," he urged, "This is the last thing we need from you. Sit down and make the call, you're close to being done."

Dr. Hayes said nothing. His face was devoid of any sign of expression. Reluctantly he lowered himself into the chair.

"Have you two gone over the plan?" Slovak asked.

"No, we've been waiting for you," Sarah answered.

"Tell Stephen where the transfer will take place."

"We'll be parked down past the apple grove by the creek. The road's a little washed out, but you should be able to make it. We'll do the transfer there."

With a flash of anger, Hayes blew up. "So, I'm just supposed to drive her there and watch as you and your thugs walk up to my car, yank her out, and take her?"

Sarah shifted back in her chair. "It'll be fast, Stephan. We'll hood her and sedate her…she'll be out within a minute."

"And then wake to a grisly nightmare…I don't know if I can do this."

"There's no turning back for any of us! You can't back out now," Slovak insisted, pushing Hayes' cell phone towards him. "Make the call, Stephen. This will be the last thing you need to do."

Sarah reinforced his demands. "It's time. Make the call."

Hayes picked up the phone and called. His stomach ached as if steel knives were driven into it. The phone rang only once, and Carly immediately picked up. "Dr. Hayes… I've been waiting for your call. Are we still on for 2:00?" she said, barely giving Hayes a chance to talk.

"Yes." Dr. Hayes said, clearing his throat. "We're all set for 2:00. See you then."

"I'll be ready."

Hayes let the phone drop onto his desk. He closed his eyes and leaned back in his chair. He never heard Slovak rise and stand behind him. Removing a wire garrote from his pocket, Slovak gripped the leather handles and opened his arms until the weapon stretched taut. He threw the thin wire around the front of Hayes' neck and tightened his grip.

Instinctively, Hayes reached for the wire, grabbing and pulling at it. Slovak held tight, as guttural sounds filled the room. Grabbing only air, his thrashing arms could not reach Slovak. In a last desperate attempt, Hayes twisted in the chair, causing its legs to become unbalanced. He pushed his weight back and the two tumbled to the floor. Slovak maintained his grip.

"Grab his legs! Sit on his legs!" Slovak choked out, as he strained to keep the garrote tight.

"Jesus Christ!" Sarah cried, then dropped to her knees and lay over his flailing legs.

The two kept their positions until the gasping sounds faded and Hayes no longer moved.

"He's dead," Sarah said studying his face. "Are you sure?" Slovak asked.

With an annoyed look Sarah lifted herself. "I've seen plenty of dead people. He's gone." She looked at Hayes urine-soaked pants. "Yeah, he's dead."

Releasing the pressure of the garrote, Slovak rose to his feet.

Standing mute, looking away from Hayes' body, he heard a phone ring. A picture of Savannah Ray with the word HOME scrolled across the screen.

Slovak raked his hand through his disheveled hair, then wiped the beads of perspiration from his brow. He reached down and picked up the phone, then pressed the decline button.

"We had to do it. We couldn't trust him." Slovak set the cell back on the desk and looked at Sarah.

"He probably would have picked Carly up and driven her straight to Welchester's PD. We couldn't take that chance. Get your guys in here and load him into the trunk before Susan gets back from lunch. I don't want to have to kill her, too."

Sarah punched a message into her cell phone. Within minutes, two men wearing J & M Carpet uniforms entered the office, pushing a cart with a large rolled rug. They removed the plastic outside wrapping and spread the rug onto the floor.

"Couldn't you have at least closed his eyes?" Józef scoffed as he bent over and with the base of his palm shut each eye.

"Grab his legs. I've got his arms," he said to the other man. "Let's put him on the end and roll him."

“Wait,” Sarah ordered as she knelt next to Hayes’s body checking his pockets until she found his keys.

“Put him in the trunk of his Cadillac. Then bring back the keys.”

“You’re the boss,” Józef said, taking the keys from Sarah and placing them in his pocket.

Chapter 25

The Cadillac rolled up in front of the cabin and remained idling. Hayes was late. Twenty minutes late. Carly snatched her keys off the counter and hurried out the door. She locked the deadbolt, rattling the door making sure it locked in place.

Carly walked down the steps. Nearing the bottom something caught her eye—the outline of the driver through the darkened windows—smaller, shorter.

While the Cadillac idled, Sarah watched, a gun resting on her lap.

"Here she comes. Wait until I lower the window and have the gun on her. Then grab her and throw her in the back floor."

Carly reached the side of the car, lifted the door handle, but it was locked. The tinted window slowly lowered, and Carly saw a square-shouldered woman with tight lips pointing a gun.

"Don't move. Make a move, and I'll kill you."

Carly stood paralyzed.

"Get her!" Sarah yelled.

The back door sprang open and Józef bolted from the car. He grabbed Carly from behind and began to shove her towards the opened door. Immediately, she fought back, sending her heel into Józef's groin with a back kick. Cupping his genitals with both hands, Józef dropped to his knees.

"Son of a bitch," Sarah thundered, bursting out of the car, desperate to get Carly under control.

"Don't move, Mother Fuckers," boomed a loud voice coming from a thicket of bushes alongside the cabin. Holding a revolver with both hands, Ahmed cautiously approached, knees bent taking one step at a time. "Drop the gun," he yelled, keeping an eye on Sarah and then back to Józef.

"Ahmed!" Carly blurted, puzzled.

Józef scrambled from his knees and jerked Carly in front of him, putting his forearm around her neck. He tightened his hold, nearly choking her. A flash of silver appeared. Józef held a switchblade to Carly's neck.

Ahmed hesitated, momentarily lowering his draw. It gave Sarah an edge, a chance to shoot. Crack! A bullet hit his chest. Crack! The other grazed his head. Red spattered the snow-covered ferns and Ahmed fell to the ground. Wasting no time, Sarah walked up to him, lifted her gun, and at point blank range pumped another round into his head.

"Ahmed!" Carly screamed, then tucked her chin tight to her chest and sent her elbow into Józef's ribs.

Sarah charged at Carly and with the butt of her gun hit her above the right eye. She then hit her again. Carly fell limp as blood trickled down her forehead.

"Fuck it. Fuck her," Sarah said. "Throw the crazy bitch in the trunk with Hayes."

Sarah opened the trunk and shoved Hayes's body further to the back. Józef lifted Carly onto his shoulder and carried her to the trunk. He dumped her next to Hayes.

"Whore ass bitch," he snarled looking down at Carly's limp body.

"Józef …get into the car! Let's get out of here," Sarah said as both scrambled to get into the vehicle.

The Cadillac fishtailed as it took off, fleeing down the drive leading away from the cabin. Adrenaline galvanized Sarah into pushing even harder on the accelerator. Józef sat gripping the dashboard with one hand and bracing his feet against the floor.

Hearing what sounded like gun fire, David bolted to his deck. Trying to see where the sounds originated from he noticed a black car driving wildly and fast. The car sped past him and disappeared around a curve. Within seconds he heard what sounded like an explosion followed by a blaring horn.

"Jesus Christ!" he said.

Flying off the steps, David followed the sound of the horn until he reached the accident. He saw the front end of a Cadillac wrapped around a tree and the hood was smashed. Windshield glass lay scattered on the snow, like greenish white diamonds. Near the rear of the car, unmoving, was a deer...a doe. Her front legs lay bent beneath her and blood dripped from her nose. David noted the vanity plate, still intact. "SAVANNA"

Son of a Bitch. It's Hayes.

David approached the car, not wanting to look inside, afraid of what he would see. When he did, he saw two bodies; a man and a woman. Both were dead in the front seat, heads twisted, eyes open, unrecognizable.

The airbags had been of little use. Shards of glass, hair, and blood spattered the interior of the Cadillac. The blaring horn showed no sign of weakening. Moving to the driver's side of the door, David found it locked. He carefully reached through the broken glass and removed the keys from the ignition, tossing them on the hood. The jammed mechanical component keeping the horn blaring dislodged and the woods became silent again.

The woods were eerie. David's heart beat rapidly as memories of roadside bombs tore through his head. He removed his cell and punched 911, then stopped. *Carly!!* He remembered.

She's supposed to be with Hayes.

Avoiding the patches of silvery blue ice and keeping to the snowy edge of the road, David ran back to Carly's cabin. He leaped up the steps two at a time and began pounding on the door. "Carly!" he yelled, grasping the handle and rattling the door. Peering through the window, he found the cabin dark.

Turning from the door David's body became rigid. He noticed a man, unmoving, lying in a widening pool of blood. Images of combat erupted in his mind. Grabbing the ax next to the wood pile, his recon skills kicked in. Step by step he worked his way down looking for any sign of movement. Once over the body, he knelt, placing his fingers to the man's neck. *Nothing.*

Inches from the dead man's hand lay his gun. Dropping the ax, he picked it up, clicked on the safety, and removed the clip. *Full.* He jammed it back into the butt of the gun and shoved the gun under his belt.

Around the body were several footprints, shuffle marks and disturbed snow. David spotted a metallic object laying in the snow. He walked over and picked it up. It was a gold locket.

Could she be in that car?

Triggered by fear, David wasted no time returning to the wreck. He pulled on the passenger's door and looked in. Seeing nothing, he slammed the door and pounded his fist on the trunk. A noise from inside pounded back. Grabbing the keys from the hood he pointed the clicker and pressed. Light invaded the dark trunk as Carly squinted trying to focus.

"David," she whispered.

"Jesus, Carly!" David said, looking down at the blood above her eye. "What the hell's going on.?"

"I'm not sure," Carly could barely get out. "Someone tried to take me."

"Take you? Like kidnapping?"

"Yes. She had a gun."

"Hold on," David said as he lightly packed a fist full of snow. Let me see your head."

He gently dabbed the wound, studying the jagged cut as he did. He took a hold of her hand placing the snowball in it. "Hold this up to your head so I can help you out of the trunk."

Carly slowly lifted her hand and took a hold of the snowball, never opening her eyes. She placed it over the cut.

"Are you ready to sit up? You might be a little woozy."

"I think so," she said opening her eyes.

David carefully placed his hand under her back and gently lifted her. Carly groaned as he raised her into a sitting position.

"I feel sick. I think I'm going to throw up."

"Okay. Just relax and breathe. When you're ready, I'll lift you out."

Carly nodded. She kept the snowball to her head.

"How did I get here?"

"I thought I heard gun fire and went to the deck to check it out. This car came flying, went around the curve and crashed. I mean it sounded like an explosion. It must have hit a deer. There's a dead one on the side of the road."

"Oh, God, no. Not one of my deer," Carly gasped, pushing herself out of the truck with help from David. "I want to see it."

Carly's feet felt heavy as she made her way to the deer. David held her arm. She stood there staring, saying nothing.

"Looks like a bomb went off. The front of the car is destroyed," David explained. "Must have hit her midstride. Took out the whole windshield."

Carly eyes were locked on the doe. "She saved my life. They were going to kill me. The woman had a gun… pointed it at me. She said she would shoot me...She would have done it...Mama Doe...she saved me. Where are the people who took me?"

In a deadpan voice, David answered. "In the car. They're dead."

"Dead!" Carly blurted, then a startled look came over her face. "We got to get back! Ahmed's there. She shot him! I have to go. I've got to help him!"

Carly pushed past David, but he stopped her by the arm. She jerked away and said, "I gotta help him. He's hurt!"

"He's dead, Carly. The guy's dead," David said, sympathetically. "When I went back looking for you, I found him, close to the cabin, on the ground, not breathing... I also found this." He reached in his pocket and pulled out a locket. Is this yours? It was lying not far from his body."

Carly felt a cold ache strike her heart, the same kind of cold ache that struck her when she heard of Artie's death. She reached out her hand and took hold of the locket.

Bewildered, she said, "Jesus, I don't know what's going on. Why was Ahmed here? Why are weird things happening? I gotta call Dr. Hayes. He can help me. He will know what to do."

David winced internally. "You can't," he told her, noting the strain on her face.

"Why not?"

Pointing with his chin in the direction of the trunk, David said, "I think he's in the trunk. That's how they got his car." David paused; a knowing expression crossed his face. "You didn't know...my God, Carly. You didn't know!! This is Dr. Hayes' car!! This is his Cadillac. It has SAVANNA on the license plate. When I helped you out," he hesitated, "I noticed a bulge in the carpet and shoes sticking out at the bottom. Crocodile leather—like the pair he always wore."

Carly stepped away from David, heading toward the trunk. David grabbed her. "Don't, Carly. You can only see his shoes. Let's leave it at that."

In a somber voice, David told her, "We have to get out of here. Go somewhere and figure all this out. If we call the police, they'll separate us... probably lock us up... They may even think we had something to do with this. The only ones that can explain what happened are dead. We need to get away from here."

"But, where will we go?"

"Town. We need a car."

David reached into his pocket and pulled out his cell phone. Handing it to her he said, “The password is PENNY. If something happens to me or if we get separated, dial 911.” He then reached behind his back and removed the pistol and placed it in his front waistband.

Carly eyes widened. “Where’d you get that?”

“Found it lying next to your friend. May come in handy. Let me take one more look at your head.”

Carly stepped closer to David and angled her head toward him. David looked closely at the wound.

“Good. The bleeding looks like it stopped.”

Reaching into his pocket, he removed his wallet. “I’ve got forty bucks. What about you?”

“Maybe two hundred. Wait… where’s my purse? I don’t have my purse. It’s gotta be somewhere.”

“Wait here. I’ll check.”

Carly watched David scavenge through the trunk. He grabbed the bottom of the rolled carpet and pushed with both hands, moving it aside. *Nothing.*

“It’s not here,” he said looking up from the trunk, then slamming it shut. “Maybe one of them grabbed it and threw it in the front.”

David went to the front of the Cadillac and looked in. He removed the stocking cap from Józef’s head, making sure Carly didn’t see him.

“Nothing in the car,” he said, walking back to Carly. “Maybe it got lost during the struggle. I didn’t see it when I was at your place. We have to go back. Maybe we’ll find it there.”

Reluctantly, David asked her, “Do you think you can make it to the cabin?”

Carly didn’t answer right away. Placing both hands on her head, she said, “My head hurts when I touch it. It even hurts when I breathe.”

“Do you think you can make it to the cabin?” David asked again. “We can go slow.”

Aggravated that she even had to make a decision, she snapped, “As opposed to staying here with those God forsaken derelicts wasted in the car?? I’d rather be locked in a cage with rats than stay with them. Let’s get out of here.”

David handed Carly the cap. “Put this on and pull it over your cut. We don’t want people wondering what happened.”

“Where do you get this?”

“Found it in the car,” David said. He didn’t mention he took it off a dead man.

Chapter 26

The snowmobile would not start. Over and over again Louis pushed the start button. The motor would not kick in. Not wanting the battery to be completely drained, he removed his helmet and lifted the hood.

Pain in the ass, he thought as he tugged on each wire, hoping to correct a bad connection.

He looked up when he heard another machine coming in off the trail. Pulling up next to him and shutting off his engine was his partner, Clinton Steele.

"So, the thing won't kick over?" he said.

"I almost wore the battery down trying to start it," Louis said.

Steele unbuckled his chin strap and removed his helmet, then placed it on the seat between his legs. He pulled back his sleeve and looked at his watch.

"Where are you going? Your shift doesn't start for another forty-five minutes."

"You didn't hear those shots?" Louis asked.

"Shots? No, didn't hear a thing. Can't hear squat with the helmet on."

"We really need to post the property better. This is the third time this month that I've had to kick hunters out. They come in off public land and don't realize they've wandered onto hospital grounds."

Louis pushed the hood of the snowmobile down until it latched in place.

"This is going to have to sit awhile," he said. "I need your machine."

"Be my guest," Steele said. "I'll let the Captain know it's time to spend some cash and get us a reliable backup. One sled just doesn't cut it."

Louis Cardello climbed onto the machine and turned the key. He let the engine idle as he donned his helmet and put on his gloves. Over the quiet purr of the engine he said, "Remind the Captain we were promised a new machine last year. Tell the old goat not to be such a push over. He's gotta be more of a hard ass when it comes to hospital administration."

Chuckling, Steele said, "I'll use those exact words when I talk to him. I'll make sure he knows those were yours, not mine."

Louis squeezed the throttle and headed down the trail, kicking up snow as he went. He steered his snowmobile by the stand of ferns that lined the road. Cruising at a low speed, he scanned the road ahead.

Rounding a curve, he saw a deer lying dead on the road. Bright red blood oozed from its body, indicating a fresh kill. Not far from the deer was a car, the front end lodged into a tree. Louis accelerated the snowmobile and stopped next to the Cadillac.

His heart pounded as he removed his helmet and got off his machine. Peering into the window, he saw the unmoving bodies.

"Damn!" he said out loud, then talked into the mic attached to his shoulder. "Dispatch... need backup. South Fork Road, just south of the cabins. Looks like a deer/car collision."

The calm, controlled voice of Dispatch answered, "Copy that. Welchester PD will be notified. Do you need EMS?"

"Yes. Two occupants. A man and a woman," Louis said, as he opened the car door and took the pulse of the closest body. "I think there're both gone," he relayed to Dispatch.

****

Carly waited while David searched for her purse in the snow alongside her cabin. The body of Ahmed lay still on the ground where Sarah took her last shot. A still widening pool of blood surrounding his head. Grimacing, she turned away, squeezing her eyes tight.

A white flash burst through her mind.... an image appeared of a man, a ski mask over his face, holding a gun. Her face flushed, her knees wobbled, and Carly grabbed a nearby tree branch to steady herself. The image faded as David ran back with her purse.

"Are you all right?" David asked, placing the strap of the purse over his shoulder. "You don't look so good."

Carly shook her head and refocused. "I'll be all right. Must be the bang to my head. Do I hear sirens?"

David paused and turned his head. A frown creased his forehead. “Sounds like they’re coming off Adams Road. It’s just a matter of time before police will be swarming this entire area.”

He slipped his arm through Carly’s and brought her in tight.

“Do you think you can walk the trail to Welchester U? It isn’t that far if we take the trail.”

Carly nodded.

The packed snowmobile trail made it easier to walk. It skirted the university grounds, then split off at the student union parking lot. As the two walked arm and arm, David noticed movement in the woods. He lowered himself to his knees bringing Carly with him.

“Might be security,” David said just above a whisper.

The noise in the distance kept getting closer. They both concentrated, hearing what sounded like branches snapping. They heard no voices. David carefully raised to his feet. Carly watched as a grin grew on his face. She immediately stood up.

“The fawn,” Carly affectionately said. “His mama would never had let him get that close to us. I think he is looking for her.”

“He’ll be fine,” David assured her. “It’s a tough world for animals in the wild. He’s old enough to make it on his own.”

The trek to the University Center took too much time. As soon as they got there, David eyed the people, while Carly contacted an Uber. The destination...Welchester’s Public Library.

“Eight minutes it’ll be here,” Carly said, looking up from the phone. “His name is Carlos. It’s a white minivan.”

Within minutes, the minivan showed up.

“There it is,” David said, pushing the door of the University Center open for Carly. The two walked to the van where the driver opened the side door and Carly and David got in.

“You’re going to the library, right?” Carlos asked.

“Yes,” David answered. “The Welchester Library on University.”

“Get you there in ten.”

Carly handed David back his phone, then retrieved hers from her purse.

“I got a text from Meghan,” she whispered. “Says there are cops all over the place and wants to know if I’m ok. Should I text her back?”

David paused before answering.

"Tell her you're in town with Dr. Hayes, and you'll get back in touch."

As Carly texted Meghan, David watched Carlos weave in and out of traffic. Once in front of the library, he parked the van and turned on his flashers. Carlos then headed to the side of the van and opened it. David exited and handed him a rolled 5-dollar bill.

"This is for you," he said.

With a nod Carlos took the five-dollar bill and tucked it into his front shirt pocket.

"Thank you," he said. "You two have a nice day."

As the van pulled away Carly asked, "Why the library?"

"I'll explain everything," David answered, taking her by the arm and walking towards the door. "First, let's get to the second floor. It will be easier to explain from there."

A half dozen people mingled outside the elevator doors. The red up-arrow button was lit, and they heard the chime as the door opened. Everyone shuffled in.

"Second floor," a man standing in the back said.

"We want a place by the window," David quietly said into Carly's ear. "It's got to be facing University Street. You'll know why when I explain."

The elevator rose to the second floor and stopped with a slight jerk. The two squeezed out and stood outside the elevator doors, looking around for a table.

"There's one," David said, leading her to a table in the mostly empty seating area.

They seated themselves at a table with a view of the Royal Park Hotel, directly across the street from the library. Pointing to it, David leaned in and said, "That's where we're gonna steal a car."

Carly's eyebrows narrowed. "Steal a car? I don't know how to steal a car."

"You will after today," David said offhandedly. "See those guys in the valet parking jackets? They have our wheels."

"You're insane. I'm not stealing a car! We're already in enough trouble with Hayes being dead and the rest of them. What's next? Robbing a bank!!"

"Just hear me out."

Carly's arms dropped between her knees and she slumped over. She focused on the grey floor tiles and then back at David.

"We are going to get into so much trouble. You and I are going to find ourselves back up on the hill. That is, if we don't get thrown in jail first."

"Someone killed Dr. Hayes and Ahmed and they went to great lengths to kidnap you. We don't know who's involved. It could even be the cops. Let's just get out of here first. We don't have time to think about anything else."

Carly paused, saying nothing, while at the same time tapping her fingers on the table. "Okay. I trust you. Where are we going to go?"

"I've got an Army buddy that lives on the west side of the state. He hates the government, doesn't trust em… long story. I'm sure he'll let us crash at his place a couple of days."

Chapter 27

Meghan Conner stepped onto the porch of the rented townhouse and stomped her boots to remove any clumps of clinging snow. She rang the doorbell twice before shoving her hands into her parka.

"Who's there?" called a voice from inside the townhouse.

"Porsche," Meghan said. "Open the door. I just want to talk. I am Agent Stacey Canter, and I work for the FBI." There was silence on the other side of the door. Again, Agent Canter spoke. "I know you came here and met Ahmed Osman. There's been a shooting."

The blind in the small window lifted and a pair of eyes stared out. Meghan pulled out her FBI identification and pushed it flat against the window.

After a few seconds, Canter heard the deadbolt click and the door slowly opened. Porsche stood, wearing a man's night shirt, hands hanging by her sides, a pistol in one of them.

"You...you're the one I watched day after day walking with Carly Fletcher," she said. "You're Meghan Conner!"

Stacey nodded her head grimly. "That was my undercover name. My real name is Stacey Canter, I'm with the FBI. I came to tell you something...there was a shooting."

"Is it Ahmed? He hasn't texted me in hours. That's not like him."

Agent Canter, in a calm voice, asked, "Can I come in so we can talk? I will explain everything."

Porsche's forehead creased as she raised her voice. "Is he dead!? Tell me if he's okay."

Stacey stared at Porsche, gathering her thoughts before speaking. "I hate telling you this. I'm sorry. He didn't make it."

"You're lying!! It can't be true. He knew how to handle himself."

"I'm sure he did," Stacey agreed. "But something went very wrong. Four people are dead, Ahmed included, and we need to find out why."

Porsche wrapped both arms around her stomach and hung her head. “I don’t feel so good.”

Noticing Porsche’s ashy face, Stacey grabbed one of her arms and guided her to the couch.

“I’m okay… I’m okay,” Porsche said to her, even though her feet shuffled and scraped along the floor. “I can make it. I don’t *need* your help.”

Stacey held Porsche’s arm tightly, not letting go, until she got her settled on the couch.

“Porsche…” Stacey started.

Porsche grabbed hold of a puffy pillow and hugged it to her chest. “Can you just leave?” she asked, her gaze on the floor. “Please…leave me alone. Just get out of here,” she said speaking in a voice that had no life in it.

Stacey removed a business card from her coat pocket and placed it on the arm of the couch. “Okay, I’ll leave you alone. There are a couple things I need to do. But, I won’t be far away. When you’re ready to talk, text me. I’m here to help.”

Porsche took the business card.

“Again, I’m sorry,” Stacey said, leaving the townhouse. “I can let myself out.”

As soon as the door closed, Porsche forced herself off the couch to get to the door. She leaned a shoulder against it and locked the dead bolt. Through a crack in the blind, Porsche watched as Stacey got into the Civic.

Her mind was numb as she walked through the hall to the bedroom. She sat on the bed and buried Ahmed’s pillow into her face. She could smell him. His hair, his sweat, his shampoo. Muffled cries filled the room as her tears soaked his pillow.

If only I had been there…

Stacey came out of the Seven-Eleven carrying a tall cup of coffee and a pack of chocolate cupcakes. In the hour that had passed, she talked to Chief Bolton twice—each time he gave her more details about what happened at Holy Oaks.

She just finished her cupcake, washing the last bite down with coffee, when her cell went off.

Porsche!

“You can come back now.”

When Porsche answered the door, her eyes were pink and swollen. "C'mon to the kitchen," she said. "We can talk there."

Canter followed Porsche to the small kitchen and took a seat at the counter.

"Can I get you something to drink? Water? Coffee?"

"Water is good."

Porsche opened the refrigerator and handed Canter a bottle, then leaned up against the adjacent counter and crossed her arms in front of her chest. Her face was unreadable. She was all business now. "Tell me what happened."

"I am an FBI agent working on an assignment involving Carly Fletcher. It's a joint operation between the FBI and CIA."

"But, I've seen you with Carly. You were a resident at Holy Oaks."

Stacey took a sip of her water. "That was my cover. Meghan Conner…the lunatic that attempted to kill her aunt. My whole background was created to get me into Holy Oaks. No one at Holy Oaks had a clue I was FBI. That's how far up the food chain this went."

Porsche listened quietly, considering what Stacey said. "Ahmed always thought we were on our own. I don't think he had a clue there were others involved, at least he never told me."

Agent Canter pulled a small spiral notebook from her pocket. She flipped a few pages then said, "So, we know Ahmed was a CIA operative and reported directly to Carly's father in Germany."

"Yes. He told me."

"We also know that Colonel Fletcher asked for Ahmed's help and later Ahmed sent for you. Am I right?"

Porsche nodded, as she took her purse from the counter and removed a pack of *Kool's.* She tapped the pack and removed a cigarette. Before lighting it, she asked, "Do you mind?"

Canter shook her head.

She lit her cigarette and took in a deep drag. Through a large cloud of exhaled smoke, she asked, "Who killed Ahmed?"

"This is where it gets sketchy. There was an accident. A deer/car collision. Two people were found dead in the front of the car. We think they are the ones that killed Ahmed. A doctor, his name was Hayes, was found dead in the trunk of his car. He was strangled. We believe the two stole his car and went to abduct Carly. It looks like

Ahmed tried to stop it, and that's when he was shot. No one has seen Carly since."

"So, the bastards that shot Ahmed are dead?"

"We think so," Agent Canter said, looking down as she reviewed her notes. "We found a gun in the car and are waiting on ballistics to determine if it was the murder weapon. All signs point that it was."

"So why are you here? What do you want with me?"

"Let me cut to the chase. We need you. We need you to share what you know about Carly and what Ahmed told you."

"Why bring me in? I never graduated from Deutsche Hochschule. When it was exposed that Ahmed and I were lovers, I was kicked out. The CIA made Ahmed resign. Having an affair with a subordinate was strictly forbidden. I'm the one who seduced him. It was my fault."

"It takes two to tango, Porsche. It's rarely one person's fault."

"Yeah. He told me that. He said if I didn't approach him, he would have come after me."

"Did you know this has to do with missing mithridate?"

"We weren't exactly sure, but Ahmed thought it had something to do with what happened back in Germany."

"I really can't discuss anything further. You'll be briefed if you come with me."

"Briefed? I just lost the man I love and you're not telling me what I need to know. Can you at least tell me where they took him? I'm like the only family he has. We were going to get married."

"The agency has Ahmed's remains, and I'm sure you'll have access to them."

Porsche put her cigarette out in the ashtray. "I'll go with you, but I'm not saying I will help. Did you say Carly is missing?"

"We think she's on the run with David Farris. He is missing, too."

"He's that big guy living in the other cabin, right?"

"Yes. Carly texted me and said she was with Dr. Hayes. Obviously, that was a lie because we found him dead. We are not a hundred percent positive, but we believe the group watching Carly realized they were under surveillance. They seemed to have hastily changed their strategy and plan. We're still in the dark with much of this. Tell you what. How about you pack and come with me?"

"Where to?" Porsche asked.

"To a clandestine site. It has sleeping quarters and you'll be safe there. I'll tell you more on the drive, but please promise not to let the chief know that I briefed you."

"Not to worry, Agent Canter. I won't throw you under the bus."

"Why don't you call me Stacey? I'll be waiting in the car."

Porsche walked out of the rented townhouse carrying two large suitcases. At the same time, Stacey stepped out of the Honda Civic and gave a wave. She walked to the back of the car and opened the trunk. Porsche wheeled the suitcases up and tossed them in. They both got in the car and pulled out of the lot.

As Stacey merged onto the highway, Porsche read the sign. *I-75 South Toledo-Detroit.*

"Is the place clean? No prints. Nothing to lead to you?" Stacey asked.

"It's the best I could do, in the amount of time I had. The rent was paid in advance, so we have six months before anyone will even enter the house. Someone can always come later and really clean if it's needed."

"Good. Would you mind if I didn't share any more information until the chief's briefing? We'll be at the compound in about forty-five minutes."

"Sure, that's fine," Porsche said, as she lowered the window and lit another cigarette. Staring off into space she became silent.

The off ramp led into an industrial area of the city. Deep in the belly of a Detroit ghetto, surrounded by a fence capped with barbed wire sat "Fort Mackinac." This was the nickname given to the Special Operation Command Center. The land was once a foundry during Detroit's industrial heyday of the 50's.

Mounted on a pedestal just outside the warehouse was a biometric, fingerprint recognition scanner. Removing her glove and lowering the window, Canter placed her thumb on the scanner. Two large gates swung open, allowing entry. The two continued to drive another 500 feet before coming to a stop next to an intercom mounted in front of a large steel garage door.

Leaning out the window and speaking into the intercom, Stacey said, "Pontiac's Rebellion 1763," which caused the large door to open. Two armed men in military fatigues stood guard at the door. She drove past them, nodded, and proceeded to park the car.

As Porsche exited the car, she couldn't help but notice the enormity of the building. A fifty-foot ceiling crisscrossed with rusted girders supporting darkened panes of glass reminded her of a butterfly sanctuary she visited as a kid.

A small, walled office sat to one side and stacks of what appeared like military equipment sat shrink-wrapped on wooden pallets. Coaxial computer cables stretched high overhead led into rows upon rows of tiered Intel data storage processors. Large TV screens were mounted on the walls and monitored by military personal wearing microphoned headsets.

"This place is huge," Porsche said out loud.

"Follow me. I'll introduce you to the chief."

Canter entered a small office followed by Porsche.

Next to the counter, stirring a Styrofoam cup of coffee was "Chief of Station" Richard Bolton. A face lined with age spread into a smile.

"Come on in, and grab a cup," he said as he licked the wooden stirrer and tossed it into the trash. "Just made it. It's fresh."

"Would you like some coffee. I'll grab you one," Stacey asked Porsche.

"Black. Thanks."

"Sit down. Take a load off," Chief Bolton said.

Porsche took a seat and scooted in her chair. She noticed a white board with pictures of Carly and David mounted to it. Other pictures mounted to the board were not familiar to her.

"I've been waiting to meet you. I read your background and you were one of the top cadets until…" Chief Bolton paused.

"Until they kicked me out," Porsche finished his sentence.

An uncomfortable silence was in the room when Agent Canter returned to the table and handed Porsche her coffee. "What'd I miss."

"I was just telling Porsche on behalf of the CIA how sorry we are with the passing of Ahmed. I heard he was a great asset in Germany. A good man."

He handed Porsche a manila folder. **Operation Arrow Fletcher** in bold letters was written at the top. "So, Porsche, you and Ahmed were watching Carly Fletcher daily. Is that correct?"

"Yes, Sir. We would take turns."

"So, you also knew there were bad guys in the field trying to get at the mithridate."

"Sort of. Ahmed knew there was something that they wanted, but I didn't know what it was until Stacey told me on our drive here."

Chief Bolton looked at Canter with a perturbed look and then back at Porsche before he continued. "Okay. Did you ever meet Ms. Fletcher?"

"Just once. We gave her a message that someone was watching and listening. It was when she was in the cabin. Ahmed said she had to go through it, so we could find out who was putting her life in danger. Colonel Fletcher's last message to Ahmed was to help Carly find Mr. Etadirhtim."

A smile grew on Chief Bolton's face.

"What's so funny?" Porsche asked.

"Etadirhtim is mithridate spelled backwards. We're pretty sure that Fletcher told her where it is or gave her some type of clue. He contacted her right before he was killed." Bolton took a long sip of his coffee, then continued. "She's on the run with that David Farris guy," he said, pointing to his picture mounted on the board. "He was the resident in Cabin One."

"Yes, I know who he is. We kept an eye on him, too."

"When all hell broke loose, they both disappeared. We know they walked to Welchester University. We followed their tracks from the crash site. We need to find her before the bad guys do. Since you've been trained by one of the finest, we thought we would bring you in. We want you to be a member of our team."

"What about Ahmed? Where is he?"

"We have his remains. If you would like to see him, I can arrange that."

Porsche paused and slowly shook her head. "No. We knew the business we were in. We both agreed if something like this happened, we didn't want our last memory to be standing over a bullet ridden corpse. Have him cremated, and I will take the ashes back to Germany with me."

"We really would like you to join our mission. Find these bad guys," Bolton said. "Besides, you've had training and probably can add a lot to this investigation."

Silence fell over the tiny office as Porsche's eyes began to water. Staring at the Styrofoam cup and twisting it nervously on the table, she looked up. "Let me know how I can help. It's what Ahmed would want."

From across the table, Stacey spoke. "Ahmed would be proud if he knew you were helping find the people who killed Carly's father and wanted to kill her, too."

Chief Bolton nodded. "Thank you, Porsche. Let me explain the operation. Not sure if Agent Canter told you that I'm fascinated with the Native American tribes that lived in Michigan. I'm a history buff. The name of this operation is *'Arrow Fletcher'.*"

"She didn't mention that."

"I'm surprised she left that out with all the other information she wasn't supposed to share with you."

He looked at Canter with a half grin. "I named this operation for Ms. Fletcher's last name. If you look up the origins of Fletcher, it's a medieval name for arrowsmith or one who fletches arrows. Word origins…another specialty of mine. I noticed you spell your first name like the car instead of Portia."

"Yes. I guess it was my dad's idea. He really loved his car. I had no say in the matter."

Chief Bolton smiled and then pointed to a photo of Carly's father. "Her father, Colonel Arthur D. Fletcher was a senior officer for us. His cover was the Chief of the Medical Corps for the Army's Human Resource Command. Secretly, he oversaw a Biological Weapons program developing a high grade of pathogens. Did Ahmed mention this?"

Porsche nodded, "A little."

"We know Ms. Fletcher met with her father the day he was killed and at the same time she lost her memory. That we know for sure. What we don't know is if he told her where the antidote is. If he did, we think she can't remember. Slovak and Hayes were trying to get her to remember through hypnosis."

The chief pulled a memorandum from the manila folder and handed it to Porsche. "Read this and we'll talk. I'm getting another coffee."

Chapter 28

The Volvo bounced and shimmied as it slowly wove its way down the two-track. Slovak gripped the steering wheel silently cursing the washed-out ruts in the road while hoping he didn't scrape the bottom of the car.

He pulled into the driveway of the log cabin, half-hidden by thick groves of pine trees, and parked alongside a black van. A metal sign hanging from a pole read Port Austin Lodge.

Where's her jeep? Slovak thought. Slovak's upper body began to tighten. Clutching his chest, his breathing short and shallow, he fumbled for the vial deep inside his khaki's and removed a pill of his nitro. Placing it under his tongue, he waited for the angina to lessen.

After a couple of minutes, Slovak felt well enough to get out of the car. Just as he reached the cabin door, it flew open. Facing him was Tatyana Nikolaev.

"What the fuck is going on?!! What's happening at Holy Oaks? It's all over the news."

Confused, Slovak followed her to the living room and looked at the television.

"Four bodies. Four fucking bodies the news is reporting. A woman and three men. No more details than that. At Holy Oaks. If that woman is Carly, you're as good as dead!"

Slovak took off his coat and hung it on a hook by the door.

"I never heard from Sarah. I don't know what happened."

He took hold of his chest and grimaced.

"Are you all right? Your face is ashy," Tatyana said.

"I just need to sit down. Would you get me a glass of water?"

Slovak went to the kitchen table, pulled out a chair and sat. Tatyana never took her eyes off him as she walked to the cupboard and got a glass. She turned on the tap and filled it, then handed it to him. "It's freezing out and you're re sweating like a pig. You better not fucking die on me."

"Thanks for the warm concern," he said as he dabbed his forehead with the top of his sleeve and took a drink of water. "I'll head back first thing in the morning. Don't know what could have gone wrong, but I'll find out. Where are you keeping Bo?"

"He's in the back room with Viktor."

"Good. He may be our last hope, a bargaining chip."

****

Carly's hands were clammy as she watched David cross University and walk down the sidewalk running parallel to the arborvitaes. He stopped, looked up at her, and walked across the lawn, soon vanishing into the sea of green. She swallowed; her mouth felt like cotton as she dialed the front desk of the Royal Park Hotel.

The phone rang four times and then went to a recording. "Thank you for calling the Royal Place Hotel. Your call may be recorded for quality assurance. For front desk and reservations, press one, all other calls press two." Carly pressed one and waited. A female voice came over the phone.

"Front desk reservations. This is Carmen. How may I help you?"

"Listen carefully. This is no joke. There is a bomb in your hotel," Carly said, and then hung up, placing the phone in her back pocket.

She waited, heart thudding, waiting for the reaction. *Nothing's happening*, she thought, watching for what seemed like an eternity. As if someone stomped on an ant hill, people began pouring out from every possible exit of the hotel. The library filled with chatter as patrons lined up at the windows watching people running from the hotel.

David was now standing just behind the arborvitaes, ten feet from the door of the valet booth. The *Keeper of the Keys* looked up from his cell phone watching people exiting the building without coats, hats, or gloves.

He stepped from the booth and stopped an elderly couple, who were arm in arm hurrying from the building.

"What's going on?"

"I don't know. Fire? Bomb?" the man said. "A robot voice came over the PA system telling everyone to immediately vacate the building and not to use the elevators. Scary as hell in there."

David made his move. He stepped next to the door, reached in and removed a set of keys hanging on the pegboard. He was gone in seconds.

Carly left the elevator and walked to the nearest trash bin. She tossed her I-Phone into it, before weaving through the mass of people on her way to meet David. She stood on the sidewalk until a silver Jeep Grand Cherokee pulled up next to her and the tinted window lowered.

"Did you toss the phone like I told you?" David asked.

"Of course, I did," Carly said giving David a miffed look. "Just because they hit me in my head, it doesn't mean I lost my mind."

"You're right. Let's go."

Carly went to the other side of the Jeep and got in. "How did you know what set of keys went with what car?"

"When the valet parks the car, they have two tickets with the same number on it. They give one to the owner and tag the keys with the other. The number corresponds with a parking spot."

"And how did you know how the valet operated? I mean, how did you know that they hung the keys in that shack?"

"I used to park cars. Made good money for a seventeen-year-old kid."

Carly watched as the first responders pulled up one after the other.

"Oh, my God. I can't believe we started all this."

"Relax. The hard part's over. We have three quarters of a tank. It should get us a couple of hundred miles. If the car's not dirty, we're home free."

"Dirty?"

"You know. Got to find out if this baby is equipped with a tracker. Like On Star. It's not a GM so it won't have On Star, but it could have another tracker. I'm going to get a few miles out of town and then take a look."

"How do you know what to look for?" Carly asked.

"My uncle had a mechanic shop. He installed systems. It's pretty simple actually. You need a power source to run the thing. I'll just follow the wiring harness and check a few of the accessories to see where they might have tapped in. There's only so many places to get power and to hide the thing. I'll look for battery trackers, too."

As Carly buckled her seat belt she said, "You're fricken amazing."

David laughed, "Jack-of all-trades, master of none."

David put on his blinker and pulled into an Advance Auto store. Once parked, he pulled the hood latch and turned to Carly.

"I'll look for it here. It's less conspicuous having the hood up. Plenty of people use the lot to replace windshield wiper blades or to add oil. The last thing we need is to have the cops pulling up on us."

Handing Carly his phone, he said, "See how many miles Traverse City is from here."

David finished his inspection and slammed the hood, then headed to the back of the jeep. He knelt, checking the undercarriage and frame.

"I think we're clean," he said as he jumped back in and started the jeep. "Let's go see Tim."

"We're about two hundred and thirty miles from Traverse City. Who is this Tim again?"

"A buddy of mine from the service. We called him Terminator Tim."

Carly raised her brows and said, " 'Terminator Tim,' that's a little concerning, wouldn't you say?"

"Naw. Tim's fine. He did what he felt he had to. We were just trying to survive over there."

"What'd he do? Tell me what he did."

"Tim was a Sergeant First Class. He was our Platoon Sergeant. You know, one of the guys. Not an officer, but an enlisted man. He had been in the Army for about 15 years. He was a lifer until he decided to quit.

"Anyway, he was the old man of the Platoon. He had all the experience, and he kept us from getting killed. We looked up to him. Even the young officers fresh out of Officer's Training School let him call the shots. One day we got orders to redeploy and I mean fast. Tim told the head brass that if we pulled out this abruptly, the locals along with the orphanage would be slaughtered."

"Orphanage?" Carly asked.

"Yeah. Tim was in an orphanage as a kid. He bounced from family to family until he was old enough to enlist. He spent all his spare time and money helping with the kids whose parents were killed. I mean he put a ton of money into that orphanage."

"So, did they listen?"

"Oh, hell no. Washington had made its mind up. We were 30 miles from the village where we had set up our new perimeter. We got word that the village was under attack. Some splinter militia group. The next day Tim left. He was gone for more than 8 hours.

"Our second lieutenant almost put out an AWOL on him. Tim had gone back to the village. Everyone was dead. Men, women and children. I mean we knew these people. I'll never forget what Tim said when he came back."

"What'd he say?"

"He said he was too late. The flies had already set up their nurseries. I don't think he ever got over those kids being killed. "

"God. That had to be horrible. Bo would tell me little bits and pieces of what he went through, he suffered with Survivor's Guilt."

"I believe it. It's a real thing." Shaking his head, David continued. "That was it for Tim. He finished his tour and didn't re-up. Said he couldn't fight for a country that he didn't respect or trust. Didn't hear from him again… until I got state side.

"He contacted me when he read about what I did to those boys who hurt Penny. He wrote to me when I was in jail waiting for my trial. Judge didn't give me bail. She wasn't sure how dangerous I was to the rest of the community. He told me if I ever needed anything to look him up. So that's what I'm doing. Why don't you lean back and try to sleep? You've been through a lot."

Carly pulled the lever on the side of her seat and leaned back. She removed her hat and folded her arms upon her chest. She turned her head slightly. "Sounds good. I'm really exhausted."

"I'll wake you every hour or so. You supposed to do that when someone has a possible concussion. Don't know why."

David did not hear Carly answer, but instead heard the faint purr of a snore.

Chapter 29

"This is bigger than I ever imagined," Porsche said. "I don't think Ahmed knew the scope of it." She looked at Agent Canter. "This memorandum explained a lot."

"It does," Chief Bolton said, returning to the office.

"So the same funding source of the German operation that killed Fletcher's son is funding this one?" Porsche asked.

"Yes, as far as we can determine. But, there's more that we don't know. We think the suspects want to carry out an attack on the West. Presumably the United States. We have intelligence that shows they want to expose a large group of the population to some type of pathogen. They killed the founders of a startup who were developing drone technology and stole two of the prototypes."

Bolton shuffled through a stack of papers and slid an article to Porsche.

"Read that. The guys we are dealing with are driven, savage, and brutal. Slaughtering a family--Mother, kids, and only God knows what they did with the father---meaningless to them."

"Drones?" she said, taking the article.

Auburn Hills Family Slain, Husband Missing

by Al Gibb

Oakland Banner

Auburn Hills, MI *–A mother and 2 small children, were found dead in their Oakland County home. Police in Auburn Hills responded to the family's home on Montroy Dr. about 9:00 a.m. after receiving a 911 call from the family housekeeper arriving to work.*

According to the Oakland County District Attorney's Office, police found 38-year-old Sally Wellington and the couple's two children all dead of gunshot wounds. Husband Todd Wellington is reported missing and a search at his office showed the building ransacked. He is the CEO and Cofounder of "Drone USA" His whereabouts at this point is unknown. Federal authorities have been brought in to assist with the case.

Porsche handed the article back to Bolton. "So, you think the attack will take place with drones?"

"Our best guess is they would release the pathogens during an outdoor activity like a football game. Something with a big crowd. They might even strike tourists walking around Washington D.C.... you know... the symbolic effect."

"How many people would this kill? What numbers are we looking at?"

"Tens of thousands. Maybe millions," Chief Bolton said. "It's a poor man's nuclear bomb. And another thing, Porsche, as far as the U.S. is concerned, our operation doesn't exist. Your participation in this doesn't exist. If you or anyone involved is killed, there will be no record of it. It didn't happen."

"A nonofficial operation."

"That's right. That's why you're here. We still get the intelligence, only POTUS and the heads of the agencies know of this. Can you imagine the panic that would set in if this got leaked? The FBI is doing a lot of the surveillance since they have jurisdiction in the states."

Bolton went to the white board and opened the binder clip holding the picture of Slovak. He held it in front of him while explaining to Porsche and Stacey.

"Now this is one bad actor. His name is Alexander Slovak. Born and raised in Serbia, he lived through the Kosovo war. He is a credentialed psychologist. We know he's personally responsible for the killings of three CIA assets. And I don't mean he ordered their assassinations. He did the assassinations. He's a killer!"

"Why haven't you taken him out?" Porsche asked.

"Same reason Ahmed let Ms. Fletcher go through all of this. We're trying to find the big boys of the terrorist cell. Slovak is high up the chain, but he's by no means the top dog."

The chief snapped the picture of Slovak back to the board and went on to Dr. Hayes.

"This poor bastard's dead," he said, tapping his index finger on the picture. "His name is Dr. Stephen Hayes. Psychologist at Holy Oaks for over 15 years. Married with one child."

"He's still a mystery to me," Agent Canter said. "I don't know his involvement in all this, but he seemed to really care about his patients. At least that's the feeling I got."

"His body was found in the trunk of his car…rolled up in a rug," the chief said. "We think he was killed and then his car was used for the attempted abduction of Ms. Fletcher. He was working with Slovak. Not sure how they recruited him. We think he was killed to silence him.

"Now this one is a gem," Bolton said sarcastically, addressing the picture of Sarah Hass. "After 911, we were scrambling for intelligence. Didn't care where or how we got it.

"She conducted rendition for the United States and used a clandestine facility in Poland. She was a mercenary and hired herself out to the highest bidder. Cold heart, I am telling you. A real cold heart. She along with one of her operatives were killed in a deer / car collision.

"This is where everything gets hazy. We know Ms. Fletcher was in the car. We have her footprints and evidence of a struggle at the scene where Ahmed was shot."

"If she was in that car, how could she have survived the impact?" Porsche asked.

"Haven't figured that out yet."

"Where do you think she went?"

"We tracked her and David Farris to the University Center at Welchester."

Porsche nodded, then said, "David Farris. He's the big guy in Cabin One."

"Yes. The two are on the run. They left the University Center by Uber and went to the Welchester Public Library. Across the street is the Royal Park Hotel. The hotel has a valet service. Ms. Fletcher called in a bomb threat and then tossed her phone. We tracked it to a trash can just outside the library."

"Bomb threat!?" Porsche asked, surprised.

"Best we can figure it was for a distraction. We have video of Farris taking keys from the valet booth and stealing a car. We have footage of Ms. Fletcher rendezvousing shortly there after. She gets into a Jeep Grand Cherokee and the two drive off.

"Damn. They're pretty resourceful," Porsche said, with a hint of admiration.

Chief Bolton returned to the table and sat. He looked first at Agent Canter and then at Porsche.

"That's where we're at, ladies. We're in the process of pinging David's phone, if he uses it. He hasn't since he left Welchester. The ping will only get us the location of the tower, but at least it'll be a starting point. Any questions?"

Both shook their heads.

"Agent Canter, why don't you take Porsche down to the squirrel cage? Get what you think you need."

His expression softening, Bolton's gaze went to Porsche. "I really appreciate you helping us with this. Ahmed was a good man. I assure you, when this is over, we will fly you and Ahmed's remains back to Germany."

Once out of the office, the two walked past the command center where large TV monitors were housed. As Porsche glanced at the screens, she saw what appeared to be aerial shots. Crosshairs hovered over buildings until they vanished in a mushroom of fire. Men and women dressed in military fatigues manipulated yokes resembling joy sticks as they sat glued to the monitors.

"This way, Porsche," Canter said as they turned a corner and entered a caged armory filled with military gear and weaponry. Behind the counter was a red-haired stocky man, leafing through a stack of papers in front of him.

"Mr. Gully, we've got an outside stakeout operation. We need some cold weather gear. Would you hook us up?"

Grabbing a clipboard hanging on the wall, Gully said, "Black and white camo. Got your size on record, Canter, but not the new face."

"I'm good," Porsche said. "I have outside weather gear."

"Do you need a weapon?"

"I'm good there, too."

"Ok, Canter. I'll pull this along with standard issue of surveillance tools. Anything special you want for the field?"

"Not that I can think of."

“Give me a half hour,” Mr. Gully said, then turned and walked down the narrow aisles of military gear.

“Let’s get some chow,” Stacey said. “Once we’re done, we’ll get your suitcases, and I’ll show you where the sleeping quarters are. You can shower and get some rest.”

****

Slovak tossed and turned on the couch, fluffing his pillow, attempting to get more comfortable. He reached down between the cushions and felt his gun. He closed his eyes and went back to sleep.

“Get up, Alex. Let’s get this over with,” Tatyana said walking from a back bedroom.

Slovak sat up from the couch. He stared at Tatyana, his face swollen and unshaven. “Give me a minute,” he said, then rubbed his temples. “All the wonderful side effects of the nitro. It should go away shortly.”

“God, you look like death warmed over,” she said. Tatyana grabbed a duffel bag along with a small tabletop tripod sitting next to the couch and placed them on the table. She unzipped the bag and removed three ski masks along with a large sheathed Bowie knife.

“This should only take five minutes,” she said, holding up the mask. “It’s got to be done. Put this on and meet me back where we have Bo.”

Chapter 30

A horrifying scream filled the tiny cabin followed by moaning and then quiet. Slovak walked from the back room and pulled off his ski mask, tossing it on the couch as he passed. His face was expressionless. He stepped to the sink and turned on the tap. Placing the bloody knife under the running water, he rinsed it off before removing the latex gloves and throwing them onto the counter. Using a dish towel, he dabbed the blood splat from his shirt.

"You cut him too deep," Tatyana laid into him, tossing bloody towels into the sink. "You damn near killed him. We need him alive!"

"We got the bleeding to stop," Slovak countered. "You worry too much!"

"Worry? Me worry too much! One of us has to worry because it hasn't been you!" she retorted.

Seizing the Bowie knife in his fist, Slovak raised his arm and stabbed it straight down, sinking it deeply into the wooden counter. "Shut up. Just shut up! Keep that damned mouth of yours shut!"

Startled, Tatyana lowered her voice before speaking. "Take it easy, Alex. All I'm saying is we need him alive." To change the focus of the conversation, Tatyana asked, "When are you leaving for Holy Oaks?"

"Now. I'm leaving now. I'll head to Hayes' office and talk to his secretary. Once I have some information, I'll get back with you. If Carly's dead, the operation is over."

If Carly's dead, your life is over, Tatyana wanted to say, but didn't.

Slovak picked up his gun and cell phone from the couch and walked to his jacket, hanging on a hook mounted to the wall. He pushed his arms through his sleeves and said, "Sit tight. Wait until you hear from me."

****

The sun was just rising above the trees while David sipped his vending machine coffee. He stood studying the map of the State of Michigan mounted to the rest stop wall. Carly and David had spent the night there, the jeep parked on the other side of a dog run.

"Did you sleep well?" David asked as Carly walked into the welcome center and headed to the deserted lady's room.

"Never better," she said sarcastically.

"Do you want a coffee?"

"Please."

David fed two one-dollar bills into the machine and watched as the cup dropped and filled with coffee. He removed his fifty cents in change and dropped it into his pants pocket.

A hand dryer broke the silence as it echoed from the lady's room. Carly walked out and stood next to David who was once again studying the map. He handed her the coffee.

"We're here and headed here," he said, tracing the path to the town of Beulah. "It's just south of Traverse City."

"You know they make great wine there," Carly said.

"Where?"

"Traverse City. Maybe one day I'll take you on a wine tour."

Using the scale on the map Carly calculated the miles to Beulah. "Does your Sergeant know we are coming?" she asked as they walked out of the lobby.

"Yep. Said he might not be there when we arrive. He's coming home today from Marquette. Never know what the weather will be like driving south from the Upper. If he's not there he said just to wait."

David pushed the glass door open and held it for her. Both of them noticed a Michigan State Police cruiser parked next to the jeep. Carly's heart began to race as the officer stepped out of the cruiser and walked towards them.

"Good morning," he nodded walking past them, heading to the vestibule of the rest stop.

"Good morning," they said as they walked towards the jeep. Neither said another word as David hit the clicker and the locks popped up. They lost no time getting into the jeep, forcing themselves to move slowly, keeping everything as normal as possible.

"Oh, my God!" Carly said as she looked over her shoulder, feeling like at any moment the officer would come barging out, hand on his gun having discovered he had just passed two fugitives.

"I hear you," David said, looking in his side mirror and backing out of the parking spot. "I can't believe that just happened."

The bright sun glared off the snow as they drove north towards Bay City. From there, they would head west on US 10 making their way to the town of Beulah. When they crossed the Zilwaukee Bridge, Carly squinted, wishing she had her sunglasses. Ice shanties dotted the frozen Saginaw River and from Carly's view, it looked like a miniature toy village.

The four-hour drive was uneventful and the two listened to the news for any information about Holy Oaks. David set the cruise control at two miles over the speed limit and stayed in the right-hand lane. The Michigan weather for this time of year was typical. Mostly sunny with the occasional snow squall. He turned down the radio as they entered the tiny town of Beulah.

"There's the Lucky Dog Saloon," David said, nodding toward a cedar-sided building with a neon "OPEN" sign in the window. "According to Tim, it's the only place in town to throw a few back. Are you hungry? He also said there is a twenty-four-hour diner in town."

"I'm good. If you're hungry, we can stop."

"Nope. All good. If I know Sarge, he'll want to feed us."

Sitting at the only light in town, David continued. "We go down about three and a half miles and turn left. Sarge said there is a cell tower about a quarter mile before the road we turn on. I forgot the road's name. It has something to do with skiing. Sky Line or Fall Line, something like that. I don't want to use my phone for directions."

David noticed a gas station and pulled into the Circle K. He parked next to a pump.

"Do you want anything?" he asked.

"No...well...how about a bag of pretzels and a coke?"

Before paying the cashier, David grabbed a couple of newspapers. The Detroit Free Press and the Detroit News. He threw them on the counter along with two cokes and a bag of pretzels. He then handed the girl $30.00.

"Would you take the papers and this stuff off and put the rest on pump 4?"

"Sure will. Do you need a receipt?" the cashier asked.

"No. All set."

David walked to the jeep and opened Carly's door. He handed her the papers and the snacks.

"See if there's anything about Holy Oaks."

The road out of town cut through the northern woods. The only things that didn't look natural were the occasional red florescent markers indicating a homeowner's driveway. The homes were tucked back and off the road, making it hard to see them.

The two passed the phone tower and turned left on Sky Line. "See," David said, "I knew it had something to do with skiing."

The mile and a half dirt road that led to Tim's house was bumpy. Snow-filled potholes kept the Jeep bouncing. David pulled into the driveway passing a sign that read, *Brown Eggs. $2.50/ Doz*. "We're here."

The driveway led to a small farmhouse badly in need of painting. Strips of white peeling paint encompassed the pillars that supported the tin porch roof. Naked ivy vines ran from the electrical pole along the wire and down the fieldstone chimney.

Woven wire fencing attached to 6-foot-high fence posts created a pen and kept the goats from wandering. Chickens scratched and pecked where they could find bare ground on their way in and out of their coop. The pen was attached to a barn. Two Golden labs with muddy noses and paws barked and rushed the jeep.

"I'm not getting out," Carly said, as she eyeballed the dogs, which were on their hind legs looking in the side windows and covering them with muddy paw prints.

"Yeah. I think I'll stay right here."

Sergeant Tim walked down the wooden steps of the farmhouse, lifted his hand in a wave, and walked toward the barn. He placed his index and pinky fingers in his mouth and when he blew a high shrieking whistle, the dogs instantly ran towards him. He lifted the latch on the barn door and both dogs ran in.

Carly's jaw dropped. "Max never listened like that!"

"All clear," Sergeant Tim yelled, then began to walk towards the jeep.

"Let's go. I'll introduce you to the Sarge," David said, as he opened the jeep door and hopped out. "You'll like him," he said before closing the door.

Carly pulled the hat down over her wound and lifted the door handle. She got out of the jeep and stood by David. Tim walked up, and the two shook hands, then immediately hugged.

"You told me you bought a farm. I thought you were just growing crops. Didn't realize you were also raising animals."

"Yeah, well, you need both to pay the bills. The eggs bring in a little money, but it's the goats that bring in the real cash." Sergeant Tim stepped back and did a once up and down on Carly. "And who is this lovely lady?"

Carly laughed and fidgeted with her stocking hat making sure it was covering her wound.

Placing his arm over Carly's right shoulder, David said, "This is my friend, Carly Fletcher. She's a patient at Holy Oaks."

"How long have you been dating this crazy son of a bitch?" Tim asked, his face breaking into a grin. "Just kidding. Hell of a guy. Best grunt I ever toured with."

Sergeant Tim was nothing like what Carly had imagined. Standing 5 foot 6 he barely came to David's shoulders. *Terminator?* Carly thought. He was stocky with a little paunch. He wore combat boots and camouflaged military fatigues. His hair was short cropped, and he sported a meticulous *Fu Manchu*.

"I finally get to meet the Terminator," Carly said, mischief evident across her face. "David has told me a lot about you." She held out her hand towards Tim.

"Oh, damn," Tim said, "and you still came!" He took Carly's hand, raised it to his mouth, and kissed it. "The pleasure is all mine, my lady."

"Sarge," David said interrupting. "We're not dating. We're just friends. She's way out of my league."

Carly playfully hit David on his shoulder. "Out of your league. I don't think so."

The three turned when they heard a ruckus coming from the pen. Two goats butted heads and then began to chase each other.

"Are those baby goats?" Carly asked.

"They're not babies, but they're goats. C'mon. Take a look," Tim said walking to the pen. "What I have here is a small herd of Nubians. They produce a lot of milk for their size. The local dairy buys it up and uses it to produce cheese and yogurt. Each one of my ladies can produce a gallon a day. At nine bucks a gallon, times my 12 milking goats… you do the math."

Sergeant Tim abruptly changed the conversation. "What the hell is going on, Farris? I thought you had less than a month before you were out."

"I did, but things changed."

"Changed!? Are you in trouble?"

"Yeah, you can say that."

"Hold that thought. Let's get you guys in and something to eat. You can fill me in on what made you leave." Tim motioned to the house. "Head inside, make yourselves at home. I'll wait here and then let Daisy and Duke out."

"Daisy and Duke? What cute names. Are they brother and sister?" Carly asked.

"No. I had Duke and I got Daisy to keep him company. Hope they have pups in the spring. I let them wander the property. Closest neighbors are a mile and a half away. Only visitors I get out here are the locals, coming to buy eggs."

"Is there a place where I can hide the jeep?" David asked. "We didn't have a car, so I had to borrow one."

"Damn, Farris. A month to go and now this. Give me the keys. I'll move it. Hope you know what you're doing."

****

Slovak drove past the yellow police tape, cordoning off the road that led to the cabins. He parked his Volvo and noticed only three other cars in the expansive parking lot.

He opened the door and with satchel in hand, followed the shoveled path to the entrance doors. He pulled on the first door and it was locked, he then tried the other. "Dammit," he mumbled as he cupped his hands to his eyes and peered in. Seeing no one he began to pound.

A white-haired man pushing a trash can on wheels finally turned the corner. He walked slowly to the door. He removed a cluster of keys attached to his belt and unlocked the door. Cracking it slightly he said, "Building is closed. Can't let visitors in."

Slovak slipped his foot just inside the door jam.

"The police have shut the building down for the day," the elderly man said. "We're not supposed to let anyone in. Maybe try tomorrow."

Slovak removed his wallet and handed the custodian his ID. "I am Dr. Slovak…I am working with the police. Dr. Hayes was a colleague of mine. I need to get to his office and retrieve some documents. Would you like me to call security to verify?" Slovak felt for his gun.

The custodian paused for a moment. He looked down at Slovak's license and then back at him.

"That won't be necessary," he said, handing Slovak back his license. "I've seen you around. The office is open, the receptionist is there." The custodian stepped aside, and Slovak walked in.

"Thank you," Slovak said, "I won't be but a minute."

The *Out of Order* sign on the elevator door made Slovak pause, and shaking his head, he headed to the stairwell. He climbed the stairs slowly, going one step at a time and resting when he felt out of breath. He had already planned what he would say to Susan on the drive to the hospital.

"Good morning Susan," Slovak said as soon as he entered the office.

Susan jumped and turned from the filing cabinet. "Dr. Slovak. I'm surprised you got in. The custodians were supposed to lock the building so no one could get in. The office is going to be closed for a few days. I'm only here because I was told to pack up some papers and personal effects. I don't know when we'll be open again."

"I thought that might happen," he said pulling up a chair from a vacant workstation and placing his leather satchel on his lap. "Can you tell me what's going on?"

Susan sat back in her chair. "I'm not supposed to talk about anything to the media or anyone while the investigation is ongoing. The police were here yesterday asking all kinds of questions. They took Dr. Hayes' computer."

"I understand how these things work. But, I'm not the media. I wanted to talk to you before I visit Savannah Ray and her mother. I plan to see them after I'm finished here."

Susan let out a deep sigh and her eyes teared. “I just saw them. They are devastated. What do you want to talk about?”

Slovak proceeded carefully. “I heard there was some type of terrible accident and Dr. Hayes was killed. The news also reported others… any idea who they were?” Slovak waited, watching Susan’s face.

“Well, you already know about Dr. Hayes. It was his car that was in the accident. That I know for sure. There were three more bodies found, but they haven’t been identified. No details have been released about who they are or why they were with Dr. Hayes. One of the security guards heard shooting and went to investigate. What happened after that, we don’t know.”

“I’m not surprised details are being withheld,” Dr. Slovak commented. “It’s pretty much the way police do investigations.”

Susan nodded in agreement. She tapped her fingers on the desk and stared at a spot above Slovak’s head. She cleared her throat and started talking again. “What’s weird is…” Susan paused, “What’s really strange is we have three patients missing. Carly Fletcher, David Farris and Meghan Conner. The hospital did a head count after the lock-down and the three of them are gone. Hospital Administration is keeping everything hush, hush. You know until the families are notified.”

Slovak’s chest pounded with the possibility that Carly was alive. In the next couple of minutes, he would know for sure. “What a terrible thing for the Hayes family…and everyone else involved. I have to ask you a big favor. I need to get into the office to get a few of my things…my notes and some medical manuals for a case I am now working on.”

Susan’s pressed her lips into a thin line and she slowly shook her head. With raised eyebrows she stared back at Slovak and said, “I’m not supposed to let anyone back there. The police want it off limits.”

“I am not just anyone. I’m sure it’s for reporters and such. I have another case. It is another girl, a lot like Carly. With Dr. Hayes gone, it will be almost impossible for me to get the papers I need if you don’t let me into his office.”

“I can’t,” Susan said, raising her hands in the air and shaking her head. “I’m afraid to.”

Slovak edged his hand inside his pocket, fingering the handle of his revolver. He leaned in from his chair getting closer to Susan’s face, close enough that she could smell morning coffee on his breath. Speaking in a voice so low that it was hard to hear, Slovak said, "I'm going to ask you one more time. Unlock the office for me. I need to get those papers."

Something in the tone of his voice made Susan feel cold. She looked into Slovak's face and saw no warmth there, only hard, dangerous eyes. And the danger was to her. Reluctantly, she opened the center drawer of her desk and handed him the keys. Avoiding any more eye contact, she said, "Please return them when you're done."

"Of course," Slovak said with a wan smile.

After unlocking the office door, he immediately went to the coffee hutch and ran his fingers along the frame finding the hidden key. Slovak opened the bottom drawer and peered in. His hands trembled as he removed what looked like a cell phone and turned it on.

A smile grew on his face as he placed his hand to his head. The device went into his pocket. He removed any file dealing with Carly, David and Meghan and slipped them into his leather satchel. He then called Tatyana. After one ring, she picked up.

"Talk to me."

"Carly is alive. I think she's on the run with David Farris and Meghan Conner. Meet me at the Park and Ride off I-75 before the Dixie Highway. We'll plan from there. See you in about an hour."

****

Tatyana pulled the black van off I-75 and into the Park and Ride. She spotted Slovak's Volvo and passed it making sure he saw her. She parked in a spot away from the other cars. Slovak lifted the door handle and reached for the satchel sitting on the passenger seat. He left his car and entered the van, placing the lather satchel behind his seat. Handing Tatyana the tracker he said, "Take a look."

"What is this? It looks like an Uber map."

"It's Carly. In real time. We have a GPS transmitter on her. Lucky she hasn't found it yet. Didn't want to take any chances. Hayes kept the tracker under lock and key in case we ever had to use it." Slovak tapped the screen and made it bigger. "Look. You can see she's on the west side of the state, about three hours away."

Tatyana started the van. “Let’s nab the bitch and get her back to where we have Bo. I’ll torture him in front of her. She’ll give up the information.”

“You sound like Sarah. You don’t get it. She isn’t hiding information from us. She can’t remember. Let’s stick to the plan and send her the video first. It might be just the thing that does the trick.”

“Whatever,” Tatyana said, as she pulled out of the lot and onto I-75 heading north.

Chapter 31

Tim pulled the Jeep Grand Cherokee into the garage. He pressed the illuminated button mounted to the wall which lowered the garage door and he went out a side door. The chain squeaked and whined behind him as he walked to the barn and lifted the latch. Duke and Daisy were waiting, tails wagging and ready to run. “Get,” Tim said which sent the labs running and playing.

Carly was surprised when she entered the farmhouse. The inside had been totally remodeled. Oak plank floors were covered with area rugs, strategically placed throughout the rooms. One rug was under the kitchen table. One led down the hall from the kitchen to the family room and a huge rug filled that room. A wood burning stove sat in the middle of the family room. In the far-right corner Carly noticed what looked like a gigantic combination safe. The safe almost reached the ceiling.

“Your place is beautiful,” Carly said as Tim walked in the front door.

“Thank you,” he said, kneeling and unlacing his winter boots. “I figured I would start with the inside and save the outside for last. Haven’t pulled any permits for the remodeling ‘cause I don’t want my taxes to go up. The government gets enough of my money.”

Sergeant Tim noticed Carly shiver. She had taken off her shoes and her light winter jacket was no match for the northern weather. “Farris, would you mind throwing another log in the wood burner? Put in a couple… it’s a little chilly in here.”

“Sure thing, Sarge. But before I do, tell me what’s up with the *Fu Manchu*?”

“What? You don’t like it?” Sarge said, stroking his mustache and looking at Carly.”

“I think it very becoming,” Carly said.

“Suck up,” David said as he went to the wood burner.

“Careful. Use the mitt. That handle gets hot as hell.”

David put on the mitt that sat on the small stack of logs and opened the iron door. He could feel the heat from the red-hot coals as he tossed in a log and then another. Flames immediately shot up as he slammed the door closed, then locked the handle in place.

"Who wants a beer?" Tim asked as he went to the fridge, bent down, and looked in. "Got Bud light or Bud heavy. How about I heat us up some chili? Just made it this morning."

"Sounds good to me. I've been eating vending machine food for the last day and a half," David said. "Bud heavy will work. It's been a couple of years since I've had a brewski."

"Carly, what about you?"

"I'll take a water if you have one and some of that chili. I got pretty banged up a couple of days ago. Beer is out for me."

Tim placed the pot of chili on the stove and headed to the table carrying a couple of beers and a bottle of water. "Come have a seat," he said, setting the drinks on the table.

Carly took off her hat and pulled the kitchen chair from the table. She showed Tim her wound.

"Damn, girl. That's some goose egg," Tim said, frowning and moving closer to examine the purple and yellow gash.

"I have some first aid supplies in the bathroom that should help. I'll be back in a sec."

Returning from the bathroom, Tim took a sterile pad and rubbing alcohol and cleaned Carly's wound.

"That should do it," he said. "Don't want to cover it. Let the air dry it out." Grabbing a kitchen chair, he turned it around and straddled it. "All right. Which one of you is going to tell me what's going on?"

David started. He described the discharge program and the sixty days alone in the cabin. He shared his concerns with the unexplained footprints. Carly explained the strange message she received from the drunk sorority girl and how she was kidnapped and placed in the trunk with Hayes. She struggled when she described Ahmed's murder.

Sergeant Tim took a slug of his beer as he shook his head. "Un-fucking believable."

"It gets worse Sarge," David said. "Tell him about your brother."

Sergeant Tim turned to Carly. "During one of my hypnosis sessions I found out that my brother was murdered. I always thought he accidentally drowned but through hypnosis I learned he was murdered. I forgot my cell phone and had to return to Dr. Hayes office. When I went back I overheard Hayes talking on the phone. He and Slovak already knew my brother was murdered and they acted surprised."

"Who is this Slovak?" Tim asked.

"The therapist who hypnotizes Carly," David said. "All I could think of was to keep Carly safe. She was in danger and I had to protect her. See why we had to get the hell out of there?"

"Why do you think they tried to kidnap you?"

"That's what we don't know. David and I went over and over it on our way here. I think they're after something called mithridate. It's a universal antidote."

"Antidote," Sergeant Tim said. "We had antidote kits when we were in Iraq. After Saddam gassed the Kurds back in '88, the Army wasn't taking any chances. Whenever we went on patrol, we always had a kit. That's what kept me up at night. Bioweapons. If the jihadists got their hands on one, they'd use it for their Holy War. That gas is some nasty stuff. Why would they think you have it?"

"I *don't* have it and I *don't* know why they think I do. There's a period of my life that is blank to me. It's like someone took an eraser to my brain. Dr. Hayes suggested regressive therapy for me where I get hypnotized and visit past events, possibly reliving them. Dr. Hayes thought this hypnosis might bring my memory back."

"How did you lose it?"

"I don't know. That's what these sessions were about. To try and figure out why I lost my memory. I have these real vivid images that pop in my head at times. It's of people being shot. Dr. Hayes at first thought I was delusional. But after a time, he thought it might have something to do with my memory loss. It was during hypnosis that I realized my dad had given me a clue."

"What kind of clue?" Tim asked.

"Find Mr. Etadirhtim and look to your brother for direction. At first, I didn't understand what it meant. A friend of mine at Holy Oaks helped me figure it out. Etadirhtim is mithridate spelled backwards. My dad had given me a locket when my brother died. There were clues in the locket spelling out mithridate."

"Tell me more about this kidnapping."

"Dr. Hayes… my therapist at Holy Oaks… was supposed to pick me up to go into town and get my driver's license reinstated. When he pulled up in his Cadillac I ran down the steps. His windows were tinted so I couldn't see in the car. There was this man and woman. They tried to force me into the car. That's when Ahmed came out of the woods to try and help and got shot."

"And you didn't know this woman."

"Never saw her before in my life. She cracked me with her gun. That's the last thing I remember before blacking out. They threw me in the trunk with Dr. Hayes."

"Damn. This is bizarre," Sargent Tim said, tipping his beer and finishing the last swig.

"Anything else that you might have left out?"

"Not really," David said. "Unless you're talking about Carly calling in a bomb threat and stealing a car."

"What the fuck Farris, you're in a world of hurt. We'll get you out of this."

Looking at the stove Sergeant Tim noticed steam rising from the pot. "Let's eat. You guys are probably starved. We can talk while we eat."

Tim left the table and walked back to the stove. He filled three bowls with chili and set them on the table. He put a box of crackers and squares of corn bread in the middle.

David reached behind his back and removed the pistol from his waistband. He sat it next to his beer.

"This tastes just like Grunt Chili," David remarked. "It will definitely stick to the ribs."

"Just eat it up, Farris. There's no complaining about the cook at this table."

As they finished their meal, Tim handed David the last of the corn bread before taking the empty bowls to the sink and rinsing them. Carly collected the silverware and box of crackers and placed them on the counter.

"Hand me the dishrag," she said.

Tim squeezed the excess water from it and tossed it to her. She wiped the table then tossed it back.

"You look a little flushed, Carly," Tim said. "Do you want to lie down? It will give me a little time to kick this grunt's ass in chess. Plus we can go over any details you might have left out."

"Bring it on, Sarge," David said confidently. "Started a chess club at Holy Oaks. Things have changed since the desert."

"Maybe I will," Carly said. "I am a little tired. Where's the bed?"

"Guest room. Down the hall on the right. The door is open."

The match was tied one game apiece and both men badly wanted the tie breaker. Tim watched David move his rook back into a defensive position. The Sarge was one move away from checkmate.

"Can I ask you something?" Tim said.

David's eyes left the board and looked at him. "Sure, Sarge."

"This Carly. How well do you know her?"

"Pretty good. We hung a lot at Holy Oaks. I'd like it to be more… but for now we're just friends."

"Just friends? You're sure about that? Have you told her how you feel?"

"I've dropped hints and at times I get the feeling she's into me and then other times I think she's just into her boyfriend."

"She's got a boyfriend?"

"Yeah. I've met him. Seems like a nice enough guy."

Tim sat back in his chair and stroked his *Fu Manchu.* A smile grew on his face.

"Dammit!" David said, slapping his knee. Whenever the Sarge set back in his chair and smiled, he knew the next move was fatal. He watched helplessly as Tim took his queen and placed it to the far corner of the chess board.

"Checkmate," his Sergeant said.

****

Carly shuffled from the guest room rubbing her eyes. Her hair was disheveled and the scab on her head had a smear of fresh blood. David and Tim looked up from the board.

"You must have scratched your head in your sleep," Tim said. "You got a smear of blood on your forehead."

Carly raised her hand to her head and gently patted her wound. "This itches like crazy, must be healing. What time is it?"

"A little after four," David said. "You slept a couple of hours."

Tim stood from the table. "You sit right down here. David and I have been talking about what happened, but I want to hear more from you. How about I make some coffee and we continue where we left off? Are you up to it, Carly?"

"Sure. That nap really helped."

Tim left the family room passing the kitchen table and heading into the tiny kitchen. He filled the coffee maker, then leaned up against the counter and waited.

"Want to give it a shot?" David asked, as he rearranged the chess pieces and set up a new game.

"Do you mind if we don't?" Carly said, then curled up crossed legged in the chair and covered herself with a quilt that was draped over the back.

Tim poured three cups of coffee from the pot and set out the cream and sugar.

He called out, "Get it while it's hot."

David grabbed the arms of the upholstered chair and pushed himself up. It took a couple pushes and groans before he was standing.

Watching from the kitchen, Tim started teasing him. "Oooh, ahhh, unhh. Old Man… need some help getting out of that chair. You act like you're 80. Did you hear his bones creaking, Carly?"

"I think I did," she agreed following David to the kitchen. "It sounded like my granny's old rocker we kept in the garage."

"Knock it off," said David. "I did that on purpose to see how you would react!"

"And you two were in the military protecting us!!! Carly chuckled. "What was everyone else doing?"

"That's the problem. None of us knew *what* we were doing!" David cracked.

The lighter atmosphere in the room lasted only a short time before thoughts turned to the grim reality.

Tim abruptly stopped talking and his forehead furrowed.

"What? What's the matter, Sarge?" David asked.

"How long would you say you guys have been here, four maybe five hours?"

David looked at his watch, "About five."

"Ya know, those dogs are awfully quiet," Tim said. He walked to the front window and pulled aside the curtain. He saw Duke and Daisy sitting at the end of his drive, like soldiers standing guard. "We may have a more immediate problem."

"What's that?" Carly asked, walking to the window. David followed.

"See my dogs sitting by the road?"

Just as he said, Carly and David spotted the two Goldens sitting side by side on the driveway.

"They'll sit there until the cows come home. About forty-five minutes ago, someone drove past my house and down the road. I heard the dogs barking. It's a dead-end. The dogs know who ever drives down that road will turn around and come back. They go bonkers when they pass by."

"So, what are you saying?" Carly asked.

"Someone is sitting down the road. They've been there for a while. Could you have been tracked here?"

"Tracked? No way," David said. "I checked the car. It was clean."

"When's the last time either one of you used your phones?"

"David had me throw mine out before we left for here… day before yesterday."

"Only used mine when I called you to see if we could come. That was day before yesterday too."

"Okay… I don't think your phone is the problem. If someone was pinging the phone, it would only get the cell tower, and they would triangulate the phones location from there. Whoever's tracking you I'm pretty sure knows you're in my house."

David went to the kitchen table. He grabbed his gun and placed it back in his waistband.

"God, David," Carly said. "Who *are* these people?"

"I won't let anything happen to you, Carly. Whoever they are, we'll be ready for them."

Carly leaned in and wrapped her arms around David. He hugged her back.

"And you told me you were just friends," Tim said, taking a quick step away from the window. "Let's figure out how they're tracking you. Carly, I want to see if you are chipped."

"Chipped?"

"Yeah. Follow me to my bedroom. I want to check your clothes."

Carly followed Tim into the bedroom. He opened the closet and handed her a robe.

"Put this on after you take off your clothes. I need to check all of them, even your undies and shoes. When you have them off, come out to the kitchen and lay them out on the table. I'll be back in a second."

Tim left the bedroom.

"What's the plan, Sarge?"

"We're going to see if Carly's clothes have been chipped. Gotta go to the pole barn and grab something."

"Should you arm yourself?"

"Always do," Tim said, smiling. "Nothing to worry about with Duke and Daisy prowling the grounds."

Carly came into the kitchen, her arms holding all her clothes—jacket, jeans, shirt, vest, socks, hat, panties, and boots. She put them on the table.

Tim returned carrying a stud finder. He walked to a wall and turned it on. It beeped, and a green light temporally tuned on, then went off. He passed it over the wall. "See how it beeps and the light turns green when you pass over a stud? Not only will this identify studs behind a wall, it picks up microchips in livestock. If I have a cow or goat that wanders on my property, I check to see if it has been chipped. If it has, I call a vet to come and read it. We can then get the animal back to the right ranch. This should work for hidden GPS sensors."

"That's amazing, Sarge," David said. "Hell, instead of Terminator we should call you MacGyver."

"MacGyver?" Carly asked.

"Yeah, you know. The guy who could use whatever he found to make tools to help him escape. He was on a TV show."

"Never heard of him."

"That's because you're a kid."

"And you're my old man because you're six years older," Carly said smiling.

"That's right, so you better listen to your elders. I've heard they made a remake of the series. Haven't seen it yet."

Tim began to scan Carly's clothes. The three watched for the green light and listened for the beep. He slowly passed over each piece of clothing, paying particular attention to heels, hems, and collars. He scanned each item once and then did it again.

"Nothing," Tim said, shaking his head. "Is there anything else you brought with you from the hospital? Anything at all?"

Carly thought for a minute, shaking her head she said, "No… nothing I can think of."

"Get your purse. Dump it out on the table."

Carly found her handbag by the couch and walked back to the table. She unzipped it and dumped the contents. Tim immediately spotted it…a key that dangled from a flashlight key chain.

"Is that a key from the hospital?"

"It's the key to the cabin."

Tim picked up the flashlight keychain. "This has to be it. There's a battery in here, and I bet my ass the GPS is imbedded."

He waved the stud finder over the keychain. The diode turned green and the unit beeped. Tim looked up from the keychain.

"There's a chance I am just picking up the battery. I don't want to mess with it. Not sure, but it may give off some type of signal if it's tampered with. You know like those ankle tethers for criminals. It's got to be it. It's the only thing that makes sense."

"I want to see that," Carly said, reaching out for the key chain. Tim handed it to her, and she examined it closely. "*Why* would someone do something like this? *Who* would do something like this?"

David looked at her and shrugged. Tim was the first to speak.

"We have no idea who we're dealing with. One thing we do know… they're dangerous. Let's not take any chances. We need a plan."

Chapter 32

Tiptoeing past a sleeping Agent Canter, Ahmed walked to Porsche's bunk. He stripped down to his boxers and slipped beneath the sheets. Startled, Porsche opened her eyes, her lips parted to speak, but Ahmed placed his index finger over them.

She said nothing as he placed his mouth over hers and they kissed. She became excited as his hands traveled over her body and settled between her legs, gently stroking her. First on the outside of her panties and then he went inside.

She felt his hardness through his boxers and slipped her hand inside them, caressing his penis.

Ahmed was fully aroused.

They said you were dead, she tried to explain between moans of desire.

"Ssshhhh," Ahmed whispered as he slipped down his boxers and then removed her panties. He climbed on top of her and she dug her nails into his shoulders as he entered and slowly began to thrust.

"Wake up, Porsche," Agent Canter coaxed, gently shaking her shoulder. "They got a ping on David. We gotta go."

Porsche's eyes opened, but she remained silent, still in the erotic throes of her dream. She felt the dampness between her legs as she closed her eyes once again yearning to go back to Ahmed. Stacey sat on the side of her bunk lacing up her government issued boots.

"Porsche," Agent Canter said more forcefully. "Didn't you hear me? We gotta go. They pinged David and Carly, chief wants to brief us in ten."

"Sorry!" she said jumping out of bed, grabbing her shirt. "I was dreaming about Ahmed."

Canter paused, then spoke to Porsche. "We're gonna get those sons of bitches responsible for Ahmed's death. We'll make sure Carly is safe, and then we'll take out the whole goddamn terrorist cell. Sweet revenge for your boy."

Porsche smiled sadly and continued to dress. There was nothing more she could do for Ahmed, but there was plenty she could do for Carly. It only took a few minutes to reach the command center. They walked side by side, heads down and their hands in the pockets of their parkas.

"Don't have a lot of time," Chief Bolton explained, as Porsche and Agent Canter entered the office. "Grab a cup. You'll have to eat on the road. A trooper spotted Carly and David at a rest area near West Branch. His name is Fitzgerald. You have a ten o'clock meeting with him at the MSP Post 32."

"Oh, I thought you pinged them. But it was a sighting?" Canter asked.

"Yes, a sighting. And Porsche…you can't go into the meeting. Officially the FBI was brought in to help with finding domestic terrorists who called in a bomb threat and stole a car. That's our cover and how I got the meeting with the trooper."

"Understood," Porsche replied.

****

Parked on a dirt road next to a frozen ditch, Slovak balanced the manila folders on his lap. He took a pen from the cup holder filled with spare change and placed it sideways in his mouth. "Find me something to write on," he mumbled through the pen.

Tatyana reached behind the driver's seat and grabbed a crumpled receipt. She flattened it and asked, "Will this work?"

"Yes," Slovak said taking it from her and placing it on the cardboard folders. At the top of the receipt he wrote, Carly and then her phone number. He then took Meghan's and David's number and did the same. Once done, he tossed the pen back into the cup holder and placed the folders in his satchel.

"We're going to wait until dark… it gets dark early, and then send the video. I'm pretty positive the three of them are at the farmhouse. Still can't believe that went sideways… Sarah was such a pro."

"Why are you fucking around? Let's nab her and take her back. Wasn't that the original plan? We'll take her back to the cabin and use Bo to get her to talk."

"I wish it was that simple. The plan changed after we were compromised. Carly still can't remember what her father told her during that walk in the park. I'm hoping the video jogs her memory. Once she remembers, then we can do what it takes to get the information out of her."

Slovak again felt a twinge of pain as he placed his hand to his chest and massaged. He removed a tab of nitro and placed it under his tongue. Tatyana watched the beads of sweat that formed on his forehead.

"That's the second time this happened. How about some fresh air?" she asked, lowering Slovak's window.

He ignored her at first then muttered, "I'll be fine. Just give me a minute."

Give you a minute? Christ.

Slovak dabbed his forehead with his open palm. He then turned to Tatyana, "ok... where was I?"

"The video," Tatyana said, emphasizing the word video.

Slovak continued. "Let's show her the video first. I figure if we send it to all three she is sure to see it. The video is the trick. The shock of seeing Bo may jog her memory. It's not going to be a walk in the park to get her. Did you see those dogs when we passed the house?"

"Dogs! I'm more worried about you having a heart attack then I am about the fucking dogs. They won't be a problem once they're dead."

"Oh and let them know we're coming. There could be a gun in that house. There could be a lot of guns in that house. Never known a farmhouse that didn't have a shotgun...or two."

"You're an idiot." She rolled her eyes at him. "I came prepared. I have a silencer. We'll take the dogs out first."

"Idiot?" he repeated in a brusque tone. "Tread easy, Tatyana. Tread easy."

Slovak reached into the console and picked up his cell phone.

"We don't know what we will be facing, but there is something you need to know—Don't underestimate Carly. She knows how to use a gun. Maybe she hasn't realized it yet, but she *knows* how to use one. I found out when she damn near killed me at the park. You think differently when you've faced the other side of a gun. A mirror reminds me of that every day.

"Now...let's look at the video...one more time," Slovak said tapping the red arrow on his phone.

****

Porsche and Agent Canter pulled down East Houghton Street on their way to Post 32. The Michigan State Police headquarters, District 3 was where her meeting would take place. They pulled into the parking lot of a building that sat high upon a bluff. Two flags, the American and State, flew at half-mast. The country had just lost its longest serving U.S. Congressman and that Congressman, Representative John Dingell, had made Michigan his home.

"What's the name again of the Trooper?" Porsche asked.

"Fitzgerald."

"So, he actually saw Carly and David at some rest stop?"

"I think so," Agent Canter said as she parked the car and handed her the keys. "I'll let you know after the meeting."

Porsche watched Agent Canter walk between the blue Michigan State Police sedans and up to the steps of the post. She placed the keys back in the ignition and turned on some music. She leaned her seat back and closed her eyes.

Fitzgerald walked into the office, gripped the four-dent pinched corners of his broad brimmed hat and set it on the table. The two of them shook hands.

"Are these the two you saw at the rest area?" Agent Canter asked, handing Fitzgerald a picture of David and Carly."

The trooper examined the pictures then handed them back to Stacey. "For sure it was the male. The female was wearing a stocking hat that was pulled down close to her eyebrows. If I was a betting man, I would say yes, that was her.

"Too bad the APB didn't get to us a couple hours sooner. I know they're driving a Jeep Grand Cherokee. I believe it was silver. I parked my cruiser next to it. Wonder what was going through their minds as they came out and saw me?"

"Anything else you can think of?" Agent Canter inquired.

"Not really. They're headed north, but east or west is a crap shoot. They didn't seem to be dressed for the weather. Light winter coats, that kind of thing."

"I appreciate your time."

Canter stood and was headed to the door when Trooper Fitzgerald said, "One more thing."

She stopped and turned around.

"Can you tell me what's going on? The FBI doesn't get involved for a stolen car. Something big has to be going down."

"Before stealing the Jeep, Ms. Fletcher called in a bomb threat. That's why the bureau was brought in. That's about all I'm authorized to share."

"Will I read about it in the paper?" Fitzgerald asked.

Canter smiled, "I hope not."

****

Tim stood in front of the gun vault bolted to the floor in the far-right corner of the family room. He punched in his code and lifted the steel handle, allowing the heavy door to swing open. Twenty-four firearms of all makes and models stood vertically side by side. Shot guns, long rifles, semiautomatic assault weapons, Winchesters, pumps… all had their specific cradle. Ammo-cases stacked one upon the other covered the floor of the arsenal.

"Damn, Sarge," David blurted, standing in front of what looked like an armory. I know you don't trust the government, but I didn't think you were preparing for Armageddon."

"I don't trust those fools in Washington as far as I could throw them. Just like in Iraq… I like to be prepared. Don't want any surprises. What's your flavor these days, Farris?"

"You know me, Sarge. I was married to my M-16 while touring paradise, but I think I need something more for close range. You got a 12-gauge in there?"

Tim pulled a 12-gauge shotgun from its cradle and handed it to David. "I think I'll join you," he agreed, removing a semiautomatic 12-gauge for himself. "Grab the ammo-case furthest to the left. Your back is younger than mine. Set it on the table."

Tim studied Carly for a moment. "Carly…you have a preference for any certain kind of gun or…" Tim stopped talking. "Carly… are you all right?"

Carly had braced herself against the counter wobbling slightly. Tim could see her straighten out her knees to keep standing and to maintain her balance. "Whoa…" she breathed. She shut her eyes tightly and shook her head. Speaking in a voice below a whisper she murmured, "One in the chamber…rounds…. Dad…Don't flinch,

Carly. Just squeeze…Good shot." *I remember being at the range. I remember how to shoot.* A secretive smile crossed Carly's face, surprising both of them. "Give me a Glock."

Tim removed the Glock from a pistol peg and handed it to her.

Carly took the pistol and pulled back the slide. She could tell by the weight the gun wasn't loaded. "You gonna give me some ammo or do you want me to throw this at the bad guys?" she kidded, then dropped the magazine in her hand waiting to load the 15 rounds.

Tim grinned, "Farris, she's a keeper." He reached into a drawer of the vault and retrieved a box of 9mm bullets. He handed them to Carly and walked back to the table opening the ammo-case. "If they come, we'll be ready. They first have to get by Duke and Daisy."

From the ammo case he handed David a box of 12-gauge buckshot shells and took one for himself.

Chapter 33

Tatyana kept the heat on full blast. She would start the van and let it run for 10 minutes, then leave if off for 20. The lake effect snow was blizzarding and visibility was little more than a hundred feet.

"It's going to be tough to take out those dogs in this weather," Tatyana said. "Maybe they brought them in or put them in the barn. Why don't we show Carly the video now? Why wait for tonight? We're running low on gas and according to the weather, this storm isn't going away any time soon. Seeing the video may even make her want to leave."

Slovak said nothing as he cleared the fogged-up window with his glove and looked out. The wet snow torrent was falling horizontally, and the power lines were coated in ice. He nodded his head, then looked back at Tatyana. "That may not be a bad idea. We wouldn't have to deal with the dogs, and we wouldn't have to spend the night in the van. If they leave, we could come up from behind, side swipe them and run them into a ditch. With the storm, they won't be driving fast, and they will be an easier target."

"I think we should kill David right there in front of Carly. If your flashbulb memory theory holds up, she would experience more trauma seeing her friend murdered then any video could produce."

Slovak paused, "That just might work."

He handed Tatyana the receipt with the numbers he had written of Carly, David and Meghan. Holding the phone in front of him, Slovak took a deep breath. "Give me Carly's number first and then the others."

"You got it," Tatyana said, reading the numbers to him.

Slovak tapped the screen and sent the video. "I'll take the first shift. We can monitor the tracker. If they don't leave by dark, we'll have to go in."

****

David sat on the couch while Tim was in a recliner. Carly could hear them conversing when she left the back bedroom. She gripped a pair of Tim's jeans by the waist while holding a belt with her other hand.

"Can you punch another hole in your belt?" Carly asked pulling the waistband out from her belly, revealing an eight-inch gap. "Pants are a little loose, don't you think?"

Carly placed the belt through the loops and held her thumb where the new hole needed to be punched. She slipped the belt back off.

"Right where my thumb is," Carly showed him, then handed Tim the belt.

"Sorry, Carly," Tim said looking at how she struggled with his oversized clothes. "I just don't want to chance it. I might have missed a chip. You gotta leave them with me." Tim took the belt. "I've got an ice pick in the kitchen."

Holding her jeans so they would not slip to her knees, she stuffed the oversized t-shirt inside the waistband, and sat next to David on the couch. They both heard a ping come from his phone.

"Who's texting you?" Carly asked with a questioning look. "Could it be Meghan?"

"I don't recognize the number," David said puzzled. "Whoever it is sent a video." He then tapped the image to make it fit the full screen.

Sergeant Tim walked back from the kitchen and handed the belt to Carly. "This should do it."

"Someone sent David a video," Carly said, as she took the belt, placed it through the loops and cinched it tight.

"Who would be sending you a video?" Tim asked, then stood behind the couch to view David's phone.

David tapped the red arrow as the three focused on the screen.

The video started, and it was at first a bit blurry and then the image became sharp. A man wearing a ski-mask, holding a sheathed bowie knife stood behind a victim strapped to a kitchen chair. The victim's head hung low, chin to chest. His body was limp, and he slouched in the chair. The camera focused on the executioner who lifted the knife high in the air and ceremoniously removed it slowly from the sheath. He placed his hand under the victim's chin and lifted his head.

"Hello, Carly," the masked man said, his voice low, his speaking rate deliberately slow.

"Any idea who that is?" Tim asked.

Carly gasped, "That's Bo. They've got Bo!"

An unshaven Bo Harris stared back into the camera. Eyes wide with panic, he said nothing. The executioner placed the knife to his neck then said, "Give us the mithridate. You know where it is. Give it to us or Bo will join your brother."

The executioner placed the knife to the corner of Bo's mouth and cut vertically towards his ear. Bo screamed. He thrashed trying to move his head, but the executioner held firm. Blood poured from the wound, immediately covering Bo's lower face and neck. A second masked man came from the side and held towels to Bo's face. They quickly became soaked with his blood. The executioner handed the knife to his accomplice and stepped from behind the chair. He removed a picture from his shirt pocket. As the camera zoomed in, it revealed a picture of Artie, the same picture Carly had in her locket.

"You have twenty-four hours to contact us. You have the number."

****

Smoking a cigarette outside the West Branch hotel, Porsche thought about Ahmed. She took her last drag and tossed the butt into a can, then walked back into the room. Agent Canter lay on the bed, pillows piled behind her back, watching TV.

"You all right?" she asked Porsche.

"No, not really. It'll be a long time before I am." Porsche walked to the other side of the bed and fluffed a couple of pillows before she lay next to Stacey. "So, how long do we stay here?"

"Until we hear from the Chief. Right now Carly and David could be anywhere in the state. Once they get a location, he'll send us on our way."

"So you haven't heard from Carly since the last text?"

"No. Remember we found her phone in a trash can just outside the Welchester Library."

"Do you think that David guy might try and call you? Do you have his number?"

Stacey reached down and grabbed her duffel bag, bringing it up to her lap. "That's a brilliant idea," she said rummaging through its contents and removing the cell phone she used as Meghan Conner. She then turned it on. "I'll have to clear it with the chief. If David answers we could ping him. I can't believe I didn't think of that. Ahmed did a great job training you."

As Stacey looked at the phone, her forehead creased.

"What? What is it?" Porsche asked.

"Someone sent me a message…actually it's a video."

Porsche leaned over to view the phone as Stacey started the video.

"Jesus Christ. Who's that guy getting cut?" Porsche asked, grabbing Stacey's hand bringing the phone closer for a look.

"It's Bo Harris, Carly's boyfriend. This video was sent to Carly, David and me. I recognize the numbers. Whoever sent this must think the three of us are together. I gotta send this to the chief."

****

Except for the icy snow spattering against the windows, the room was quiet.

"What the hell was that?" David gasped, "Reminds me of an ISIS beheading!"

"Follow me to the kitchen, Farris, and bring your phone." Sergeant Tim ordered. "The light's better in here. Gotta see that again."

Carly shuddered momentarily, then brought her knees to her chest and rested her head on them. While David and Tim watched the video, her mind went to that place of nothingness. She slowly closed her eyes as foggy half memories began to present themselves. Before long the fog lifted, and Carly saw herself sitting in a different living room that was much too empty. Max was lying across her feet. Bo was gone and probably not coming back. Ever!

"Your dad is a real jerk, Max. A real jerk."

Max lay there quietly, not moving his head. His tail thumped slowly on the floor.

When her cell phone rang, she sat in the chair, who would be calling this early? She looked at the caller ID.

"Dad! Are you in town?"

"Yes, Carly. Just got in."

"Are you going to come to my place and visit this time?"

"Can't do that now. I really need you to come to Belle Isle. Can you make it? I'll be on the Trail of Tears."

"Is everything okay, Dad?"

"No, not really. I need you to come here. Bring your camera and all your gear. There are bird watchers everywhere. I don't dare come to your place."

"Okay… Got it. I 'll be there."

Birdwatchers…Grab my gear.

Carly crossed the kitchen to reach her bedroom. She took the few steps to the dresser and paused to look at the picture of Bo and her—smiling and sitting on a bench in Cadillac Square. She touched the frame, then placed it face down.

Bending over, she pulled out the bottom drawer and pushed aside some sweaters. She removed the pistol from the drawer, pulled the slide to chamber a round, then placed it in her waistband.

On the way out of her bedroom, Carly stepped on Max's tail. He let out a piercing yelp.

"Max! Jesus Christ! Stop getting in the way."

Carly snatched Max's leash and he wiggled with excitement waiting for her to attach it to his collar. She lifted the camera from the counter and threw the strap over her shoulder.

"C'mon, boy. Let's go see Grandpa."

Carly guided Max down the steps to her white Impala parked on the street. Max waited patiently as Carly unlocked the door and opened it for him.

"Okay, Max," Carly said. "Let's go."

Max leaped onto the seat and immediately lay down. Carly checked the street before getting into the car. Nothing looked out of place. A few people stood at the bus stop waiting for the Woodward bus. The usual cars were parked in their places.

The engine sputtered before it started. She drove down Jefferson which led to the bridge that crossed the Detroit River.

As she drove to Belle Isle a knot formed in her stomach. Something was not right with her father. Why else would he want to meet in the park and have her bring her gun? As the scenery whipped past, Max nervously paced from window to window. His panting causing the windows to fog up.

"You're such a good boy," Carly said, checking her rearview mirror. "We're almost there."

She named the footpath "The Trail of Tears" after Artie stepped on a bee and cried like a baby. It was his own fault. Dad always warned him to wear shoes.

Max recognized his surroundings when Carly parked her car. His tail wagged from side to side and he began to whine even louder. This was not his first walk in the woods.

"Sit," she commanded, taking the pistol from the passenger's seat and placing it in her waistband. Max waited until Carly opened the rear door.

"C'mon," Carly said grabbing the leash still attached to Max's collar and helped him from the car. "Let's go find Grandpa."

Carly stood in the parking lot, checking to see if she had been followed. Cars pulled in and families jumped out. Kids so happy to be heading to the sledding hills. When she felt comfortable, she began to walk the trail, snapping pictures as she went, making everything look as normal as possible.

"Now don't go chasing squirrels," she said to Max as he walked next to her. Suddenly, he lifted his ears. Out of nowhere, Carly's dad appeared.

He held out his arms as Carly got closer.

"Dad!" Carly blurted as she hugged him, not wanting to let go. "What's going on? You sounded weird on the phone."

Fletcher held his daughter tightly as he nervously scanned the woods and the path.

"We don't have a lot of time. You have to listen very carefully. Walk with me."

Carly listened, absorbing the strange ramblings of her father. She could see the concern in his face and hear the urgency in his voice.

"Don't trust anyone until you know they can be trusted. If anything happens to me, you have to find Mr. Etadirhtim and look to Artie for direction."

"Dad," Carly said, but her father cut her off.

"Just listen, Carly," her dad said forcefully. "Please, just listen."

Carly's father abruptly stopped when he noticed two individuals walking further down the trail towards them.

"Dad, we're not the only ones in the park. Other people walk this trail."

"Right," Carly's dad said hesitantly. "Just stay close to me and listen. Mr. Etadirhtim is in Canada in case you need to find him. He's living in the basement of a house Grandpa built. You can see it from the viewing deck. He'll be waiting if you need him."

Carly heard Max growl and then a shot rang out leaving her disoriented. Two men wearing ski masks had drawn their guns. Carly's dad pushed her to the side then drew his pistol. Seeing Max lying motionless in the snow, Carly also drew her weapon. Another shot rang out. It was her father striking the man who shot Max.

Eyes wide, Carly witnessed her father take a round to the head. Blood mist filled the air and then rained down covering the white snow. His knees buckled, and he fell to the ground, never letting go of his pistol. Reflexively she raised her gun and popped two shots.

The forest became eerily quiet. Carly stood motionless, vacantly staring at the carnage around her. "Dad," Carly whispered as she dropped to her knees next to her father. As she knelt she saw two men wearing masks and guns drawn running towards her. Carly jumped to her feet and fled into the woods.

Tim and David walked back from the kitchen and stopped in front of Carly.

"Carly, what's wrong?" Tim said. "I heard you say Dad. What happened?"

Carly slowly looked up from her knees. "I remembered that day in the park. It came right after seeing the video," she said. "My father is dead. Slovak was there."

"What did you remember?" David asked softly.

He sat down next to Carly and put his arm over her shoulder. She nuzzled her head into David's chest.

Carly reached into her t-shirt and removed her locket. She gave it a gentle kiss then pressed it up against her heart. "I remember what my father told me. It came back to me when you were in the kitchen.

"I was walking in the park with my father and before we knew it, two masked men with guns drawn were in front of us. Max growled and … they shot him. My dad drew his pistol and hit one of the men before he was shot himself. I fired my gun and the last guy fell. I saw two more men running towards me, so I ran into the woods. I *know* it was Slovak. I recognized his wrinkled khaki pants and voice from the video."

Carly's expression hardened, "That fucker's responsible for killing Artie, my dad, and Ahmed. "I can't let him kill Bo too. We have to find the mithridate."

David nodded. "Did your dad tell you where it is?"

"Not exactly. But he gave me clues."

She repeated what her dad said. "Mr. Etadirhtim is in Canada in case you need to find him. He's living in the basement of a house Grandpa built. You can see it from the viewing deck. He'll be waiting if you need him."

Carly went silent, then spoke again. "It was me."

"What was you?" David asked.

"It was me that shot Slovak. There was no stray missile that caused his disfigurement. It was my bullet."

Tim and David exchanged glances. "Farris," Sergeant Tim said. "I told you she's a keeper."

Chapter 34

The boom of a high-powered rifle echoed outside the farmhouse. A blue-white flash illuminated the yard followed by a loud explosion. Inside the house, lights flickered. David instinctively pulled Carly to the floor. Another blast rang out. Sergeant Tim grabbed his 12-gauge from the side of his recliner and rolled to the window.

Getting to his knees, he stealthily looked out the corner of the window, puzzled as to why the dogs were not barking. The lights momentarily went out then within seconds came back. Carly drew her Glock and aimed it on the front door.

"I've got the back door," David yelled. Then he crouched and made his way until he had a clear view of the back door. He waited, his shotgun fixed, ready for any intruder.

"Damn!" Tim said, when he pulled up the shade. "It's the goddamn transformer. I can see it arcing from here."

"Oh, my God," Carly burst out getting to her feet. "What the hell happened?"

"Power lines are covered in ice. Looks like the weight pulled the wire down. Lucky for us I have one of those natural gas generators that turns on automatically when the power goes out. Can't chance my security system going out with all this firepower in here."

Shaking his head on the way back into the family room, David said, "You have to admit, Sarge, it felt like we were back in Iraq for a minute."

"Yeah, it did. The good old days," he said smiling, settling back down in his recliner and laying the shotgun on the side of his chair. "Who is this Mr. Eta- what?"

"Etadirhtim," Carly said. "It's mithridate spelled backwards. It's that clue my father gave to me…hidden inside my locket, a locket he gave to me and my mom the day we buried my brother."

"Oh, that's right. You told me about it. What did your old man do for a living?"

"He was a doctor. But the more I'm finding out, the more I'm realizing he might have been more than that."

Tim paused, then spoke. "Okay, so what are these clues you remember now?"

Carly sat back on the couch followed by David. Her brow narrowed as she spoke. "Mr. Etadirhtim is in Canada in case you need to find him. He's living in the basement of a house, Grandpa built. You can see it from the viewing deck. He'll be waiting if you need him."

"So, where's this viewing deck your dad's talking about?" Tim asked.

"It's gotta be my grandparent's lake house."

"Is it in Canada?"

"No. That's what doesn't make sense. It's in Lexington, Michigan."

Holding up her hand she showed him the Michigan mitten. Carly pointed just below the knuckle on the outside of her thumb. "You can see Canada across Lake Huron. But the lake house is in the states."

"Was your grandpa a builder?"

"Grandpa Wiebelhaus? No. As far as I remember he was some big shot with a manufacturing company. A VP I think. Something to do with chemicals. He did have a wood shop though. He'd putz in there and made things."

"Like what?"

"You know like…umm…Christmas ornaments, a lot of Christmas stuff. He once made this manger and my grandma made figurines that went into it. She had a kiln and was really artistic."

Carly stood up from the couch. "The viewing deck my father was talking about is definitely at the lake house. Only problem is my grandparents sold the house years ago. They sold it and moved to Arizona. We have to get there. You heard what Slovak said. We've only got 24 hours and we're wasting time."

David slapped both hands on his knees, got up, and stood next to her.

"Hang on, Bonnie and Clyde! Don't be so quick to leave. We need a plan. Sit back down. Let's talk."

Reluctantly Carly and David sat back down.

Sergeant Tim leaned forward sitting on the edge of the recliner. He began to stroke his *Fu Manchu*.

"What are you thinking, Sarge?" David asked.

David, Carly and Tim bagged all of her belongings. Tim made sandwiches and packed a couple bottles of water along with a half can of cashews for their trip. Carly stuffed tissue into the toes of a pair of boots and Tim gave her a winter parka.

"I want you guys to keep the guns," Tim said as he placed a pistol in his waistband.

Sergeant Tim removed five one hundred-dollar bills from his shirt pocket. He held out his hand and gave them to David. "Don't use your credit cards. They can track you with those." David took the cash and smiled.

"Thank you, Sarge. You've always been there for me."

"Remember, Farris, what I taught you in Iraq. You have the upper hand with the enemy. You're now in control. Use that to your advantage."

Chapter 35

With little effort the Jeep Grand Cherokee plowed through the six inches of snow, kicking up a blizzard behind it. The unplowed roads made it a challenge to maneuver, but the four-wheel drive kept the jeep steady.

Soon head lights could be seen, coming up from behind.

"These roads are fucked up," Tatyana said, keeping both hands on 10 & 2 while the back tires struggled to grip the icy roads. "I can feel the ass-end fishtailing."

"Don't worry if you can't keep up. If we're lucky, they're headed to the mithridate as we speak. We've got the tracker. Just keep tailing them until we get on some better roads."

Tatyana nodded.

The two had been on the road for little over a half hour when the tracker started to ping. Concern filled Tatyana face as she watched Slovak tap the screen until the pinging stopped.

"They're not moving," he said studying the tracker. "They're three miles ahead and it looks like they've turned off the main road. Keep going, I'll tell you where to turn."

The van slowed, and then stopped in front of a two track. "They're about a quarter mile down this road," Slovak said. "If you stay in their tire tracks the van shouldn't get stuck."

Making a left Tatyana followed the tire tracks. "I don't like this," she said as they slowly made their way down the two track.

"Stop!" Slovak said in a raised voice. "Something has to be wrong. The tracker says they're twenty yards ahead and I see nothing." He pulled his gun. "Let's walk from here."

Tatyana parked the van and lifted her gun. The two stepped out and followed the tracker until they came upon a black garbage bag. A shot rang out and Slovak and Tatyana dropped to the ground. On a ridge they saw a man with a *Fu Manchu* jump into a Silver Jeep Grand Cherokee and drive off. Neither said a word as they walked back and saw the flattened rear tire.

****

Carly and David hurried out the door to the attached garage. David laid the shotgun in the back seat of Tim's Blazer and put the food beside it. They both then hopped in.

"I'm going to take it nice and easy. With this weather, it may take us five hours or more. Lexington is a little less than 250 miles away. We'll be traveling from one Great Lake to another. Michigan to Huron."

Carly kept nervously turning around to see if they were being followed.

"I think we're good Carly," David said. "The Sarge's plan worked perfectly."

Feeling a little more at ease, Carly's mind drifted to the summers she spent with her grandparents. "You know when we drove from Detroit to the lake house, my dad would always refer to I-94 as 'The Ditch'. When I was a kid, I really did think it was a ditch. The way the high walls cut through the city seemed massive.

"Who's ready to take 'The ditch' to Grandma's house," Pops would say, sticking his head in our room getting us up for the trip. Those years we lived in Michigan were some of the best of my life."

David turned the blower higher when the windows began to fog. "I need you to tell me everything you can remember about that lake house. I want you to start from when you would pull out of your driveway until you arrived at your grandparents. Describe everything to me… don't leave out a detail. Even if it seems trivial. You never know what could answer those clues."

Carly unzipped her oversized parka and took off her stocking cap. Keeping herself buckled, she turned slightly, and leaned her back against the car door. "Okay, you ready?"

"Yep."

"Like I said, the highway always reminded me of a ditch. It was a boring ride until the first sign of water. Winding our way along Lake Huron, you would see cabin after cabin overlooking the lake. The water was a sapphire blue."

"Sounds beautiful. I've never seen Lake Huron," David said.

"You've got to be kidding. You've lived in Michigan your whole life and you've never seen Lake Huron?"

"Nope. Never."

"Wait till you do. It won't be as pretty as in the summer, but it's still beautiful. We would drive the road until we would see the water tower. That's when we knew we were there.

"Can you picture this? Am I giving you enough detail?"

"Yes! Perfect. Don't leave out a thing."

"My dad would pull down a dirt drive lined with spruce and birch trees. It would snake through the woods and end at a high bluff overlooking the lake. That's where the house was. My grandparents were as happy to see us as we were to be there. They'd come running out as soon as we pulled in. We'd each pick one and go running into their arms. Then we would switch and get squeezed by the other." Carly smiled. "Grandma and Grandpa Wiebelhaus spoiled the hell out of us."

"So, the lake house… is it all by itself?"

"No. There was this other cabin on the property. Artie called it the country store. It had a wooden deck that was flush to the ground. A cedar shake awning covered a picnic table where my uncles would play cards and smoke thick cigars for hours. An old stand-up Pepsi cooler sat next to the door, and I can tell you it was not filled with pop. When my cousins came into town, the adults would stay in the big house and us kids got to sleep in the cabin."

"And where is this viewing deck?"

"There's this cliff. Actually, it's a really high ridge that overlooks the lake. Have you heard of the Mackinac Race?"

"The sailboat race?" David asked.

"Yeah. All the boats in the race would sail past the house. We would sit on the deck and watch as the boats with their different colored masts sailed by. My grandparents would have a big party during the race weekend. Anyway, there are steps that lead all the way to the shore. Halfway down, 17 steps to be exact, is a seating platform. I remember counting them as a kid. It sat on the side of the steps and had bleacher seats and a railing. That's where we would watch the race. On a clear day you could see all the way across the lake to Canada."

"That was one of the clues. You could see the house your grandpa built from the deck and the house is in Canada. How many miles is it across the lake?"

"Not sure, maybe twenty-five or so."

"So how then can you see a house from the deck? It doesn't make sense."

"I know. That's why we have to get on that deck. From there maybe we can figure out what my dad was saying. If we can't, they're going to kill Bo."

David quit talking. He stared straight ahead.

"What?" Carly asked. "What are you thinking?"

David cautiously started. "What if Bo is already dead? I mean, the only thing we have is a video. I don't want to get you upset, but they cut him pretty bad. Maybe after the taping, they just finished him off. Remember what the Sarge said before we left. The ball is in our court. We have the advantage. Let's text Slovak and demand that you get to FaceTime with Bo. You can tell him that you know who he is."

For a moment neither one spoke. David watched as Carly reached for his phone on the center console.

"I see how you stayed alive in Iraq," Carly said. "The Sarge would be proud of you." With a determined look she began, reading her text out loud as she typed.

****

Tatyana and Slovak sat in Bubba's Restaurant and Bar in downtown Traverse City. They had recovered the tracker Sergeant Tim had tossed on the side of the road. Traces of black too stubborn to wash off still covered Slovak's hands. Changing the tire took over an hour. A Shania Twain song played on the jukebox. Tatyana took a bite of her burrito and washed it down with a Bud. Slovak wiped his face, removing the fixings of his Shrek Burger that dribbled down his chin.

"You got a heart problem and you order that monster burger," Tatyana snapped at him. "You should be eating salads and drinking almond milk."

Slovak squirted Ranch dressing all over his French fries. "You know Tatyana, there's a reason you've never been married. You'd drive a man to suicide."

"I was married… and for your information, he did take his own life."

Slovak did not respond. He sipped his coke and swallowed before he popped the last of the burger into his mouth and finished off the fries. Tatyana shrugged and took another swig of her beer. She muffled a small burp, then said, "It was a long time ago. I was young."

The tension was thick, and Slovak quickly changed the subject. "Clearly, they're on to us. Everything Carly had, including the GPS sensor, was stuffed in that bag we found. I just don't understand how they figured this out."

"Are you that freaking dumb…that you can't see this? We've been compromised! You said it yourself. They gotta be working with someone. CIA, Homeland Security, who knows. You better have a plan because no longer are we dealing with just one person."

Slovak's cell phone vibrated on the table. He recognized the number. "It's David Farris."

Tatyana watched as Slovak read the message. His eyebrows furrowed, and his face tightened. He put the phone on the table and said, "It seems the little mouse wants to play."

"What is she saying?"

Slovak handed her his phone.

"Read it."

I know it was you, Slovak (or whatever your real name is) in that video. I remember everything! You killed my father. I also know where the mithridate is. You must give me proof that Bo is still alive. Let me have some FaceTime with him. If he is still alive, I will trade the mithridate for him. If I do not get proof, I will take the mithridate to the authorities. You have an hour to make it happen.

****

Chief Bolton watched the edge of the knife glide across the screaming man's face. He knew it was Bo before the masked man gave his message to Carly. "Now we know where Bo went," the chief said to the field officer sitting across from him. "Poor sonofabitch. He lived through one war, just to die this way."

"You know chief, I was thinking. Didn't you say Agent Canter got pretty close to Fletcher when she was undercover?"

"Yes, she did. I almost thought too close. I kept telling Canter to be careful, not to get too-emotionally involved."

"So, Fletcher trusts her."

"Absolutely."

"Why don't we have Canter get in touch with her. We could have her call that David guy. If they are as close as you say, she may let Canter help her."

"That's not a bad idea. For a rookie, Huntington, you're impressing me."

"That's my job, chief."

****

Stacey and Porsche were watching the local news when the call from the chief came in. Stacey swiped her screen and put it on speaker.

"Here, chief. You're on speaker."

"Any luck figuring out what was familiar on the video?"

"Not yet. There's something there, but I can't put my finger on it."

Stacey stood up from the bed and walked to the window. From habit, she peeked out and checked the parking lot.

Bolton continued. "What do you think about getting in touch with Carly?"

"You want me to call Carly?" Canter said raising her eyebrows at Porsche. "Would I get in touch as Meghan Conner or me?"

"I think it should be you. You need to convince her that you are on her side, and it's the best thing for Bo."

Agent Canter paused. "I think FaceTime would be the best way. I can show her my ID and at the same time she can see how sincere I am… I really do care about her, you know. We became sisters."

"Good. Then get it done."

Chapter 36

Tatyana's expression hardened. "Don't get yourself all worked up. Who gives a rat's ass if she knows who you are. Even if she is working with some type of law enforcement, we can still make this work. She knows where to find the mithridate and we have Bo. We just have to be smarter than they are."

Slovak pushed himself away from the table. "Order us some food to go. I need to make a phone call."

Tatyana watched him weave his way through the tables to the back part of the large dining room, out of hearing distance from any other diners. She saw him press a number into his cell phone and hold the phone to his ear, his body moving very little while he spoke.

The waitress in the black t-shirt came to the table the same time Slovak returned.

"Your carry out is almost ready," she said. "Would you like to pay now?"

"Yes, please give it to me," Slovak said, then opened his leather billfold. He removed three twenties and handed it to her. "Keep the change."

Tatyana waited until the server was almost to the kitchen. "Are you listening to me? Did you hear what I said?...Who gives a damn at this point if she knows who you are? The important thing is she knows where the mithridate is."

"So she says," Slovak said thoughtfully. "So she says. The game has changed. We may need a different trap for this one."

Tatyana let his words mull in her brain.

"We need to call Viktor," Slovak told her. "He needs to clean Bo up. Give him a fresh shirt, comb his hair, and make sure the blood is off his face. Tell Viktor to take it easy on him. No more bruises."

"I'll call right now and have him set up the FaceTime."

****

After the call ended with Chief Bolton, Stacey placed her phone on the nightstand and sat down on the edge of the bed. She placed both hands on the top of her thighs and said, "You heard the chief. We gotta convince Carly to stop running so we can help."

"I think that's a great idea," Porsche said.

"Easier said than done. Think of how you felt when you realized I was an FBI agent and not Carly's best friend."

"That's true. When you were standing on my porch, I had no idea what the hell was going on. It all was such a shock."

"That's what I mean. Carly and I grew very close; we were like sisters. She's going to think those feelings were just part of my cover."

"Then tell her," Porsche said. "I can see the worry in your face. Tell Carly you did deceive her, but you were following orders. Say you weren't truthful at Holy Oaks, but you care for her and will do anything to help her."

Agent Canter took her purse from the floor and removed her wallet. She stood up from the bed and placed her FBI ID under the lamp on the desk. Using the phone, she took a picture of her ID and then one of Porsche.

"I can't imagine the betrayal she is going to feel. But I can't think of any better way to go," Stacey said.

"I agree. Let's do it."

Stacey fluffed some pillows up against the headboard of her bed and stretched out. Porsche did the same and lay next to her. She brought her knees to her chest, balanced her hands and began to type.

Carly, I'm not going to even try to understand what you are going through. I truly am your friend. **.** *I am and always have been here to help you. I truly care about you. I am not Meghan Conner. My real name is Stacey Canter. Agent Stacey Canter. I work for the FBI. Your father was a CIA Officer and Ahmed reported to him. You should recognize the woman in the picture as the one who had a message written on her palm. Her name is Porsche Berliner, and she was Ahmed's girlfriend—called by him to come here and help. Your father contacted Ahmed when he knew you were in trouble. I need to*

FaceTime with you. It will be easier to explain face to face. Please FaceTime me back.

As David merged onto US 10 east, a message came over his phone. Carly turned to David and asked, "Do you think that's Slovak?"

"Only one way to find out," he said, then took his phone from the front console and tapped on the message. "It's Meghan," he said handing Carly the phone.

"Megan's probably worried sick," Carly said.

David looked at Carly and then quickly back to the road. He noticed her eyebrows knitted together as she read the text. "What does she say?...What's she want?"

Carly did not answer right away. She then said, "I must be in some kind of nightmare. This is bizarre."

"What's bizarre?"

"This text message is bizarre! Meghan said she's really not Meghan. She's an FBI Agent."

"FBI? What??!"

"Can you pull over?" Carly asked. "You really need to read this and look at these pictures. Meghan isn't who she said she was. She's an FBI Agent. There also is a picture of that drunk girl who gave me that message on her hand."

David took the next exit and turned right onto a blacktop paved road. He eased the SUV onto the dirt shoulder and placed it in park, keeping the engine running. Carly handed him the phone.

David read the text and enlarged the pictures to get a better view.

"Jesus Christ, Carly. This keeps getting worse and worse. Meghan is Agent Canter of the FBI and that Porsche Berliner was the girl on the porch. What the hell!"

"I know, right. Meghan was my best friend and now I find out it was all a lie—a deception. She probably doesn't give a rat's ass about me. It was always about finding the mithridate."

"Hang on for one minute. I saw how you and Meghan were. She *was* sincere. You can't fake those types of feelings."

"Feelings?" Carly said voice raised. "How could I or you for that matter possibly know her feelings? She's a goddamn FBI agent. They're trained not to have feelings. It's all an act. They become someone else. She played on my weaknesses and I bought it."

"Do you think your father had feelings?"

"What does that mean?"

David took a hold of Carly's hand. "If your dad was CIA as Meghan said, he would have had similar training. You know who your father was. He could love. He could care. You don't lose what makes you human just because you become an agent. I think you should FaceTime her. At least hear what she has to say."

Carly reached out her hand. "Hand me your phone."

****

Viktor could hear the metallic cling, cling, cling of Bo's shackles as he shuffled out of the back room to the shower.

"Now be a good boy and wash up," Viktor said sarcastically. "We want you looking pretty when you FaceTime your girlfriend."

Bo flipped him the bird as he stopped in front of the bathroom door.

"Are you taking these ankle bracelets off or am I going to take a shower with my pants on?"

Viktor reached into his pants pocket and removed a key. He tossed it in front of Bo then drew his gun.

"Don't waste your time trying to get out the window. It's been bolted shut. If I hear glass break, I'll come in and shoot you. There's a razor. Use it. Fresh clothes will be outside the door when you are done. Put them on and then re-shackle. Leave the key right there on the floor. If you try anything, I'll continue the scar that Slovak started."

Bo crouched to the floor and grabbed the key, his eyes searing into Viktor's. He removed the shackles, stepped into the bathroom, and shut the door.

****

Stacey's heart pounded when she heard the distinct sound of her FaceTime ring tone. "That's gotta be Carly," she said as she jumped to her feet and accepted the incoming call.

Carly's face appeared on Stacey's phone.

"Oh, my God, Carly, what happened to your head?"

"You're asking about my head?! That's the first thing you say to me! I trusted you. I shared my most personal thoughts with you, and now I know you betrayed me. You never really cared about me…it was all fake. Whatever it took to get the mithridate." Carly stared at Agent Canter.

Stacey began to walk the room, her arms animated as she spoke. "Carly, please let me help you. You're right. At first when I went undercover you were just an assignment. But, then, I got to know you and care about you. You no longer were just my assignment. You became a little sister. One that I loved and still do."

Carly turned to David, then back at the phone. "Why should I believe you when all you have ever done was lie. Your whole life has been a lie. Your mom kills your dad to save you and then takes her own life…all a bunch of sick lies."

"The agency made up my background, so I could get admitted to Holy Oaks. I had nothing to do with that. I had to lie to make it seem convincing. I was acting when it came to Dr. Hayes. I was not acting when it came to you."

David interrupted, "Give me the phone."

"Hello, David," Stacey said as he appeared.

"What's this stuff about Carly's father being CIA? Carly tells me he was a doctor working with wounded vets. She was there. She saw him working."

"He was both. He worked as a physician but also for the agency. Please meet with us. I can explain everything much easier in person. Porsche can explain why she was here with Ahmed."

Carly abruptly shouted, "Tell her we'll get back in touch with her."

David began to repeat what Carly said when Agent Canter stopped him.

"I heard what she said. That's understandable. You two talk and then let me know. You are dealing with some very dangerous people. Don't try this alone. The people holding Bo are ruthless. Please Carly!! Let me help you."

David ended the FaceTime. He turned to Carly and said, "I think we need her. I believe Meghan or Stacey—whatever her name is. I could hear it in her voice."

"Oh really. You can hear it in her voice, huh.?" Carly said, clearly annoyed. "You're not the one that spilled your guts to someone whom you trusted."

"I'm just saying. We're dealing with killers. Look what they did to Hayes. I think she could help. Remember what the Sarge said. The ball is in our court. I doubt Slovak knows the FBI is involved. If what Meghan says is true, I would feel a whole lot better having them on our team. It's your call, Carly. I'll go with whatever your decision is."

David pulled the Blazer back onto the road, did a u-ey and headed back onto the freeway. "Just give her a chance, Carly. Try to keep an open mind."

Chapter 37

Green reflective eyes glowed in the headlights forcing David to tap the brakes and swerve slightly. The three deer leaped back into the woods as the Blazer passed by.

"Holy shit," he said, feeling his heart pound. "We don't want to hit one of those."

"Wow!" said Carly, as she turned down the radio. "That was close...Do deer have a death wish?"

David's phone sat in Carly's lap. She heard a text come over the phone.

Within an hour we will have Bo FaceTime you. After you speak with him, we can set up a meeting where we will trade Bo for the mithridate. You can get on with your lives and never hear from me again.

After reading the text to David, Carly said, "I'm going to text Meghan and let her know where we are headed. If we decide to meet her, it will save time. We have less than 22 hours."

****

Bo knelt just outside the bathroom door and reattached the shackles, leaving the key on the floor as he stood. The shower had been his first in a week. He felt refreshed, energized.

"Well I barely recognize you. Didn't realize you were such a pretty boy," Viktor said, then waved his gun towards the bedroom.

"Are you a switch hitter?" Bo said with a grin. "I don't let just anyone suck my dick."

"Go." Viktor said, clearly agitated.

Bo delivered a sharp salute, with a forceful "Yes, Sir," before once again flipping him off. Shuffling to the middle of the bedroom with the chain dragging between his legs, Bo was surprised to see a padded chair. The kitchen chair had been replaced. "Sprucing up the place I see," Bo said sarcastically.

"Lock it up."

Bo lowered himself to the chair and fumbled with the chains. He placed the padlock through the eyehook attached to the floor and secured the shackles. Viktor placed the revolver in his back waistband and removed a phone from his front pants pocket. He handed it to Bo.

"Don't say anything stupid," Viktor said, then picked up a pair of pliers sitting on the top of a chest of draws. "Make the call. Don't say anything you'll regret, or you won't have any toenails on either foot."

Bo held the phone. It felt warm in his hands. Viktor removed a folded piece of paper from his shirt pocket and began to read off a number. Bo punched it in.

The sound of the FaceTime ring tone caught David's attention. He watched as Carly held the phone in front of her so both of them could see. A gaunt Bo Harris stared back.

"Bo. What happened to you? I had no idea you were a prisoner."

Bo said nothing at first, wiping away a couple of tears that began to run down his cheeks. The sight of Carly and the sound of her voice overwhelmed him. He swallowed and cleared his throat. "Carly, I'm sorry… I'm sorry for leaving you. What happened to us was my fault. Professor Nikolaev is behind my kidnapping."

Instantly the view of the cell phone left Bo's face. Images of the room appeared haphazardly on the screen. Carly could hear Bo being struck and moaning. She yelled into the phone. "Don't hurt him, you bastard! If you hurt him, you won't get the mithridate."

The beating stopped.

"Listen, Slovak," she screamed into the phone. "If you hurt him, the deal is off."

"No need for that. It won't happen again."

The voice Carly heard was unfamiliar to her. "Put Slovak on the phone!"

Hesitation. "He's not available at this moment. Like I said, it won't happen again."

A disheveled Bo reappeared on the screen.

"Bo, I'm going to get you out of there. I've got what they want."

Bo began to speak but the connection was lost. The screen went blank. Carly turned to David, "We have to find the mithridate."

"We will, Carly. Who is this Professor Nikolaev?"

"Hang on," Carly said, frantically texting Slovak.

I just FaceTimed with Bo and some goon beat him. If this happens again I'm going to the cops!!! Tell that bitch Professor Nikolaev I've got her number too.

Carly looked from the phone to David. "I'm sorry. What did you say?"

"This Professor…who is she?"

"She was a Professor at Wayne State. Bo had her for a class and she offered him an internship that was only for returning vets. We were so poor, and this was a paying job. We were so happy when he got it. But there was something I didn't trust about her."

"What? What was it?"

"It was the way she looked at him. Not the way a teacher looks at a student. It was something more personal. I convinced myself it was all in my head, but it wasn't. I loved him a ton, but that didn't matter. He left me…for her. The weird thing is he kept coming to visit me. He then probably left and went back and banged her. What a prick!!"

David could not look at Carly, keeping his eyes on the road and tapping his fingers on the steering wheel. The words *I loved him a ton* echoed in his head. "It's awfully nice of you to still care for a guy that did that to you."

Carly noticed David's torn expression and reached over and took his hand. "We have a past, David…that's all."

David abruptly changed the subject. "Tell me more about the lake house."

"Well, I remember in the spring the waves would churn up the water and make it a sandy gold color. But as you looked further out onto the lake, it turned a teal blue. The contrast of the colors was so beautiful. As you pulled up to the house, the first thing you would notice is the tall peaked gabled roof. Brick pavers ran up to the front porch, but it was the back porch that made the house. Overlooking the lake running the entire length of Grandma's house was a massive porch. White pillars held up a slanted wood awning. The whole place looked like it belonged in a magazine."

"That's it," David said.

"What?" Carly asked.

"That's how we are going to get on the property. We are going to tell the new homeowners that we are from a magazine that specializes in beautiful homes on the lake. We'll tell them that their house may be chosen to be in an upcoming issue of the magazine. We simply need to walk the grounds and take a few pictures. No addresses will be given."

"What if they say no?"

"You'll first go to the door and ask. I'll stay in the Blazer. If you get the green light, you come and get your assistant. If not, we'll try another plan and they will not have seen me."

"That could work. We need to buy a camera and case when we're in Lexington. We also need to get a *Beautiful Homes* magazine to give to them for authenticity. I think we can make this work."

David focused on the oversized clothes Carly was wearing. Her belt was cinched tight forming gathers around her waist. The winter coat Sergeant Tim had given her engulfed her thin frame. Her boots looked like canoes. With a slight grin he said, "We need to get you some clothes. I think if you went to the door in that outfit, the homeowners would call the police."

Carly pulled down the visor mirror. "Oh, for God's sake," she said as she checked out the gash on her forehead, trying to arrange her hair over the wound. "I'm going to need a shower and I'll have to bring my bangs down over the gash. A little mascara and blush would help."

"I think you're beautiful just the way you are."

With a smirk, Carly said, "Quit lying, Farris."

David turned on the intermediate windshield wipers. The snow had stopped an hour ago and it began to mist. The outdoor temp showed 40 degrees.

"What happened to all the snow?" Carly asked. "They hardly have any here. What a difference from one side of the state to the other."

"Do a weather check. See what the temperature is going to be."

Carly tapped the weather app on David's phone. She read the daily weather. "God, it's going to be beautiful. The high today is in the mid to high-forties and sunny. Two days from now the high is only twenty-two and the lows are in the teens. You can thank El Nino for this crazy ass weather."

"Is that what the App says?...Crazy ass weather."

Carly smiled but said nothing.

****

Porsche cracked a window and lit a cigarette. She took a drag and exhaled, fanning the air with a magazine.

As Stacey came out of the bathroom she said, "So, it's about two and a half hours to Lexington."

"That's about right." Stacey replied. "We just have to wait until we get the pseudo antidote."

"Let me get this straight. We're waiting for a fake antidote to be made."

"Yep. You know we can't let Slovak take the mithridate if Carly actually finds it. There's no chance of that."

"I figured as much."

"Whatever Carly gives him; he is going to test. He just won't take Carly's word for it. My guess is he'll have test strips for all kinds of poisons, you know like cyanide or anthrax. As long as he gets a positive result for any pathogen, he'll think it's the real thing. The lab has been synthesizing a pseudo antidote for the last couple of days. The compound is mildly toxic and should give a false positive."

"Did you come up with that?"

"Nope. Can't say I did. That came right out of Fort Mackinac. None of this will matter, though, if Carly doesn't let us in."

"She told you she was going to be in the Lexington area. Seems like she wants you nearby."

"True. I hope you're right."

****

"*Cause I've got friends in low places, where the whiskey drowns and the beer chases...*"

For the last half hour, Garth Brooks songs floated out from the jukebox across the room. Tatyana cringed. She hated country music. It was getting on her nerves. She watched Slovak read the latest text from Carly. "Come on...What did she say...Did she FaceTime with Bo?" Tatyana nagged.

He sat expressionless until she saw him fighting a smile. "Oh, she did."

"So, tell me what she said."

"Seems our little mouse knows who you are. So much for the ski masks!"

Tatyana leaned back in her chair. "Son of a bitch."

****

Viktor returned from doing his outside perimeter check when the text from Slovak came in.

"You stupid Son of a bitch. I told you to take it easy with him. If this goes sideways, I will cut your throat myself!! You better have him ready for the swap."

Viktor texted back. "*I will.*"

Chapter 38

Carly and David entered the little town of Lexington just past midnight. The village was asleep. Not a shop or store was open. They passed Ava Maria Parish where Carly attended Sunday services as a little girl. "Keep going," Carly said, "and we will hit Fort Gratiot."

"Fort what?" David asked.

"Gratiot. It's another town about six miles down the road. We should be able to get something to eat there."

David drove the narrow two-lane road which twisted and turned following the shoreline. The lake was calm and black except for the occasional reflection of the moon breaking through the clouds. He pulled into a twenty-four-hour Coney Island and backed into a spot lined with arborvitaes and parked. "Don't want anyone to see the plate."

"This is Tim's car," Carly said grinning. "It's not stolen."

"Oh. What a dumb ass."

Carly arranged her bangs one more time before leaving the Blazer. Through large glass windows they watched two waitresses scurrying from customer to customer, filling coffee mugs and delivering food.

"It looks pretty full," David said. "Probably full of drunks this time of night."

Please Seat Yourself the sign read as the two stepped through the doors. Carly scanned the restaurant and spotted one empty booth near the back. She took David's hand and led him there. A waitress looking in her mid-twenties placed two paper placemats filled with historical facts about Fort Gratiot in front of them. She laid two sets of silverware wrapped in paper napkins on the placemats. She then took their orders.

David was on edge. He scrutinized every face that was in the restaurant and any new people that walked through the door.

"So what's this Slovak guy look like?" David asked.

"He's got a short-cropped beard and gray shaggy hair. Sort of reminded me of a hippie. Just under his right eye is disfigured. Like his cheekbone is sunken in."

"That's where you shot him."

"Yep."

"That's so bizarre!!" David said, "And all the time he was hypnotizing you…you never knew."

"Could you imagine if I found out while I was laying on the couch. I mean how would I have reacted. Not sure I would have kept it together. This whole thing is so messed up."

The waitress strolled to the table with their food. "Can I get you anything else?"

Carly noticed the pink ribbon; Kim was wearing just under her left shoulder. "Can I ask you something?"

"Sure."

"Who are you wearing the pink ribbon for?"

"My baby sister, Jana. She passed from breast cancer last month. She had two kids and was single. I have both of them now and one of my own. That's why I'm working the late shift. Got two more mouths to feed."

"Sorry about your sister. And two kids… Wow."

"Oh, they're good kids. Not sure what God's plan is, but it's sure testing me. They really miss their mom…as much as I miss my Baby Sis."

David turned his face away as Kim spoke. He took a long drink and cleared his throat.

"I'm all set," David choked out.

"Me too," Carly said with a smile. 'I'll take the bill"

David got up to leave when Carly grabbed his arm. "Sit for a minute. I have a change of plans"

"What?"

"Why don't we first go to the lake house and ask if we can walk the property. I will say my grandparents used to own it, and I have great memories as a kid. I'll tell them I don't want to come into the house, but it would mean a lot if I could walk down the steps-to the beach and share my memories with my fiancé."

David thought about it momentarily. "Fiancé…I like it."

"What? The plan or being my fiancé?"

"The plan, of course. I did that once. I took a girlfriend to a farm my uncle used to own and asked if I could go back by the pond and show her where I harvested my first buck. They were fine with it."

"Okay, that's what we'll do," Carly said. "I am going to look for a place for us to stay tonight."

"You do that. I need to use the bathroom."

Carly began to search the local hotels. She found the Comfort Inn. Reserving a room with a credit card was out of the question. They would have to pay with cash.

"We passed a 24-hour Walmart a couple miles back," Carly said as David returned. "We'll go shopping first and then head to the Comfort Inn."

Carly grabbed the bill and headed to the cashier. She noticed David place two twenty-dollar bills under his plate. She smiled.

****

Agent Canter spotted the red sedan parked in the Meijer grocery parking lot. The prearranged meeting was hastily set up but came together perfectly. She pulled next to the car where Porsche lowered her window. The female driver did the same.

"Morning, Canter," the woman said handing a brown paper bag to Porsche. "Here are the goodies."

"Thank you, Gideon…I appreciate you driving all the way from Detroit."

"My pleasure, Canter. Be safe. Get the bad guy."

"I'll do my best."

Chapter 39

Tatyana waited behind the wheel in a Traverse City Gas and Go. Slovak swiped his card then pushed the button for the cheapest blend. He shoved the nozzle into the tank and clicked the handle. With his hands in his pockets, he waited.

They call you the best. Tatyana thought. *I think your best days are behind you.*

Slovak returned the gas handle to its cradle and pressed no receipt. He then walked to the other side of the van and got in.

"Now what??" Tatyana said, indignation in her tone. "We are sitting in this fucking gas station in BFE and you have no idea where Carly is. She's the one setting up where and when we trade Bo for the mithridate, and it should be us. Don't you see a problem with that?"

Slovak sat in silence. He knew she was right. His operation had gone sideways, and he was well aware of what happens when operations go sideways. He didn't trust her. Who was she texting?

"I'll turn this around. I already have a plan in place for the swap."

"How, Alex? How could you possibly have a plan when you have no idea where she is?"

"It doesn't matter. This plan will work anywhere. Already got the go ahead."

"Without discussing it with me first?"

"You forget Tatyana, this is my operation. It has been from the start. Drive to the middle of the state. Hopefully we will be a little closer when Carly calls."

"What if they drove north? We'll be further away."

"Just drive goddammit and shut the fuck up!"

Tatyana started the van. She pushed the petal to the floor and sped out of the Gas and Go, sending a car swerving and blaring its horn.

****

David entered the deserted Comfort Inn and walked to the counter. No one was there. He stood at the counter, then called out. "Hello. Anyone home?"

"I'm sorry, Sir," an attendant said as she rubbed her eyes walking out of the back-office. "I didn't hear you come in. Hope you haven't been waiting long."

"No. Just got here. Could I get a room?"

"Absolutely," she said as she shook the mouse, waking up the computer. "What brings you to Fort Gratiot?"

"Just visiting. My girlfriend spent a lot of summers here and she wanted to show me the town."

"You'll have to come back in the summer. You really can't appreciate how beautiful this place is until you see it in full bloom."

David paid for the room with cash. The attendant pulled a small map from under the counter and laid it in front of him. She pointed to the main lobby. "You are here. Drive around to the back. You are in room 64. Complimentary Continental breakfast is from 7-10am. Is there anything else?"

"Nope. That should do it," he said, taking the cards and paperwork.

David stepped out the front doors of the lobby and went to where the Blazer was parked.

"All I can think about is a shower," Carly told him as soon as he climbed in.

They drove around back. David passed two vacant parking spaces just in front of their room. He backed the SUV into a spot, up against a fence.

"We're in Room 64. I feel better not parking right in front of it. I'm sure they don't know what we're driving, but why take a chance? Should you text Meghan and let her know where we are?"

"You mean Agent Canter?" Carly said bitterly.

"You know who I mean. I'm telling you…she cared about you. I saw it with my own eyes."

Carly did not answer.

"I'll tell her we are at the Comfort Inn in Lexington and to come to our room at 8:00am This way everyone can get a little rest."

An hour later Stacey and Porsche pulled into the Comfort Inn. It was just past 3:00am. Stacey entered the lobby and reserved a room.

As she got back into the car, Stacey said, "Read me the text from Carly again."

"Meet us in room 64 at 8:00am," Porsche read. "We'll talk there."

Canter circled the parking lot, looking for anything out of the ordinary. "Let the chief know we are in a town called Lexington. Tell him we've contacted Carly and a meeting is set for the morning."

****

Three CIA officers dressed in camo studied a map of Michigan. The town of Lexington was circled. Bolton handed them a briefing paper; Operation Damsel in Distress.

"*Damsel?*" Banneker said incredulously. "A helpless young female who requires a male hero to rescue her. I didn't realize that in 2019 we still used that word."

The chief tried to hide a smile. "You know when I started in the early 60's, we had very few ladies in the agency. I'm old school. When you become chief, you can name the operations anything you want. You have a problem, Office Banneker?"

"No, Sir. Perfectly acceptable, Sir."

"Are you going to let Canter know we're coming?" asked an officer whose eyes were lined with crow's feet.

"I have to. She needs to know we want these people taken out. They killed some of our own. Canter's job is to get the mithridate. Your job is to get Slovak and whoever is with him. I'll keep you informed where and when this swap will take place."

The officers looked at each other.

"Sir, there may be collateral damage," Officer Banneker remarked.

The chief nodded; his expression grim. "I hope not."

Chapter 40

The sun barely broke through the cardboard gray skies in the shoreline town of Lexington. Agent Canter and Porsche stood just outside room 64 at the Comfort Inn. It was 7:59am and Stacey took a deep breath before she knocked on the door. "Here we go," she whispered to Porsche.

Nothing happened. No movement. She looked at Porsche who looked puzzled. She knocked again.

"Who is it?" a male voice called from the other side of the door.

"It's us, David. Stacey and Porsche."

Stacey watched the doorknob turn and the door open. David cracked it slightly and peeked out. He then fully opened it. Carly stood in the center of the room, her arms crossed, her eyes searing into Stacey.

"Hello, David," Stacey said while she and Porsche entered the room.

"Hey," he replied in a low voice.

Porsche walked by Carly who was standing in front of a small table. She sat on one of the chairs. Stacey focused her attention on Carly, then said, "Your head!"

Carly said nothing.

"Will you let me explain before you jump to conclusions?"

"What's there to explain?" Carly said in a terse voice. "You did your job. I trusted you. You betrayed me… End of story."

"Carly, there's so much more to the story. I was there to protect you."

"Oh, save it," Carly snapped. "You were there for the mithridate."

"Yeah…It was an assignment at first, but once I got to know you… that changed. Everything changed. We became like sisters. I really believe that. The chief threatened to take me off the case because he said I was getting too close to you. I pleaded with him not to do that."

"Yeah right," Carly said." I don't have time for excuses. Let's just concentrate on-finding the mithridate and getting Bo back."

Stacey kept talking. "There are things you don't know. I was brought in on the case when your father was killed, and you were placed at Holy Oaks. Your father was a CIA operative."

"My father was a doctor!" Carly retorted. "I volunteered with him. I saw him working with the vets. You don't know what you are talking about."

"Give her a chance, Carly," David cut in. "Let her explain. We're on the same team."

Reluctantly Carly dropped her arms and let out a huff as she turned her back on Stacey and took a couple of steps away from her.

"Please...Keep going Stacey," David said.

"He *was* a doctor, but so much more. He worked on a program so important to the safety of our country that it was top secret. His job was to create antidotes in case of biological attack. The US wasn't so worried about foreign governments as they were terrorists. A bioweapon in their hands is like a nuclear weapon. They could start a pandemic... killing millions. The mithridate could be reversed engineered into a biological weapon. The CIA believes a terrorist cell in Germany used your brother as ransom and it went terribly wrong. Artie wasn't supposed to die."

At the mention of Artie's name, Carly turned back around.

"Ahmed blamed himself," Porsche interrupted. "He was assigned to watch over you and Artie. He was there when your brother was kidnapped. He never forgave himself. It haunted him until the day he died."

Carly's attention drew to Porsche. "*You're* that girl. That girl who had to pee. You had the message written on your palm."

Porsche chuckled. "That was me and I really did have to pee. I came here to help Ahmed. His loyalty to your father brought him to the United States. Your father was his former CIA boss. I'm Ahmed's girlfriend, Porsche... Porsche Berliner."

"Tell her what you told me," Stacey said to Porsche.

"According to Ahmed, when Artie was kidnapped and murdered, your father became crazy paranoid. He really believed that at some point terrorists would get and use a bioweapon. He wanted to protect you and your mom. Although your father never specifically said so, Ahmed believed your dad hid some antidote in case of an attack."

Carly took a step forward. "That's why we're here. I think he hid it at my grandparents' lake house."

"Why would you think that?" Stacey asked.

"Because I remember what happened the day my father was killed."

"Your memory is back!?"

"Slovak killed my dad. Did you know that?"

"Slovak killed your father?' Stacey said slowly, surprise in her voice. "We found out that he was involved in Hayes' death and Bo's kidnapping. But... killing your father...we didn't know."

"Well, now you do. My dad had me meet him at a park by my house. As we were walking, he kept putting his hands in and out of his pockets, and he talked fast. He wouldn't let me talk. He kept telling me to listen. Then, he gave me a clue."

"What kind of clue?" Porsche asked.

"He told me that Mr. Etadirhtim is in Canada in case you need to find him. He's living in the basement of a house Grandpa built. You can see it from the viewing deck. He'll be waiting if you need him."

Stacey's mouth dropped. "So, you know where it is!"

"Not really," Carly said. "The clue doesn't make sense. The only thing you can see in Canada from the viewing deck are these huge wind turbines. It's got to be over twenty miles across the lake."

"This must be related to the locket in some way," Stacey thought out loud.

"It's gotta be," Carly answered. "David and I were planning on heading to the lake house this morning to try to make sense of it. I'm not as worried about the mithridate as I am about Bo. I told Slovak that I had it and would trade it for him. Problem is... I don't. We were hoping to find it but had second thoughts about giving it to him. We really don't have a plan. That's why we called you."

Stacey walked to the nightstand and reached in her purse. "Slovak is no rookie," she said. "He won't take your word that it's the real thing."

She removed what looked like a pipe bomb with screw caps on each end. She unscrewed a cap and tipped the tube. Two plastic bottles resembling moisturizing spray for a dry mouth fell into her hand. Each 2-inch bottle had a pump spray top.

"This is what you are going to trade for Bo. It's a dummy antidote and it should fool Slovak into thinking it's the real deal."

"How will it fool him?" David asked.

"I'm sure he'll have some type of test kit. These kits test for poisons. The ones I've seen look like a type of litmus paper."

Holding up one of the bottles Stacey continued. "This has pathogens in it. If it tests positive, he'll think he has the real McCoy."

Stacey placed the bottles on the table in front of Carly and sat on the edge of the bed. Carly picked up a bottle and examined it.

"Is this poisonous?" she asked, then placed it back on the table.

"No," Stacey said. "There are toxins in it, but the amount is so minute it's harmless."

"So… what's this plan?" Carly asked, knowing David was listening to every word.

"Slovak did not get where he is in this business without being cautious. I imagine that he will want to meet in an open public place, but also one where he and his people can observe what's going on."

"Our best advantage is to pick the place for the swap," Porsche said, looking at Agent Canter for agreement. "It will give us some control over the operation."

"Yes… for sure," Stacey said. "When you talk with Slovak, you have to convince him that *he* is picking the place. You have to make him believe *he's* in control. Are there any parks or malls in the area?"

Carly thought for a moment. "There's a park by the Blue Water Bridge. You know, the bridge that connects Michigan to Canada. There's a boardwalk that runs along the St Clair River. On the other side of the river, a couple thousand yards or so is Canada. It's wide open."

"That could work. I need to check it out first. Why don't you and David head to the lake house and Porsche and I will go to that park. We can meet back here and plan our next step."

Carly walked to the mirror, applied some lipstick then grabbed her coat from the chair. "You ready?" she said to David, ignoring Stacey and walking to Porsche. "I am so sorry about what happened to Ahmed. I loved him too. He was like a big brother."

Carly turned to David. "Let's go."

Chapter 41

Bo got up from the chair and stretched his legs as far as his shackles would allow him. He heard the engine of the approaching car and knew it was him. The whine of the Honda engine was unmistakable. Viktor was back. Like before, he listened for the cabin door to open and fantasized as to how he could kill him.

Grab the neck and cock the head back. Stick two fingers into an eye socket and gouge. Bite down on the jugular. Pull the pistol from his waist band and...

Who was he kidding? Viktor was too smart. He would never get that close and Bo would never get the chance.

"You're one lucky son of a bitch," Viktor said as he entered the bedroom holding a Best Buy bag. "You're going to FaceTime with your girlfriend one more time."

"And then what?" Bo asked.

"I'm not going to kill you, if that's what you're worried about. I am just a soldier following orders."

"Soldier… my ass," Bo said. "You're a goon."

Viktor dumped the contents of the bag onto the bed. A black and silver box came tumbling out. He removed his gun from his waistband, then drew it on Bo.

"I don't read good English," he said, handing Bo the box. "You set this up for me."

Bo took the box and read the contents out loud. "*Z-tech wireless Nanny Cam*. What? You going to watch me take a shower, you perve!" Bo said.

"What you mean perve?"

"Forget it."

"You set this up. I have my orders," he said, waving his gun at Bo.

Bo removed the camera and unfolded the pamphlet of directions. He read the first few lines then looked up. "We need a phone and the password for the Wi-Fi. It should be written on a welcome sheet when you first checked in. Do you know what I'm talking about?"

"No."

"You got information when you first checked in. Bring me anything in writing that you can find about this place." Bo spoke to Viktor with contempt.

"This is all I can find," Viktor said, returning from the living room, holding up what looked like an information sheet.

"Good job, Sherlock," Bo mumbled.

Viktor's dark eyes and face remained impassive, not even a twitch of understanding revealing itself. He stood and stared.

"I need your phone so I can download the app," Bo said, holding out his hand toward Viktor.

Viktor went to hand Bo his phone then abruptly stopped and stepped back. A smile grew on his face. He once again drew his gun from his waist band and held it on him.

"If you call the police, I will kill you and leave. Boss will understand I had no choice."

Bo downloaded the app and connected to the Wi-Fi. He added the new online device then looked up at Viktor. "It's all set. Turn on the camera. Let's see what we got."

Viktor turned on the camera and Bo saw images of the room. He held the phone showing Viktor it was working.

"Hand it to me," Viktor ordered. Bo then handed him the phone.

"Now you get to talk with your girlfriend," Viktor said, closing the nanny cam app and tapping on the number for Carly. "FaceTime her."

Viktor handed the phone to Bo who held it, waiting for Carly to answer.

The phone rang and rang and then it stopped ringing.

"The call dropped off," Bo said.

Viktor snatched the phone from Bo and called the number again.

This time, Carly answered right away.

"How are you?" Carly said, staring at the long gash on the side of Bo's face. "I'm working on getting you free."

Bo said nothing, as Carly anxiously waited for a response.

"Say something. Tell me you're ok."

"I'm okay," Bo finally said. "I lost my way, Carly. I hope you forgive me."

"Don't worry about that. Let's concentrate on getting you out of there," she said. "Have they beat you anymore?"

Carly noticed Bo look away at someone standing close to him. He then looked back into the phone. "I'm fine."

"Enough talk now," Carly heard a voice in the background say.

"I gotta go. Don't give up on us." The image of Bo froze as the connection was lost.

****

The drive from the hotel was less than three miles. They passed the Lighthouse Creamery with the big ice cream cone on the roof where Carly, her grandparents, and Artie would stop for ice cream.

David turned into a driveway with a five-foot blue and white light house at the entrance. From inside the car Carly saw the winding driveway, the white birches, the blue fir trees and then the beautiful lake. Everything looked the same.

"I don't see any cars," David said, driving slowly toward the house.

"Good. I hope nobody's home. It will be a lot easier for us."

Carly pulled down the mirror and checked her appearance. "Here goes," she said as she left the SUV climbed the steps and knocked on the door. She turned and looked at David when no one answered the door. Carly waved for him to join her as she walked back down the stairs.

"Let's get to the deck and see what we can find," she said.

David saw the little cabin and porch just as Carly had described. In the distance a white and red freighter plowed through the water, heading south.

The two walked to the bluff and then down 17 steps to the viewing deck. They sat on the bleacher-style seats and looked over the lake.

"See," Carly said pointing to the windmills off in the distance. "That's Canada. There's no way to see a house from here."

"I see what you mean. Give me the clue again."

"The house Grandpa built is in Canada and Mr. Etadirhtim lives in the basement. You can see it from the viewing deck."

David pondered the thought. "I got nothing. It doesn't make sense."

"Maybe the house is by one of the windmills we can see. You know like a house close to a windmill. Maybe the mithridate is in Canada." Carly struggled to piece it together.

"In a house Grandpa built? Surely, he didn't go to Canada to build a house. And, if your dad hid it when you guys buried Artie, do you think he had time to go to Canada?"

"You're right. That doesn't make sense."

David stood. "How about we go to the beach."

"Can't hurt."

David and Carly held hands to steady each other as they walked down the steep steps. Their feet sunk slightly into the sand as they stepped onto the beach. They both heard a text alert coming from David's phone.

"Who's texting you?"

"Don't know," he said removing his phone from his coat pocket. "It's T-Mobile. They texted that Canadian roaming charges may apply."

"Canadian roaming charges," Carly repeated. "Oh, yeah. See that wooden post sunk into the beach?"

"The one with the birdhouse?"

"Yeah. If you go past that and use your phone, a Canadian tower will pick it up and you'll get charged as if you *were* in Canada. My grandpa Wiebelhaus put that post in so my aunts and uncles knew that if they passed it and used their phone, they would get this huge phone bill. It happened to him. As kids, we used to say that we were in Canada if we ran to the other side of the post. If we were playing tag, it was a safe place, because you were in another country."

David's eyebrows raised. His attention focused on the birdhouse that was mounted on the post.

"Carly… I think I know what your dad meant. Who built that birdhouse?"

"My grandpa built all the birdhouses on this property," she answered.

Realization crossed Carly's face. "Oh, my God, David. That could be it. My dad might have hidden the mithridate in that birdhouse."

"CAN I HELP YOU!" a voice yelled from the top of the bluff. "WHAT ARE YOU DOING ON MY PROPERTY?"

A silvered-haired man in a fleece jacket moved unsteadily down the stairs.

"Oh, God, David. It's the homeowner."

"Stick to the plan about spending summers here and showing me the property. Tell him that you knocked on the door to ask for permission and didn't think anyone was home. Work your charm. I think the mithridate is in that birdhouse. Go to the stairs and distract him."

"How's my hair? Can you see my cut?"

"No. It looks good."

Carly hurried to the bottom of the steps. She watched as the silver-haired man held on to the railing taking one step at a time. He stopped at the viewing deck and sat, catching his breath. Carly scampered up the steps, rushing to meet him.

Wasting no time, David hurried to the birdhouse and focused on it. He examined the church-like birdhouse mounted to the top. *Living in the basement.* He tapped the sides and tried to look through the gothic windows and steeple, careful not to touch the bird splat. He saw nothing then lowered his head and looked underneath. That's where he spotted two hinges along with a slide latch bolt which kept the bottom secured in place. A false bottom.

He slid the latch to the side and the bottom dropped an inch. As he stuck his finger in the gap and pulled, he heard the rusty hinges creak. A small brown envelope with a gummed seal fell to the sand. David quickly picked it up and tore it open. Inside were glass vials holding a yellow liquid.

Reaching the last step to the viewing deck, Carly stood in front of the man. A little out of breath, she began. "Hi. My name is Carly… Carly Fletcher. My grandfather's name is Ray Wiebelhaus." Carly noticed two gray hearing aids in the elderly man's ears.

"Is that your car in my drive?" he asked, scowling. "Who are you?"

Realizing he had not heard, she started over. "I'm sorry. My name is Carly Fletcher. My grandparents, the Wiebelhaus's, used to own the property."

"Ray Wiebelhaus?"

"Yes. He's my grandpa. I spent many summers here with my grandparents and wanted to show my fiancée how beautiful this property is."

By this time, David had come up the steps and stood by Carly. He nodded and gave Carly a grin.

"This is David... David Farris," she said. "I talked so much about this place that he wanted to see it for himself."

"John Cabazon," the old man said, and shook hands with David.

"We knocked on the door to ask if we could go down to the beach, but nobody came to the door. I hope you're not mad."

"Oh, no. Not at all. The granddaughter of Ray and Lorraine Wiebelhaus is welcome at my home anytime. Believe it or not, I met you one summer. You were just a little thing, maybe four or five. My bride and I have lived in this area for over 40 years and have been friends of your grandparents for almost as long. Shame they had to move. We really miss them. When we found the place was for sale, we jumped at it.

"I better get back and tell the missus everything is fine before she calls the cops. You two take as long as you like."

"Actually, we have to get going. I so appreciate you not getting upset with us. Everything is just like I remembered. We'll follow you up," Carly said.

Carly, David and Mr. Cabazon were now at the top of the bluff standing next to the long porch. Mrs. Cabazon had come out to join them.

"Your grandparents are fine people," Mrs. Cabazon said. "We've known them for years."

"They are," Carly said talking extra loudly so Mr. Cabazon could hear. "I couldn't have asked for better grandparents."

"When is the wedding?" Mr. Cabazon asked David.

"Umm...In....

"August," Carly quickly answered. "We are having a summer wedding this August coming up."

"Yes. August," David agreed, looking to Carly with a straight face.

"Honey, we better get going," Carly said to David. "Don't want to be late for brunch. We're meeting my maid of honor. She and her boyfriend are driving here to spend the day with us."

"Well, feel free to bring them by," Mrs. Cabazon said. "You don't even need to knock, just head to the beach. Best of wishes with the upcoming wedding. Tell Ray and Lorraine we said hi."

"I sure will," Carly promised.

David and Carly shook hands with the Cabazon's and headed to the Blazer.

****

Carly could barely contain herself as she jumped into the Blazer. "Let me see it," she said holding out her hand.

Looking in his rearview mirror he gave the Cabazon's one last wave. Carly turned and did the same. "Careful, they are glass vials," David said removing the envelope from his shirt pocket and handing it to Carly. Dropping the vials of yellow liquid into her hand she took one and brought it close to her eyes.

"This is what everyone died for," she said, turning it up and down, watching the bubbles rise to the top. "Artie, my Dad, Ahmed. It's just so unfair."

"Life's not always fair, Carly," David said as he passed a car on the two-lane road and then weaved back into his lane. "That mithridate probably kept you alive all these months. If Slovak thought you knew where it was he would have tortured it out of you long ago and you might be dead. Your dad's plan worked. He was a smart guy."

Carly smiled slightly then said, "You're right. I'm going to call Stacey."

Even before Stacey said hello, Carly rattled off, "I think we found the mithridate. David thinks so, too."

"Oh, my God. That's fantastic!" Stacey said, mouthing the words at Porsche, *"They found it."*

"I'll explain everything when we get back. We're on our way. Are you back at the hotel?" Carly asked.

"Not yet. We're almost there. We'll meet up at your room."

Stacey placed her phone in the center console.

"Aren't you going to call the chief and give him a heads up?" Porsche asked.

"I will, but not just yet."

Porsche gave a confused look. "Why."

"You know Slovak has killed three of our own, right."

"Yeah. The chief said that in the briefing."

"Well. If he knows we have the mithridate he is going to want to take out Slovak ASAP. Bo may not be his top priority. I'll let the chief know once we have a meeting set up and in place."

"Oh I get it," Porsche said. "If you tell the chief now he will have that park staked out and when Slovak goes to check it out he may nab him and blow the whole swap for Bo."

"You got it," Stacey said.

"You're one smart agent," Porsche said.

Carly stared at the envelope holding the vials of mithridate lying on the table next to the lamp and hotel phonebook. She reached out and touched it. "It may sound odd, but I wonder what my dad felt when he hid this."

"He probably had no idea that what he hid would lead to this," David commented.

A knock at the door prevented him from going any further.

"David, it's Stacey. Open up."

David cracked the door and looked before opening it fully. "It's just a habit I have to check everything out," he said to Stacey as she walked through the door.

Porsche came into the room, a black shoulder bag hanging over her shoulder.

Carly picked up the envelope. "This is what you wanted. This is what everyone wanted. Now you have it," Carly said, handing it to Stacey.

Stacey squeezed the envelope slightly and peered inside. As she tipped the tiny packet, two vials of a yellowish clear liquid fell into her palm. She looked up from her hand.

"You don't know the significance of this. Getting this back into the hands of the CIA could save tens- of-thousands." She then placed the vials back in the envelope.

"Have a seat. I'll explain what the plan is."

Carly and David each took a chair at the small table near the window.

"The CIA will want to take this terrorist cell out. Slovak killed three of their people. Bolton will want him dead. I'll do everything I can to get Bo back. You can trust me on this."

"The first priority better be Bo," Carly shot back. "Then I don't care. Kill the sons of bitches."

"Bo will be the top priority. The park will work. It's plenty open, and I think Slovak would feel comfortable there. The only problem is he has to think he is the one setting this up. Carly, that's where you come in. You have to lead him in that direction without him realizing it. Do you think you can handle it?"

Carly nodded. "I have to. I have to do whatever it takes. So, when I call Slovak, do you want me to suggest we should meet at the park?"

"No. Not at first. You've got to lead him into it. Act a little unsure of yourself. Get the ball back in his court."

"I can do that."

"Let him start asking questions and then feel him out. He's good. Like I said he has been doing this a long time. If he feels you're being coached, he'll walk, and you may never see Bo again."

"Carly, you can do this," Porsche said.

"She's tough when she needs to be," David offered. "But you guys are putting her at risk."

"We'll protect her," Stacey said, looking at David and then at Carly.

"Okay, okay," Carly said. "Continue with the plan".

"You're going to have to tell him you are with David and me," Stacey said. "He sent us the video, so he already believes the three of us are together."

"I can do that."

"Let him know you are in the Port Huron area. He will probably start asking questions about it because I doubt that he's ever been here. That's it. It's all up to you now."

Nodding and looking at all three of them Carly said, "I'm ready." She then hit re-dial.

"You got this," David encouraged.

She heard the ring and tapped the speaker, then placed the phone on the table. David, Porsche, and Stacey listened on.

Chapter 42

Slovak opened his eyes and pulled the latch on his recliner when he heard his phone. He looked at Tatyana and gave her a nod. She quickly grabbed her purse sitting next to the hotel bed and removed a pen and paper.

"Slovak here," he said in a calm voice, placing his phone on speaker and setting it on the coffee table. "Where are you?"

"I'm in the Port Huron area…by the St. Clair River."

Tatyana opened a map of Michigan and found the coordinates for Port Huron. She followed the longitude and latitude lines until her fingers crossed. She circled the lower part of the thumb of the Michigan mitten.

"I talked with Bo, and he seems okay. I'm ready to make the swap."

"How can I be sure you have the mithridate?"

"How can I be sure that Bo will still be alive?

"You will see him before we make the swap. I expected you would need assurance that he was still alive." Slovak paused briefly. "Tell me where the mithridate was hidden."

Carly looked at Agent Canter. *"Tell him how you found the mithridate,"* Stacey said silently.

"I found it on property my grandparents used to own. That's where my dad hid it. There were two small plastic spray bottles hidden in a birdhouse. Before you killed him, he…" Carly paused. Porsche gestured to keep going. "Before my dad died, he gave me clues to where it was, never saying exactly where it was hidden. It was up to me to figure it out. When my memory came back, David and I put the clues together and found it."

Slovak pursed his lips and glanced at Tatyana. "Are David and Meghan with you?"

Carly looked at Stacey. She nodded yes.

"Yes. I want David to come with me when we do the swap."

"I want *you* to come alone," Slovak declared with a voice of authority. "The swap will happen in a public place, so you won't be alone."

Carly sighed. "I'll come alone. Where do you want to meet?"

"I'm not familiar with the area. I want a public place. Nothing indoors. I want people to be there. Some kind of Farmer's Market or something like that."

"I don't know of any Farmer's Markets this time of year. There's a park by the bridge to Canada. Will that work?"

"An amusement park?"

"No. A regular park where families go for picnics. It's by the Bluewater Bridge. There is a boardwalk that runs along the river. It's full of joggers and fishermen. That kind of park."

Stacey gave Carly a thumbs up.

"What's the name of the park?"

"Blue Water River Park," Carly said.

Tatyana wrote it down and then looked it up on her phone.

"Well, I'll have to check this out and get back with you. It may or may not work. You'll hear from me in a few hours. Do you understand?"

"I do," Carly said. She opened her mouth to say something more, but Slovak was already gone. There was only silence.

Carly checked to make sure the call had ended.

"Yes!" Stacey said. "You did great. I can't be a hundred percent sure, but I think Slovak believes he's back in control. Now the wait begins. We can't do anything until he gets back with us."

****

"As far as I can tell the bridge is about two-hundred miles, give or take," Tatyana said, studying the map.

"Okay. We'll rendezvous there with Viktor. I had him set up another FaceTime between Carly and Bo."

"Another FaceTime!" Tatyana exclaimed. "I'm getting tired of not knowing everything that is going on! When are you going to tell me about this awesome plan you have? When it's all over?!"

Slovak looked at Tatyana, a smirk on his face. "You really think my better days are behind me, don't you? You really think that I don't have it anymore, that I am not up to the job."

"I don't know what you're talking about," she lied. "You're older, but that doesn't make you less dangerous, less threatening to carry out this operation. But it's not me you need to impress now, is it?"

Slovak analyzed what she said. "I *have* held things back from you, but once we get to the park, I'll explain everything. Do you have your passport?"

"Always."

****

The room was silent except for the occasional clinking of his ankle shackles which were bolted to the floor with short chains. Bo squirmed in his chair, trying to ease the ache in his back. He waited, wondering when Viktor would return. He sipped his water trying to quench the pain in his stomach. Bo had not eaten since the day before. His hunger pangs were quickly replaced with an adrenaline rush as he heard the Honda pull up.

Like before, he listened as the cabin door opened, waiting for his captor to barge in. Viktor entered the bedroom and handed Bo a large bag from the local grocery store.

"So you don't starve," Viktor said. Bo looked in the grocery bag and saw bottles of water, bread, lunch meat, and chips. Viktor then handed him a bucket. "Better than pissing your pants.

"This is where we part ways, my friend." He turned on the nanny cam and tapped the app on his phone. "Look at me and smile for the camera," he said, taunting him. "I've enjoyed your company these past few days."

"Fuck off, Viktor," Bo said as he used his teeth to open a package of salami.

"Until we never meet again," Viktor said, amused with his own joke. He then closed the app and walked out of the room

Bo rolled a couple of slices of salami and ate them. He heard the Honda start, then pull out of the drive.

****

David, Porsche and Carly were finishing their Taco Bell carry-out when Stacey walked back into the hotel room. Dangling from her hands was a braided belt with a silver oval buckle.

"You're gonna wear this," she said to Carly. "It's actually a wire, with a camera and microphone. Doesn't matter if you meet at that park or someplace else. We want to hear and see what's going on."

Carly took the belt and examined it. "Not my taste, but we aren't dealing with taste." She fastened the belt and then said to Stacey, "I'm taking my gun."

Stacey started to protest, then changed her mind. "Just make sure it's well hidden."

"I just want to get on with it," Carly said. "This waiting is driving me crazy."

"Slovak should be calling any time now. It's been over three hours. He is thorough. I'm sure he will walk the grounds and get a plan in his head before he calls. That may take some time."

****

Tatyana drove under the twin spans of the Blue Water Bridge. Canada was in the foreground on the opposite side of the St. Clair River

"Let's go for a walk," Slovak said, picking a spot for Tatyana to park. "I'll let you know the plan as we look the place over."

Three hours passed and then four. Slovak had yet to call. The TV hummed in the background, but no one was watching it. Tension in the room was high.

Carly grabbed David's phone when she heard it ring. She placed it on speaker and answered.

"Hello," she said.

"Listen very carefully. That park will work. I want you to meet me there tomorrow at 1:00 in the afternoon. You need to follow these instructions exactly."

"I'm ready."

"When you enter the park, you will see a statue of Thomas Edison. Walk to it and sit on the bench next to it. Make sure you have David's phone. We will be watching. If all is good, and you are alone, I will call you with further instructions."

"Will you have Bo with you?"

“Yes, he will be there. I will test the mithridate, and if it’s the real thing, I will give the order to release him. Just to let you know…there will be crosshairs on you the entire time. If this is some kind of set up, both you and Bo will die.”
“There is no set up. I just want Bo back.”
“I’ll see you tomorrow. Come alone, and don’t be late.”

****

The suite was brightened by light streaming through the huge picture window. Slovak wearily eased himself into the leather chair in front of the window. He reached for a cheese square on the fruit tray Tatyana ordered from Room Service.

"What happens if she doesn't show? Or if she is late?" Tatyana mused out loud.

"I know how this girl thinks. She'll be there."

Slovak helped himself to another piece of cheese before speaking. “Call Viktor,” he said. “Have him get a jogging suit and running shoes. Tell him we will fill him in when he gets here.”

Chapter 43

Stacey pulled down a knitted cap over her head and put on the quilted jacket that was stuffed into her duffel bag. Her stomach was queasy as it always got when a sting operation was about to happen. She knew there would be officers in the field. She had called the chief and informed him where the swap was going to take place.

David stood at her side, watching her in the mirror, pleading to be a part of the operation.

"So, I'm just to stay here, while you three go and do this?"

"It's not my call. I've been keeping the chief posted on everything, and he was adamant about keeping you out of the operation. Besides, you heard what Slovak said… he wants Carly to come alone."

"How can I sit here and do nothing?" David said, his voice raising.

Carly sensed David's frustration. "Stop it, David. You can't come with us," she said firmly. "If I don't follow Slovak's orders, he might kill Bo…and me too. Please… just sit down. No more discussion."

She glanced at Stacey with a stern look and then back to David. "I just need to get this over with."

David knew his pleas would go nowhere; the decision had been made. He sank into his chair and then asked, "What's going to happen with me and Carly? I mean we called a bomb threat in and stole a car. Are we going to jail?"

"I don't think so," Stacey said. "The CIA has a way to make things go away. You'll have a fresh start."

Carly listened to those words. "I'm sure *you* know all about making things go away. Remember when we talked about a fresh start? I was going to head back to Corktown and then once you were discharged, you were going to come and live with me." Shaking her head, she added, "I was so gullible."

Stacey defended herself. “You’re right. I did say those things. I hope someday you will understand that I was doing my job.”

She knew how Carly felt and that it would take a long time before there was any forgiveness. Maybe never.

“Whatever,” Carly said, then looked at the clock on the nightstand. “12:15. I think we should go.”

David jumped up from the couch and wrapped his arms around Carly. “You come back to me. Do exactly what Stacey says and no more.”

Carly looked deep into David’s eyes. She saw his concern. Her thoughts, however, were only of Bo. “I promise.”

Breaking away from David’s grip Carly looked down at the silver belt buckle and asked, “Is this thing on? Do I have to do anything?”

“Let me show you,” Porsche said, pulling the mini iPad from her shoulder bag. Pointing at the buckle she said, “You’ll see a little black slide switch on the inside. Turn it on.”

Carly unhooked the silver buckle and found the black switch. She slid it to the side, then re-buckled. “Done.”

Porsche tapped the camera icon holding the iPad for Carly to see. A picture of the room instantly filled the screen.

“Move around. Check it out.” Porsche directed.

Turning at the waist, Carly panned the room. “Pretty amazing.”

“I’ll be able to watch and hear everything,” Porsche said. “Are you ready?”

“Ready as I’ll ever be.”

Carly walked to David and took ahold of his hand. “I’m going to do what Slovak says. Stacey and Porsche will be there with me and I’ll be armed.”

David began to protest one last time, but Carly placed her finger to his lips. “It’s got to be this way.”

****

Carly’s stomach tightened as she got closer to the River park. She turned onto Huron Street and saw the twin spans of the Blue Water Bridge. Slowly she took in deep breaths, calming herself. With her blinker on, she waited for the traffic to clear, then pulled into the lot and parked.

Lifting the gold chain from her neck, she placed her thumbnail into the slit and opened it. Artie stared back with a grin from ear to ear. She snapped the locket closed and dropped it back in her shirt. *Payback time, little brother.* Then she adjusted her pistol in the back of her waistband and stepped out of the Blazer.

"Enjoy the show, Porsche…revenge time for Ahmed and my dad."

Porsche looked away from the screen of the iPad and out the window of the car. A flicker of grief crinkled her forehead as she heard Carly's words.

Carly felt for the two plastic spray bottles in her pockets before shutting the door of the SUV. *Crosshairs on me,* she thought as she walked over the train tracks and passed the train station museum. In the distance, a bronze patina color monument of Thomas Alva Edison welcomed guests as they entered the river park.

An elderly woman snapped a picture of a family posing with the statue. The bench next to Edison was empty. Carly waited for the family to leave and then, as instructed, she made her way to the bench and sat down. She looked at David's phone and then at her watch. She was right on time.

Minutes passed, and then more minutes. Carly squirmed on the bench and waited.

A jogger wearing a maize and blue U of M hoodie stopped and sat on the far side of the bench. He placed a small box next to him as he leaned over and tied his shoe. Once finished, he continued his run, leaving the box behind. David's phone immediately rang.

Slovak kept the binoculars to his eyes as he spoke to Carly on the phone. The windbreak fisherman's tent set up on the St. Clair River along the Canadian shore was a little over two thousand yards away. Slovak had the perfect view. The windbreak blended perfectly with the other tents at the water's edge. Fishing poles with bells on their tips sat in their rod holders like solders at attention. The anglers, protected from the wind, sat in their tents, listening for the ring of the bell as they sipped from cups and thermoses.

Carly answered. "Slovak?"

"Go sit at the end of the bench and grab the box."

"Where's Bo?" Carly asked, sliding to the far end of the bench. She placed the box on her lap.

"You'll see Bo shortly," he said. "Inside the box is a phone and a test kit. I am going to call you on that phone. When it rings, place the phone on speaker. You will get all further instructions from that phone." David's phone went silent, the phone in the box immediately rang.

As instructed, Carly placed David's phone in her pocket and answered the call. She tapped the speaker. "Now what?"

Take out a test strip and spray it with the mithridate. If it's what you say, it will change color." Porsche spoke into the mic of Stacey's headset and to the other CIA officers in the field. "They have made contact. Carly is talking on the phone and has been given what looks like a cigar box."

"Copy that," the CIA officer posing as a fisherman on the U.S. side said into his coffee mug. "I have a visual on Damsel."

Carly lifted the clasp on the cigar box and opened it. Gripping the plastic test kit with one hand, she used her palm to unscrew the cap. Gently tapping the container a few strips fell into the bottom of the box. She recapped the bottle and placed it back in the box.

She removed a spray bottle from her pocket. Using her index finger and thumb she pinched a strip and held it in front of her, spraying a generous amount at the bottom. *Please turn color.* Carly watched as the bottom half of the white strip turned a deep purplish red.

She picked up the phone. "It's done. It turned a purplish-red," she said, keeping any excitement out of her voice.

"I need confirmation. Take a picture of the strip and send it to the only contact on that phone. Do you understand?"

"Yes."

Porsche communicated with the field agents. "She has tested the mithridate."

Carly held the strip away from her and snapped the pic. She went to the contact and selected the photo. "It's sent," she said.

"Wait until I see it," Slovak said. Stay on the phone." After what seemed like an eternity, Slovak returned. "Well done, Carly."

"I've held up my end," Carly said, impatience in her tone. "You said Bo would be here. I am not giving you the mithridate until I know he is free!"

"Relax and I'll explain," he said, keeping his voice calm, but stern. "Keep the box with you and walk down the boardwalk until you reach the Dog Howling at the Moon statue. There is a bench. Sit on it and you'll get more instructions."

"Carly is on the move," Porsche said to the field officers. "Sounds like she's getting instructions as she goes."

"I'm en route," Canter said, hurrying from the playground where she had been sitting with the other mothers watching their kids jump and run on the playscape.

"Stand down, Canter," the lead CIA Officer ordered. "We have visual and nothing is going to happen that we won't be aware of. Wait for further instructions."

"But…" Canter protested, then stopped and leaned up against the aluminum rail fencing following the river.

Carly kept the phone to her ear as she walked toward the statue. She could hear Slovak speaking with someone as she reached the bench and sat. Looking from side to side she saw no sign of Bo.

Frustrated, she asked, "Where is he?"

"You'll see him now. We are watching everything and remember there are crosshairs on you. I am going to hang up. Once I do, find the icon "Nanny Cam." Open it, and you can talk with Bo. You will see that he is fine. There is an envelope in the box with instructions on how to release him. Follow them. When he is released, I want you to stand up. I will call you back."

The phone went silent. Carly tapped the Nanny Cam. A live picture of Bo appeared on the screen. He sat slouched in a chair, his chin to his chest and both arms dangling to his side.

"Bo!" Carly cried.

Startled, Bo looked around. "Carly?"

"Yes. It's me. I can see you. You are on some sort of camera. I am in the process of getting you free. But you're supposed to be here. Here at the park."

"Park? What park?"

"Hang on. I need to get more instructions."

"Instructions for what?"

"On how to get you out of there. Hang on. I gotta set the phone down."

Carly took the envelope out of the box. She ran her finger through the gummed flap tearing it open. She unfolded the note and read it to Bo. "There's a key, on the left side of the padded chair. Run your fingers along the bottom seam until you feel stitching. Tear through it and find a key to unlock your chains."

Carly watched as Bo ran his hand along the seam. Not able to look, only able to feel.

"I feel the stitching," he said to the camera.

Bo dug his fingers into the loose threads and pulled. Little by little he could feel his fingers penetrating the fabric. Buried within the soft foam he felt the metallic key. "I got it," he said, holding up the key to the camera.

He quickly bent at the waist and inserted the key. The Master lock sprung open, and he removed his shackles. Bo vaulted to his feet.

"Go! Get out of there," Carly said urgently. "Get help. I can't help you anymore."

"Be advised," Porsche relayed to the field officers. "Bo has been released."

Bo shuffled from the bedroom; his legs too weak to run. He pulled the front door open, then quickly closed it.

He took a deep breath and reopened the door, then hobbled down the steps one step at a time. *Gotta get into cover,* he thought, his military training taking over.

Staying out of sight, but following the road, Bo came to a log cabin with a screened in porch. A man and woman were loading suitcases into the trunk of their car.

Breathless, and still within the cover of oak and pine, Bo waved his arms and shouted.

"Please help me. I'm not going to hurt you... Call 911... My name is Bo Harris and I was kidnapped. Please. Call 911." And then he collapsed onto the pine needles covering the ground, exhausted.

"I'll call right now," the man told Bo, waving for his wife to come join him. "You stay right there."

Never taking his eyes off Bo, he removed his cell phone from his pocket and made the call for help.

****

Carly stood up from the bench. The phone immediately rang. "What you do next will determine if *you* live or die," Slovak told Carly. "I'm serious, Carly. Very serious." Slovak glanced at Tatyana. She was looking through the scope of the sound suppressed sniper rifle balanced on a shooting tripod. "Now," Slovak said.

Tatyana fired two quick shots. The silencer attached to the muzzle kept the blasts quiet. For Carly, the bullets seemingly came from across the river…spraying and scattering several stones into the air only feet away from where she stood.

"Be aware shots fired," Porsche informed the field officers.

Carly jumped! "What the fuck! Are you trying to kill me?"

"If that's what I wanted, we wouldn't be having a conversation. Now do exactly what I tell you. Go over to the angel," Slovak continued.

"What angel?" Carly asked.

"Look out onto the lawn. Can you see the sculpture of the angel with wings? It is quite large. You can't miss it."

Carly looked over her shoulder and scrunched her eyes searching for the angel. "I see it."

"Go now," Slovak told Carly.

Crosshairs on me.

"Be advised… Damsel is on the move. She is walking on the lawn," the fisherman relayed to the field officers.

"I see her," Agent Canter said. "There's not one person in her vicinity."

Carly reached the angel. "I'm here," she said, surveying the Canadian shoreline looking for what tent Slovak may be in.

"Face the angel and kneel."

Carly faced the sculpture and lowered to both knees. Her back was now to Slovak.

"You'll see a drone under the left wing…place it to the right of you."

Smaller than a dinner plate, the aircraft resembled a tarantula. Four curved legs tucked under an oval body held four sets of fragile propeller blades. Carefully she picked up the drone then jumped from her knees and bolted behind the granite statue.

"I can't see her!" Tatyana snapped as she looked up from her shooting tripod.

Slovak's chest tightened as he helplessly peered through his binoculars. "Carly!" Slovak yelled into the phone. "I will kill you and Bo. I will track you to the ends of the earth."

Slovak could hear Carly breathing, but she was not speaking. He then heard Carly speak in a calm, haunting voice.

"Do you know the pleasure I get knowing it was my bullet that turned your face into a monster. Do you think of me every time you look in a mirror or notice a child staring at you in horror, then crying for his mother? Do I consume your daily thoughts?"

Slovak gripped his chest. "Fire a shot," he yelled to Tatyana, just fire a shot."

Tatyana fired a round. The bullet hit the 4-inch-thick granite statue causing a fracture and large chip to drop to the ground.

"Shots fired," Porsche relayed. "Shots fired."

"Really," Carly said. "You'd need a fifty caliber to pierce this granite. Even someone who isn't an Army brat would know that."

There was a long pause before Slovak continued. "Seems that we have a stalemate. If you give me the mithridate, I will let you live."

"Hate that you have to change your plans, but I can live with that. What do you want me to do?"

"Place the mithridate under the Velcro band. Make sure it's secure."

Carly reached into her coat pocket and removed the mithridate, setting it to the side of the drone. Gripping the Velcro strip and pulling, she heard the ripping sound as it released. She placed the bottles under the strip making sure each bottle was secured. "It's done." She told Slovak.

"There is a green button. Push it."

Carly pressed the green button. She heard the whine of the rotors and saw a blinking green light. The light changed to red and the aircraft lifted and hovered. Carly looked to the sky as the drone tilted slightly, then soared over the water toward the Canadian shore.

Chapter 44

The fisherman watched helplessly as the drone screamed across the short distance to the opposite shore of the river. He watched as Slovak and Tatyana ran to the drone and fled.

"Damn," he whispered, then alerted Central. "Abort operation and meet at rendezvous site. Damsel is unscathed. Target is running. Alert Homeland Security and the Canadian authorities."

Carly noticed Stacey running towards her. "We did it," she said, running up, slightly out of breath. "We fooled the son of a bitch."

Carly walked from behind the statue. She stood staring out over the St. Clair River. She smiled slightly, filled with satisfaction that Slovak had been outsmarted. She took her gaze from the water and focused on Stacey. "Once Slovak realizes he was tricked, he'll be back. He didn't kill me, but the next time…" her voice trailed off. "The next time he'll try to put a bullet in my head. When he does, I'll be ready for him."

Carly removed the pistol from the back of her waistband and tucked it into her side. Her jacket covered it. Something looked different about her. Her eyes were hard, dark, and distant. Her face tight and stern.

"I wish it weren't true," Stacey said, "but you're right. Slovak is a bad actor, but there will be other Slovaks, other bad actors hunting for you. You need protection."

"But we found the mithridate already. Put the word out. Let them know it's gone," she said, her voice agitated.

"I wish it were that easy. The CIA will leak the whole operation and how you found the mithridate, but will the bad guys buy it? They'll think it was all part of the operation to get Bo. They are shrewd and …"

Carly interrupted. "I was going to kill him today. It wouldn't have mattered if Bo was saved or not. I was going to kill him the minute I saw him."

In all the months Agent Canter had known Carly, she never saw this side of her. It made her feel uneasy, unsure of what to say next.

"Carly," Stacey said, reaching out and taking a hold of her arm. "You've been under a ton of pressure. What you've gone through the last few days would have put anyone over the edge. Let's get you back and see how Bo is doing. You saved him, Carly. You saved Bo's life."

"So, he's safe?" she said, returning to herself.

"Yes. The chief texted me, the State Police have him. The chief also wanted me to speak to you about witness protection."

"Witness protection?" Carly snapped. "You think that is an option? You really think I am going to hide for the rest of my life?! I'm not that confused patient at Holy Oaks anymore!"

"Carly, I'm serious. You and Bo need to be in the protection program. For you, it is obvious why. For Bo so they can never use him to get to you."

"When can I see him?"

"Let's get back to the hotel. I'll call the chief on the way and see where he is. You can talk with David. He'll need to go into the program, too. Everything you two would have been charged with has been erased. It's like it never happened."

Carly was silent as she and Stacey walked back along the boardwalk. She watched a huge Canadian freighter splash through the water as the crew hustled about on deck. Distant sirens of an EMS vehicle could be heard as the two came upon a crowd. Lying flat on the ground was a jogger. A man kneeling by his side was pushing onto his chest, while another blew air into his mouth. The maize and blue hoodie was soaked with red.

"He was the jogger that gave me the box." Carly whispered to Stacey. "Did the CIA take him out?"

"Hardly. Had to be Slovak. That's what they do. Once you're no use to them, they eliminate you. The less people know about what went on the better. I'm sure they also wanted a distraction."

"He would have killed me too had I not jumped behind that statue. I'm sure that was his plan all along."

"You're probably right," Stacey said. "He's a ruthless son of a bitch.

"Porsche's in the back lot waiting for me. If David wants to be with you, he has to be in the program. He'll have no choice. He will never see you again if he isn't."

Carly nodded her head slowly, absorbing the graveness of her words.

"Do you want me to ride with you?" Stacey asked.

"No. I'll be fine. I need to be alone. I have decisions to make and not a lot of time to make them. I'll see you at the hotel."

Carly found it odd to see Stacey and Porsche standing outside of her hotel room when she pulled into the Comfort Inn. Seeing Carly in the Blazer, Porsche dropped her cigarette to the asphalt and stepped on it.

Carly stepped out of the Blazer, confused. She asked, "Isn't David here? Did you knock?"

"A few times," Stacey said.

Carly slipped the magnetic card into the lock and quickly removed it. Watching the blinking light turn green, she pushed open the door.

"David?"

The room was empty. There was no sign of him.

"That's weird," Carly said. "Where could he have gone?"

"Looks like he left a note," Porsche said, picking up an envelope lying on the table and handing it to Carly. "It's addressed to you."

Carly took the note from Porsche and held it. "This can't be anything good," she said, then tore the flap from the envelope and read the note to herself.

Carly,

I hope you can forgive me for what I have done. You will understand when you read the letter your father left for you with the mithridate. It is under the pillow of the bed. Read it when you are alone. I really do love you. It was never an act. I had to leave. It's better if I don't tell you where I am. No matter what happens, I will find you again.

Love, David

Carly's face was blank as she folded the note and placed it in her pocket. She looked at Stacey and Porsche, then said, "David's gone. I don't know where he went. He said he would find me when the time was right."

"Son of a bitch," Stacey said. "David's on the fucking run?"
"Looks that way," Carly said, shaking her head in disbelief. "Where should I go from here?"

Stacey handed Carly a document.

"What's this?"

"A chance at a new life. A new life for you and maybe Bo. It explains the Witness Protection Program. You would be re-united with your mother."

"My mom?"

"She's been in the program since the death of your father. I'm sorry the CIA used you, but we had to get the mithridate. In the wrong hands, it could have been re-engineered to kill millions. We couldn't let that happen. You're a hero, Carly."

"Hero?" she said. "My dad, Artie, and Ahmed are the heroes, not me."

The conversation was broken when Agent Canter's phone rang. She reached into her purse. "It's the chief."

"Canter, here," Stacey said into the phone. Her eyes went to Carly. "I just shared the program with her. She is thinking about it and is going to let me know her decision. I also have to tell you Farris is gone. Looks like he's on the run." After a slight pause Canter said, "Got it. Thank you, Sir."

Stacey dropped her phone back into her purse. "Bo has been taken to a hospital a little over an hour from here. If we leave now, I could have you there by 6:00. 6:30 at the latest."

Carly looked at the clock. "Give me fifteen minutes, and I'll meet you in the parking lot."

"Sounds good," Stacey said. "See you in fifteen."

The door closed, and Carly immediately went to the pillow. She pulled back the covers and removed the letter.

My Beloved Family,

If you are reading this, I hope my worst nightmare has not come true. If a pandemic has begun, do exactly what this letter tells you to do. I was not able to save Artie, but I made damn sure that I could save you. Enclosed are three vials of mithridate. I hid one for each of us. Swallow it and within twenty-four-hours your body will start making antibodies to combat the pathogen. It will take months before the government starts giving the antidote to the public. Don't worry about me. Since I'm not there with you, you have to believe I'm with Artie. One day we will all be together again. God Bless. Love, Dad

Carly dropped her hands; the letter fell to the floor. *Three vials? But... David only gave me two......*

David paid the cabbie with cash and walked into the pub. He scanned the bar and spotted Sergeant Tim. As he walked toward him, Tim smiled and stood. "Has the eagle landed?"

"Yes, Sir," David said, putting his hand in the pocket of his jacket, letting his fingers feel the smooth glass of the vial. "Just like in the desert, I follow orders." He handed Tim the vial.

Epilogue

By the time the driver dropped David off at the Comfort Inn, it was too late. He saw the Blazer parked close to the room, but they were gone. What seemed like a good plan at first with his Sargeant no longer did. He needed to get back to Carly.

He still had his key card which he ran through the slot. He opened the door hoping to find some note or clue where he could find Carly. The room was empty.

David saw the pillow had been moved, and the letter was gone. He hoped it was Carly who found it, not Stacey or Porsche. He wanted her to know everything. He should have shared the letter with her when he first found it, but he couldn't; it would have exposed Tim's plan.

On the way to the Inn, he planned what he would say to Carly, if she would even listen. She was gone now, and he didn't know how to find her. He didn't know if she was alive. For all he knew, the plan to save Bo may not have worked, and she could be dead.

In fact, "Carly Fletcher" was dead. She "died" in an auto accident, a massive one, when a semi plowed into several stopped cars on a Colorado highway. The semi burst into flames engulfing several other vehicles. "Carly" was in one of those cars, and though her body was badly burned, DNA helped to identify her.

The CIA now calls her Ava Winters, and she sells her pen and ink sketchings along with her photographs at an open market just outside the Dusseldorf Art Academy. "Tom Higgins," her boyfriend, helps her set up her booth when he has time off from his job as a software engineer. He wants to marry Ava, but he has not asked her yet. He is confident she will say yes. Both of them have been through a lot together and blend in perfectly with the international art scene.

In a small cemetery just outside the city, Ava's father and brother rest. It was the least the CIA could do. Ava and her mother are not allowed to visit the grave site. They can take no chance that their identity will be compromised.

Across the street from their apartment, lies a park with winding paths, benches, and plenty of fresh flowers. Ava and her mother often sit on the balcony outside their apartment. They watch people wandering along the paved walkways—young couples, laughing teen-agers, and the elderly with their canes and walkers.

Tom, who lives with them, has brought Ava a stack of mail. There are catalogs, a free newspaper, and a padded eBay envelope from the U.S. She has been waiting for this envelope to come and quickly opens it.

Dear Ava,

There is no news about Slovak. He has not been seen. We do know that someone is looking for you, but we have been unable to identify the source. Rest assured, we are always doing what we can to keep you safe.
Love, S.

An older man with a faded scar below his right eye, focused on the screen in front of him. His fingers deftly typed the name "Carly Fletcher" and he waited for the search results. He knew the odds were against him, but he held hope that one little mistake or one little forgotten detail would lead him to her.

Several Carly Fletchers popped up on the screen. Carly Fletcher—Facebook, Carly Fletcher--Twitter, Carly Fletcher-Linked in...none were her.

The CIA had most likely scrubbed her name and history, leaving nothing to lead to her. That was how they operated. He also knew it was possible to find her, but it would not be easy. There was business to be settled.

About the Author

James T. Byrnes was born in Detroit Michigan. He enlisted in the Marine Corp in 1977. He graduated from Oakland University in 1984 and taught for 30 years. He and his wife have two sons, a daughter-in-law and two grandchildren. Operation Arrow Fletcher is his debut novel.

www.byrnesgroup.net
Facebook.com/JamesByrnes
jamesbyrnes@byrnesgroup.net

Book Club Discussion Questions can be downloaded at
www.byrnesgroup.net

Made in the USA
Las Vegas, NV
01 November 2022